For single parents, life 
than dating. But for th
a whole lot more than a fling . . .

Colm Cleary lost his wife just moments after his son Aiden's birth, and it's been just the two of them ever since. Dating is his very last priority—until he spots gorgeous Monica Rayburn on the playground with her little girl. Suddenly finding a woman sympathetic to the demands of single parenthood seems like a great idea—especially if they agree to a no-pressure, no-strings date . . .

Dazzled by the hot "Saturdaddy" who asks her out, Monica doesn't get around to mentioning that little Emma is her niece. She's in commodities, not children. A gambler to the bone, she's going to take a chance on an adult evening with Colm—and worry about the details later. But when their casual connection deepens into something more solid, the truth will have to come out—and both Colm and Monica will have to throw caution to the wind to hold on to a future together . . .

Visit us at www.kensingtonbooks.com

Books by Maggie Wells

Coastal Heat series
Going Deep
Flip This Love
Love & Rockets

Worth the Wait series
Three Little Words
A Will and A Way
A Bolt From the Blue

Play Dates
Play Dates
Published by Kensington Publishing Corporation

Play Dates

Play Dates

Maggie Wells

LYRICAL PRESS
Kensington Publishing Corp.
www.kensingtonbooks.com

Lyrical Press books are published by
Kensington Publishing Corp. 119 West 40th Street New York, NY 10018

Copyright © 2017 by Maggie Wells

All rights reserved. No part of this book may be reproduced in any form or by any means without the prior written consent of the Publisher, excepting brief quotes used in reviews.

All Kensington titles, imprints, and distributed lines are available at special quantity discounts for bulk purchases for sales promotion, premiums, fund-raising, and educational or institutional use.

To the extent that the image or images on the cover of this book depict a person or persons, such person or persons are merely models, and are not intended to portray any character or characters featured in the book.

Special book excerpts or customized printings can also be created to fit specific needs. For details, write or phone the office of the Kensington Special Sales Manager:
Kensington Publishing Corp.
119 West 40th Street
New York, NY 10018
Attn. Special Sales Department. Phone: 1-800-221-2647.

Kensington and the K logo Reg. U.S. Pat. & TM Off.
LYRICAL PRESS Reg. U.S. Pat. & TM Off.
Lyrical Press and the L logo are trademarks of Kensington Publishing Corp.

First Electronic Edition: October 2017
eISBN-13: 978-1-5161-0349-2
eISBN-10: 1-5161-0349-1

First Print Edition: October 2017
ISBN-13: 978-1-5161-0352-2
ISBN-10: 1-5161-0352-1

Printed in the United States of America

I married a man just like my father. I'm still not sure why my mother recommended against doing that, because I think it was the best choice ever. This is for Bill, do-it-all single dad who captured my heart many years ago. Your domestic skills only enhanced your hotness.

Acknowledgements

Enormous thanks to my editor, Marci, I love working with you! To Martin, Renee, Michelle, and the whole Kensington/Lyrical team, my deepest gratitude for your continued faith in my work. For Sara, Julie, and all my Super Cool Party People. My life would suck without you.

Chapter 1

Monica Rayburn inched closer to the picnic tables littered with diaper bags and juice boxes and lifted her cell a centimeter higher. The angle was perfect. Her subject was centered in the frame. This was a skill she'd honed during years of after-work happy hours and had finally mastered—the sly snapshot.

A quick look at the enormous play structure mounted in the center of the playground verified that her niece, Emma, was safely ensconced in one of the numerous hamster trails leading from one slide to another. Wiggling her thumb over the screen as if frantically typing a text, Monica tipped the phone up to adjust the angle a smidge. The whir of a fake shutter marked her success. She gave the photo a surreptitious glance as she lowered the phone.

Perfection.

All she had to do was determine if the handsome hunk of a man leaning against the wide trunk of an oak tree was parent or predator. If he was the latter, she had a great picture for the police. If he was some lucky kid's daddy, there was a good chance she could snag the prize for best "Spotted in the Wild" photo on her friend Sarah's photo blog. There were many beautiful specimens of manhood in the urban jungle, but few rocked the whole package like this guy did. He was tall, a bit brawny, and sported the right amount of scruff shadowing his jawline. Wavy black hair set off skin so creamy a cartoon princess would put in a call to her dermatologist.

But all those tasty tidbits weren't what kept her riveted. There was something about the way he stood. Yes, those broad shoulders were touching tree bark, but there was a readiness in his stance. Like he could spring into action at any moment. Like a jungle cat. Her heart did a little stutter-step. She focused on her breath until the pounding organ tripped into a semi-normal rhythm. Judging by the number of drive-by glances he was racking up from the mommy brigade, every woman within a hundred-yard radius was thinking the exact same thing.

Exhaling long and slow, as her yoga instructor taught her, Monica tore her eyes off the man of the minute to run a munchkin check. Emma had made her way to the twisty slide and was patiently waiting her turn in line. With her lopsided nut-brown pigtails and solemn expression, her niece resembled Monica more than her own mother. Melody was as fair and light as her name. Petite. Easy-going. The popular girl. The fact that her niece resembled her was an odd, and probably petty, point of pride for Monica, but she couldn't help feeling smug. Melody's only offspring took after her. Score!

She'd been the gangly girl who wrecked the curve.

Though she was older, for most of her life Monica felt like her sister's negative image. The one who got all the miscellaneous traits. Like her parents couldn't get everything right the first time. She had their dad's boring brown hair and lean build. Mel claimed to envy her sister's fast metabolism, but Monica would have happily swapped a few hundred calories a day for a little more, uh...endowment. The only feature she shared with her sister were the blue eyes they'd inherited from their mother. Well, the blue eyes and the residual effects of their parents' miserable marriage.

Emma called her name and Monica veered away from those disturbing memories. She'd collected dozens of self-help books over the years. Enough to start a library. But she'd have to think about her many manifestations later. Today was about Emma. She waved as her niece showed off her swinging skills. And Melody wouldn't screw her baby up the way their parents had messed with them.

Smiling, she watched as her niece proceeded to school a kid nearly twice her size on proper slide protocol when he tried to shove ahead in line. At nearly six, Emma was all arms and legs, like her Aunt Monnie. Mel claimed her daughter inherited Monica's bossy streak as well, but Monica didn't see herself or her niece as bossy. They were both naturally orderly people. And perhaps they were a little assertive about maintaining order, but self-control was no sin.

"If Barbara Walters ever asked me what tree I'd be, I'd pick that one," one of the ladies parked at the picnic table said, heaving a gusty sigh.

The sentiment was greeted by a round of appreciative groans and one reverent "Amen."

Monica chuckled at the mild blasphemy. She couldn't blame the woman. If they were talking about the guy she'd been checking out earlier, the view was worth possible damnation. Lifting her phone, she pretended to text as she zeroed in on the big oak tree on the far side of the playground once more. This time, her dishy daddy wasn't alone. Two other men had joined him. The tall, angular man had burnished copper hair, horn-rimmed glasses, and impatient red-haired twins pulling at each of his arms. The third was more serious looking. He was shorter than the other two, but was manhandling a double stroller with impressive skill. A kicking toddler and a boy, who clearly thought he was too old to be pushed around, jabbered at him, eager to be turned loose.

"Lord, I love the Saturdaddies," the woman closest to Monica said, propping her chin on her hand.

"Saturdaddies?" Monica asked, unable to stop herself.

The cluster of yummy mummies tore their attention from the trio under the tree to give her the collective once-over. The one who was nursing an infant under an enormous giraffe-patterned tent made no attempt to be subtle as she checked Monica's bare left hand. Turning to one of the others, she gave a grudging huff. "No ring."

Another shrugged and sighed. "Someone might as well get a little play out of them."

The nursing mother tilted her head to look Monica in the eye. "Saturdaddies are men who only have time to bring their kids to the park on Saturdays. Usually divorced or never-marrieds."

"The married ones never come to the park," another grumbled. "Too tired after working *so hard* all week long."

The sarcasm in the woman's tone was tough to miss. The top notes of bitterness rang through Melody's request for Monica to take Emma for a few hours. Normally, she wasn't really the babysitting kind of aunt, but Mel's husband was heading out of town for a conference, and her sister swore the only thing keeping her from divorcing her steady, reliable dentist husband was the possibility of hot monkey sex. And for hot monkey sex to be a possibility, she needed someone to remove the inquisitive six-year-old from the premises.

With the words hot, monkey, and sex flashing through her brain, she turned to the trio under the tree. "None of them are married?"

"Widowed, divorced, never legal," another mother reported, nodding to each man in turn as she rummaged for a juice box for her whining son.

Monica wanted to ask how she knew this and which was which, but Emma came tearing across the grass as fast as her spindly legs could carry her shouting, "Monnie! Monnie!"

Acting purely on instinct, Monica shoved the phone into her pocket and dropped to one knee to catch the tiny human missile. Damp seeped through the knee of her designer jeans. The Marc Jacobs tote she'd repacked with the supplies Mel provided slid off her shoulder and hit the ground. She didn't care. There was no way in hell she would trudge around town carrying a Dora the Explorer backpack. No way. No how.

Brushing thoughts of fashion sacrifices aside, she peered down into Emma's pointy little face. No tears. She couldn't feel any broken bones. No sign of blood. Only a shallow furrow of worry bisecting the girl's wispy brows gave any indication something might be wrong.

"What? What happened?"

"I found her at the bottom of the slide." Emma took a step and held up a grubby princess doll as if presenting Exhibit A to a jury. "Someone *losed* her."

Monica didn't bother suppressing her grimace as she eyed the doll's grimy face and dirty dress. "Lost her," she corrected gently.

"We gotta give her back. That's what you do when you find somebody else's stuff," Emma said, all wide-eyed sincerity.

Swallowing an unexpected lump of pride, Monica nodded and took her niece's free hand as she rose. "You're right. We'll ask around and see if we can find her mommy."

Emma blinked. "Mommy? Her mommy is Queen Cassandra. I didn't see a Queen Cassandra doll."

"Queen Cassandra?"

"Princess Clarissa's mommy." The little girl nodded, obviously happy to share her knowledge with an ignorant grownup, but her frown returned. "But she's not here. She lives in the Crystal Palace."

"Well, maybe we can find whoever brought Princess Clarissa here," Monica amended. She straightened and looked over at the women crowded around the tables. "Did anyone lose a, uh, Princess Clarissa?"

There was a flurry of activity as they rifled through bags. "No, I've got Eden's."

"Maribeth's is here."

"We didn't bring Laurel's because I told her I wouldn't buy another one if she lost one more."

The nursing mother looked up from her one-handed search, her mouth set in a grim line. "Sophie's isn't here." She craned her neck to get a good look at the play structure. "Great. She's camped out in the tube again. God, I hate that thing."

Monica looked over her shoulder and spotted a dark-haired girl sitting cross-legged in the giant plastic tunnel while other kids crawled around and over her to get to the other side.

"I'll go *aks* her," Emma volunteered.

Monica didn't have the heart to correct Emma's pronunciation. Her niece was practically vibrating at the thought of having a mission to accomplish, and Monica knew exactly how she felt. Giving her niece's hand a squeeze, she smiled at the harried young woman camped out under the nursing tent. "We'll go check with her."

About halfway to the playground, Monica gave up on restraining Emma one second longer. The girl sprinted toward the nearest ladder and started to climb. Monica's shoes sank into the recycled rubber mulch. She ducked under the plastic tunnel as Emma launched herself into the tube. They both froze in place when they spotted the pristine Princess Clarissa doll clutched in little Sophie's hands. A second later, Emma popped out of the tube onto a platform, waved the doll over her head and shouted, "She's not hers!"

Emma's mouth dipped at the corners as she squinted down from between the rails. Her baby blue eyes were wide but dry. Her lower lip trembled as she clutched the gnarly doll to her chest and hugged the nasty thing protectively. Recognizing the first signs of panic, Monica shifted into crisis management mode.

"Okay, okay. Come on down and we'll ask around," she coaxed, lifting her arms as if she expected her niece to catapult right into them.

Thankfully, Emma had sense for the both of them. She nodded once, and made her way to the wide, flat slide kids were hurtling down two and three at a time. Monica collected her at the bottom. Holding her hand tightly, they began to weave their way through the maze of activities, stopping to ask every little girl who crossed their path if the doll belonged to her.

As frustrating as receiving no after no was, the search went a long way to eroding Monica's cynical outlook on life. All of the girls they questioned were scrupulously honest, even the ones who eyed the grubby doll covetously. Monica promised herself she would purchase a dozen Princess Clarissa dolls and donate them to whatever charity gave out toys to kids in need. They scored another no as they rounded the corner near the swings, and Monica mentally upped the ante to two dozen dolls. She could afford the expenditure.

Hope wore thin as they approached monkey bars anchoring the far end of the equipment. Taking a deep breath while she eyed the kids hanging from the maze of tubular steel, Monica turned and squatted in front of Emma. All the noise of the morning faded away as she stared into the crystalline blue eyes so like her own. Keeping her voice steady and logical, she held her niece's earnest gaze.

"How about we leave the doll on one of the picnic tables and maybe whoever she belongs to will come looking for her later?"

"But we have to make sure they get her back," Emma insisted.

"I'm sorry, sweetie, but I think we've asked everyone," she said, calling off the search gently but firmly.

"We didn't ask the boys."

Monica blinked but somehow managed to hold off a snort when she looked down at the doll's sequin-strewn gown. Smiling, she tightened the more bedraggled pigtail and ran a soothing hand over the girl's soft cheek. "You're a sweet kid."

"We can ask them," Emma insisted, nodding to the red-haired twins Saturdaddy Number Two turned loose on the world.

Monica eyed the boys skeptically. They looked to be all boy, through and through. "Most boys don't play with dolls, honey."

"Some do," a deep voice interrupted.

Gripping Emma's arms to steady herself, Monica whipped her head around. She knew instinctively who was speaking. Saturdaddy Number One. Mr. Spotted in the Wild. He stared straight at her, his chin lifted high and his eyes narrowed to slits. Pride and defiance etched lines into his forehead. Cripes, he was even more gorgeous up close. A rugged-looking male model born to pose propped against a faux rock climbing wall.

He held a boy dressed in baggy jeans and a shirt declaring him a one-man wrecking crew on his hip. The little fellow peeked at them from the crook of his father's neck. The shock of wavy black hair matched, but the resemblance ended there. Whereas her hunk had green eyes the color of an old Coke bottle, the little boy's were nearly black and glassy with misery. At least some of those tears managed to overflow the fringe of lashes to streak down cheeks as brown as burnt caramel. Slowly, as if she were the predator she'd thought him to be a short time ago, he lowered the loose-limbed boy to the spongy ground.

"Go thank the little girl for finding P.C.," he said gruffly.

"P.C.?" Monica blurted.

When he raised a challenging eyebrow, she laughed and shook her head. She watched as Emma handed over her prize as though the grungy doll were the Holy Grail.

"Not very P.C. if you can't even call the doll by her proper name."

"Not very P.C. for you to ask only the girls if the doll was theirs," he countered.

"Touché." Monica inclined her head in acknowledgment of the hit, but she wasn't about to let opportunity slip away. "Hi, I'm Monica Rayburn," she said, extending her hand.

He clasped her hand. "Colm Cleary." He nodded to the boy who'd returned to his side so quickly she wondered if the two of them were magnetized.

"This is Aiden," he said, running a protective hand over his son's head.

She smiled down at the shyer of the Cleary men. "Hi, Aiden. I'm Monica."

Colm cast a pointed look at Emma. Startled from her trance, she laughed and placed her hand on her niece's shoulder. "Oh! This is Emma."

"Hello, Emma," Colm said, dipping his head in greeting. "Thank you for finding our friend for us." He turned his attention to the boy clinging to his side. "Aiden, did you thank Emma?"

"Thanks," the little boy murmured.

"You're welcome," Emma replied primly. "Monnie, can I go up to the slides again?"

Monica gave one of the lopsided pigtails a tug. "Sure, kiddo. Knock yourself out."

Emma took three steps and skidded to a stop. Spinning around, she fixed her eyes on Aiden. "You wanna come?"

In a flash, all vestiges of shyness disappeared. With Princess Clarissa dangling by her tattered tulle overskirt, Aiden took off after Emma without a backwards glance for his father. Colm exhaled long and loud, stuffed his hands in the pockets of his jeans, and dug the toe of his shoe into the recycled rubber chips.

Amused by his undisguised relief, she turned to him, her lips curving as she spoke. "Crisis averted?"

"We're talking Charlie-Sheen-level meltdown averted. Without the swearing. Or the drugs. Or the hookers."

"Ah, well...winning." She grinned.

He rolled his eyes but rewarded her with a smirky smile. The lopsided flash of teeth packed a wallop.

"So, uh, Colm," she began, hoping her voice didn't sound as high and squeaky to him as it did to her, "has Aiden always been a big Clarissa fan?"

In an instant, the smile was gone and the squinty-eyed stare was in place. "Is there a five-year-old who isn't?"

Monica searched her memory, trying to access the detailed wish list Emma had presented to all members of the family at Christmastime. She seemed to remember a few items with a royal theme, but frankly had no clue if they had anything to do with the scraggly doll Colm's son clutched as he climbed the rungs to get to the slide platform.

Kid stuff was way beyond her areas of expertise. She could talk to him about buying and selling. Debate the ins and outs of various retirement plans and speculate on commodity futures. If he asked, she'd tell him to sink whatever extra cash he had on hand into pork belly futures. After all, there's no safer investment than bacon. But if he asked her what Princess

Clarissa's story might be, she'd be toast.

"So, what do you do?" she asked, scrambling to find a safe topic. She didn't want this big, beautiful beast of a man to grow bored and wander into the trees.

He answered the oh-so-innocuous question with a husky chuckle. The smirky smile made another appearance as he cocked his head and peered down at her. "I'm a partner in a security company. Trident Security. What do you do, Monica?"

She chose to ignore the taunting edge in his tone. "I'm in commodities."

"Commodities?"

He didn't bother masking his confusion, so she launched into the canned spiel she usually saved for alumni events. "I advise people on what futures to buy and sell. Like stock investments, but I deal more with livestock, grain, and currency futures."

"Yeah, I know what commodities are. Cornering the orange crop like in *Trading Places*, right?"

"Don't forget the pork bellies." She grinned. "Sexy stuff, those commodities."

He ran his hand over his jaw, and Monica found she was as pleased by the rasp of his stubble against his palm as she was the note of wonder in his voice.

"You don't..." He trailed off, dropping all pretense of subtlety as he let his gaze travel over her. "I didn't peg you for the high finance type."

She crossed her arms over her chest and swung her weight onto her right leg. "I didn't peg you for the type to let his boy play with dolls."

Her assessment scored an honest-to-goodness laugh. When she spotted the dimple, all hell broke loose. Heat flared in her cheeks and her heart did a girly flutter she'd swear she hadn't felt since Jeremy Lansford asked her to go to the Spring Fling dance in eighth grade. She didn't want to think too hard about the effect the perfect little indention was having on some other bits of her anatomy.

"You have to pick your battles, right?" He gave his head a rueful shake. "I admit I fought it to start, but you realize it doesn't matter. I mean, girls play with trucks and Legos and stuff, right?"

"Were you trying to sound less sexist?"

He had the good grace to wince. "Came out better in my head." Rocking on his heels, he cast her a sidelong glance and dropped his voice to a conspiratorial whisper. "I haven't done this in a while."

She turned her most innocent gaze on him. "Engaged in conversation?"

"With a woman."

His blunt answer chased away the impulse to tease. "Any woman? Don't you have to talk to Aiden's mother?"

"No, I don't. She's dead."

Her hand flew to her mouth. "Oh! I'm sorry."

Cringing, she felt her ears go up in flames as she let her palm slide down her throat until her fingers came to rest in the hollow at the base. All in all, a much better position to choke off any other embarrassing assumptions.

Clearly regretting his blunt answer, Colm grimaced apologetically as he slipped his hands into his pockets once again. "She passed a long time ago."

"I am sorry, though. What I said was a stupid...I was trying to be all cool and clever," she admitted, wrinkling her nose. "Never works for me."

He shot her a sly look from under thick lashes. "Really? I'd bet you do okay with your husband."

She grinned at his not-so-gentle probing. "Yeah. No husband."

"Boyfriend?"

"Nope."

"Good." Colm chuckled and gave a helpless shrug. "Okay, well, now that we've got the ground work laid...If we're going to keep trying this flirting thing, one of us has to pretend to be good at it."

Always quick on the uptake when she saw something she wanted, Monica pounced. "I think, you being the man and all, you should do the heavy flirting. You need the practice, right?" She answered her own rhetorical question with a nod. "So, you go on and flirt, and I'll do my best to fall for your lame lines."

He lifted his head, skepticism hardening the planes of his face. But instead of agreeing right away, he scanned the play area until he spotted the kids, then heaved a resigned sigh. "Okay, well, you've been warned."

* * * *

He couldn't stop staring at her. Which was crazy, really, because she wasn't at all his type. She was all sharp angles and straight edges. Not like Carmen, who should have had a "Dangerous Curves Ahead" sign hung around her neck. But, the last thing he needed was another woman like his late wife. Monica Rayburn with her pointy chin and ruthlessly straight brown hair were strangely appealing. She was so unlike Carmen. Plus, there were those amazing blue eyes. No way could anything dark or mysterious lurk there. They were as clear as the autumn sky. And drilling holes right into him. Holes so big all his brains seemed to leak right out. Knowing he had to say something, anything, he clutched at the only info she'd fed him so far.

"Do you like working in, uh, commodities?"

She smiled. The tiny tilt of her lips should have told him he'd failed spectacularly, but for some reason it didn't feel like he had. Dark lashes brushed her cheekbones but did nothing to sweep away the sparkle of amusement in those vivid eyes. "Yes, I enjoy my work very much."

"Why?"

A smooth fall of light brown hair cupped her cheek as she slanted her head to look up at him. A hard fistful of lust and longing landed right in his gut. He wanted to brush the wispy strands away from her face, his fingers all but itching with the need to know if they were as silky as they looked. "Why do I like my job?"

Shocked by the inanity of his own question, but too far gone to backpedal, he pressed on. "Yeah. What makes you want to buy and sell...pork bellies, was it?"

"I've loved bacon since I was a little girl," she answered with exaggerated sincerity.

Instantly defensive, he flexed his shoulders and straightened to his full height. "It's not a stupid question, you know. Why people do what they do says a lot about them."

She blinked. "Oh, I agree. Tell me, what made you decide to open a security company? A burning need to see how many five-digit passcodes your clients could come up with?"

"I was a cop," he said bluntly. "I quit the force not long after Aiden was born. Couldn't take the chance of leaving him an orphan." A surge of masculine pleasure raced through him when her pretty pink lips parted with what he hoped was admiration. "My buddy, Mike"—he nodded toward the tree where his friends congregated—"is a genius with the business side, as well as equipment and those pesky passcodes, but he needed someone with some street smarts and credibility."

"And that's where you came in," Monica supplied with an understanding nod.

Colm nodded as he watched his friend and business partner bob and weave behind the abandoned stroller. Mike had one hand cupped under his daughter's bottom while she nuzzled into his neck, upset over some playground infraction. Colm smiled as he watched his friend do his version of the white-boy-gone-hip-hop dance all parents master within weeks of holding their offspring. They'd seen each other through a lot over the last five years—good, bad, and downright tragic—but their friendship never changed. Their bond was as strong as it had been since junior high. Stronger.

James made their pack a trio when he came on to handle sales. Unfortunately, he also got mixed up in handling Mike's younger sister, Megan—the mother of the two redheaded hellions wreaking havoc on the playground, and the flakiest girl on earth. Through a wacky blend of desperation, crowd-sourcing, and plain old trial and error, the three of them had managed to keep their business, themselves, and all five of their offspring alive. A feat. A minor miracle.

"We're partners."

She flinched. The movement was slight, but the little jerk of her shoulders cut straight through his usual haze of male oblivion.

"Not partner-partners," he hastened to add. "Business partners. The three of us." He turned his head to nod toward James. "We're business partners."

This time, she didn't bother trying to hide her shock. "And you're all Saturdaddies?"

The label shook a sharp laugh right out of him. "Saturdaddies?"

"You know. Divorced...or widowed," she said with an incline of her head. "Guys who take their kids to the park on Saturdays."

"Or working fathers." He crossed his arms over his chest, leveling his most challenging look at her. "Like those women over there." He gestured to the mommies gathered at the picnic tables. "Do you ever see them here Monday through Friday?" When she didn't answer, he forged ahead. "No. They're making up for nanny time."

"Is that what you're doing?"

"Of course." He shot her a scornful look. "Tell me you don't have a thousand other things you ought to be doing." The assertion seemed to give her pause. "But no one wants to be all 'brush your teeth' and 'eat your green beans,' do they? And so, we're here." He spotted the furrow of concern between her brows and sighed, letting some of his defensiveness go with the converted carbon dioxide. "Sorry, I just..." He shrugged and looked away, searching the playground for his son and the words he needed to explain. "Everyone thinks it's all single moms out there, you know?"

"So, you're all single dads? I mean, you're all raising them on your own?"

The undisguised surprise in her voice spoke volumes. Turning to meet those brilliant blue eyes head-on, he nodded. "All full-time dads." He pursed his lips, waiting patiently as she processed the information. "There are more of us than people think."   •

"I suppose there probably are," she murmured.

Without saying another word, she turned and started searching out her daughter. Convinced he'd been doing better with the awkward conversation than the soapbox, Colm resuscitated his opening gambit. "You never answered me. Why do you like doing the commodities thing?"

"Risk-reward," she answered, scanning area after area of the structure, not even glancing in his direction. "I'm a gambler. I like the payoff when

I take big chances."

"They've moved on to the swings."

Monica pivoted, her restless gaze seeking out the chain-linked seats. Her shoulders dropped when she finally caught sight of Aiden and Emma swaying side-by-side. He knew how she felt. He experienced the same profound relief each time he thought too hard about how close he'd come to never knowing his son. He was grateful for the doctors who jumped in to save a helpless infant and the friends who stood by his side while he groped his way through those mind-boggling months of fresh grief, terrifying responsibility, and heart-stopping betrayals.

He'd been holed up for too long. Both Mike and James had been after him to start dating, but who had the energy for all that crap? But the woman beside him? This stranger with her impossibly direct gaze and self-admitted gambling problem? She tempted him into thinking he might want to try again. At least a dinner. After all, everyone had to eat, right?

"Listen, my folks have been keeping Aiden for a while on Saturday nights," he began without taking a minute to think too hard about what he was doing. "It's new and hasn't always worked out." Okay, so he'd only had to pick his boy up once, but he didn't have to give her an accounting. She also didn't need to know the lack of success was because he pined for his son more than his kid did for him. "But if you can get free tonight, maybe get a sitter—"

"Oh!" Her eyes widened as she caught on to where he was heading. "Oh, Emma isn't—"

"Yo, Colm!" James approached, a twin tucked under each arm. He was herding the boys with nudges of his bony knees and looking more like a nutty professor than a smooth salesman at the moment. "Dude, pancake time. Gather the sprout and let's hit it. One of them's gonna gnaw my arm off."

Colm noted his friend spared only the barest of nods for Monica. Typical. If ever there was a man unnaturally attracted to the crazy, that man was Jimbo. And Monica Rayburn, with her sharp blue eyes and smudge-free but delightfully form-fitting blue jeans, was sanity incarnate.

"Pancake time?" she asked, blinking at the man approaching them.

"We go to the park and eat pancakes for lunch." He twisted his lips into a self-deprecating smile. "This is what us Saturdaddies do, you know… screw with routine." Turning to James, he nodded toward the swings. "If you can pry him loose, we'll go."

Monica laughed as James lumbered away. "Good for you. Routines are for sissies."

"So let's break ours. Have dinner with me tonight," he insisted. "Do you think you can find someone to watch Emma?"

"Oh, not a problem. My sister—"

"Monnie! Monnie!"

She yelped and staggered when the little girl rammed into her legs full-force. "Ah! Emma!" Catching her balance, Monica gently disentangled herself from her little girl's grasp. "I swear, we're going to get you a job busting kneecaps for the mob when you grow up."

"Aiden's gonna eat pancakes! Can we eat pancakes?"

Colm saw a spark light Monica's eyes, but she shook her head. "No, sweets. We have a reservation at Girlie Girls for curls and crumpets, remember?" She pulled her phone from her pocket and dragged her thumb across the screen to wake it. "Almost time for us to go, anyway."

The photo on the screen gave him hope. A picture of him filled the background. She'd zoomed in and caught him in a close-up as he leaned against the tree. And the best part was, she must have snapped the picture long before Princess Clarissa waved her matchmaking wand and brought them together. She was every bit as interested in him as he was in her. "Nice shot."

A peachy-pink blush colored her cheeks. She kept her head down, hiding behind a curtain of glossy hair as she quickly switched to the home screen. "Must have been an accident. I was taking pictures of Emma."

"Wow. You're good. Perfectly in frame. Most of my pictures come out in a blur." Emboldened by the photographic evidence, he plucked the phone from her hand. "Maybe you should give up the pork rinds and think about going pro."

"Pork bellies," she muttered. Lifting her head, she shook her hair out and squared her shoulders. "And if you must know, the picture was no accident. I'm sure you'll be a big hit on my friend's blog."

"Blog?"

"She posts pictures of hot guys spotted around town."

He couldn't repress the twitch of his lips. "You think I'm a hot guy?"

Monica huffed and he chuckled, more than happy to let her off the hook once he had an advantage.

Opening the contacts list, he typed in his name and number. "Listen, see what you can do about the crumpet here, and let me know. Okay?"

"Colm, I'm not—"

"Daddy, I'm *soooooooo* hungry," Aiden whispered, holding his belly for emphasis.

Swooping his boy up, he settled Aiden squarely on his shoulders. "Call if yes. Text if you're rejecting me," he said, backing away. "I'm sure you don't wanna hear a grown man cry."

"Would you?"

"Yes."

"Are you an ugly crier? I bet he is," she confided to the little girl at her side. "I bet he gets all snotty and gross. Boys are, you know."

He grinned, barely minding when Aiden sank his fingers into his hair and yanked. Hard. "Call me, and you won't have to worry about things getting ugly."

Chapter 2

"Seriously? So you didn't tell him? You let him believe Emma was your kid?"

Monica thought she'd prepared herself for confession and interrogation, but Mel was in rare form. She was also incandescent. Monica chose not to dwell on what caused her sister to glow as if lit by a candle. If only she could bleach the memory of her brother-in-law Jeremy's too-wide smile from her brain.

"I tried, but we kept getting interrupted, and the next thing I knew, he was gone," Monica explained, trying to control the exasperation in her tone.

"Like, poof! Presto! A big puff of smoke and nothing left but a scorch mark on the grass?"

Raking her hand through her hair, Monica dropped onto the sofa. "Not quite, but close." She hefted her overstuffed Marc Jacobs tote to the coffee table and started extracting all evidence of her day with her niece. "*Well*, you know…His friends were there, and the kids were whining, I wasn't going to stand there and scream, 'Hey, hot guy! I'm not this kid's mom!' in the middle of the park." She turned to glance at her niece, who was kneeling at the side of the table inspecting every juice box, hair band, and baggie Monica dropped to its surface. "No offense, kiddo."

Unperturbed, Emma held up a bag of cheese crackers shaped like bunny rabbits. "Can I have these?"

Monica blinked, visions of the overpriced sandwiches and petit fours the little girl had left uneaten thirty minutes ago dancing in her head. "I thought you said you weren't hungry."

Emma shrugged and hopped to her feet. "I am now."

Luckily, Mel's husband was adept at avoiding sisterly conversations. He scooped up Emma, his I-got-some smile stretching into a grin as the little girl squealed and squirmed with delight. "C'mon. We'll rustle up a

PB&J to go with those."

The kitchen door barely swung closed. Mel was on her again, her flyaway blond hair even more flighty than usual. "So are you going to call him?"

Shifting her tablet a little to the left to make room for her paper planner, she tucked the tiny spiral notebook she kept on hand at all times into the side pocket of the tote. Sparing her sister a glance from under the curtain of her hair, she mumbled, "I want to."

"You're going to have to tell him," Melody said, fixing her with a disconcerting stare.

Somehow, Monica always managed to underestimate the amount of steel in her free-spirited sister's spine. Mel seldom showed the tougher side of her personality. She preferred to go through life as if the whole world were populated with rainbow-colored unicorns. Even in the weekly yoga class they took together, Melody soaked up the plinky new-age music and threw herself into the deep breathing exercises and Oms. Monica usually spent most of the relaxation portion of the class figuring out subtle ways to throw a few Pilates moves in to save herself the time of taking another class. Hard to believe a woman clad in faded yoga pants, a tie-dyed Peace Frogs T-shirt, and a pair of fuzzy socks she claimed were infused with shea butter or aloe or some such nonsense kept a stare so potent stashed in her arsenal.

"I'll tell him." Monica returned the stare with what felt like an adequate amount of gravitas but had a hard time fighting the urge to smile. "But can I wait until after?"

Mel blinked. "After? After what? The date?"

Monica waggled her eyebrows but held her sister's gaze as she gave her head a slow shake. "No…after." Without breaking eye contact, she woke her phone from its electronic slumber and tapped the button to open the camera app. She held the phone out but kept her focus locked on her sister even after Melody's gaze dropped to the screen and she gasped.

"Holy cra...crêpes," she corrected at the last second.

"Crêpes?"

"Last week, I heard Emma tell some poor kid at tumbling her somersaults looked like crap, so I have to watch my language." Mel darted a glance at the kitchen door, then lunged for the phone. Cradling the cell in both hands, she openly gaped at the picture of Colm. "This is him? For real?"

"For real." Sinking into the couch cushions, Monica let loose with a gusty sigh. "You see why I want to delay the inevitable a bit?"

Mel stared at the phone for a moment longer. Tapping the button to close the app, she handed the cell over. "What makes you think the inevitable is bad? Most guys would be happy to find out the woman he's interested in isn't saddled with a kid."

Wrinkling her nose, Monica gave the possibility a moment's consideration. "I don't think so," she said slowly. "For some reason, I get the feeling the kid thing is part of the appeal for him."

"Like he has a mommy fetish?"

Monica laughed, tickled by the leaps her sister's mind made. "Maybe he's looking for a new mommy for Aiden."

Melody's eyes widened as she barked a laugh. "You?"

Her sister's ready dismissal of her potential stung a little, but Monica couldn't truly disagree with the assessment. "No, not me. Definitely not me."

Motherhood had never been a part of her life plan. Marriage was a possibility, but she always saw herself more as a half of a power couple than a cozy nester couple like her sister and Jeremy. Either way, their lifestyles were a one-hundred-and-eighty-degree turnaround from the chaos they grew up in.

Jeremy was a dentist with a thriving practice and a well-respected reputation. His success allowed Mel the freedom to be a full-time mommy and artist when she felt like it. The arrangement suited them both to perfection. But Monica always saw herself as a mover and a shaker. While she might be moved to dally a bit with a smoking-hot single-dad, she wasn't the type to take on personal commitments. Sadly, she had the distinct impression Colm was the commitment sort. But she might be wrong. And what better way to get a feel for someone's preferences than a friendly little dinner date?

"You're going to do it, aren't you?"

She jerked her head up to find Melody giving her the slitty-eyed stare. "What?"

"You're going to go out with him and you're going to let the poor man go on believing my baby is yours."

The sheer dramatics had Monica rolling her eyes. "How have you never added theater to your artsy-fartsy repertoire?"

"Stage fright," Mel answered without missing a beat.

"Listen, I'm only going to have dinner with him. How often does a girl like me have a shot at a hunk like that?"

"You always sell yourself short," Mel interjected. "Some guys like the put-together-so-tight-I-squeak thing you have going on."

"You flatter me so," Monica replied with a smirk. "I promise I'll do my best to avoid the topic of kids if at all possible. I just want to see if…"

She trailed off, making a slow circle with her hand and inviting Melody to fill in the blank however she saw fit. As always, her big sis didn't let her down. "If he can make you squeak?"

"Exactly."

Melody ran her hand over her bed-rumpled hair and fell into the oversized armchair with a huff. "Well, I'd be a first-class hypocrite to begrudge you hot sex. But I'm fairly sure I'm not supposed to let you use my kid to score. There has to be a section in the mommy handbook about not using your kid as a beard."

Grinning, Monica caressed the smooth screen of her sleeping phone with the pad of her thumb. "She won't be helping me score. She'll be my convenient excuse for why this can't go on after I'm done lapping him up like a saucer of milk."

"Saucer of milk?"

"He has the most gorgeous skin."

"Either way, I'm not sure I should let you use Emma as an excuse, either. There has to be at least a subsection."

"I won't be using her, per se," Monica argued. "She'll be a teensy part. Barely any…I'm busy. He's busy. We both have jobs and…other responsibilities. Better we keep things casual, uncomplicated. Right?"

"God, you're a horrible tramp, and I'm so jealous." With the speed and agility Monica always forgot Mellow Mel possessed, her sister launched herself from the chair and landed on the couch beside her, bouncing them both. "Call him. I want to hear what he sounds like."

Monica smirked, but a flush of pleasure warmed her cheeks as the backlit screen sprung to life. "Okay, but you have to swear you won't say anything. Let me have my way with him this once, and I promise I will never let your daughter pimp me out again."

"Oh, hush. Don't say such things about my baby." She shuddered delicately. "Dial."

Monica opened her contacts list and swiped his number. As they waited for the call to go through, she turned to her sister. "I'm buying Em a fur coat and a pimp hat for her Halloween costume."

"Over my dead body."

"She'll love the hat. A great big feather and—" *Oh crêpes indeed*, she thought as a low, melodious baritone cut her off at the knees.

"Hello?" Colm repeated.

"Oh, uh, hi," she managed at last.

"Please tell me this is Monica."

"Yeah. Hi." Beside her, Melody vibrated with barely contained mirth. Monica swatted her sister, scooted away on the sofa, and tried to recover

her cool. "Yes, this is Monica."
Melody was plastered right up against her side. Luckily, Colm was quick on the uptake.
"So, this is a yes," he said briskly. "I'm taking this as a yes, because you aren't texting."
"It's a yes."
Mel grabbed her arm and gave a jiggle-squeeze of excitement. When Monica tried to reclaim the rapidly numbing limb, her sister whispered, "He even sounds hot."
Thankfully, there was a clatter and commotion on the other end of the line. After a bit of fumbling, Colm asked, "I'm sorry, did you say something?"
"No, nothing." She shot Mel a warning glance. "Uh, and yes."
"Great."
Funny how a guy could convey a kazillion things in one little word. In her head she heard relief, anticipation, a touch of cockiness, and what she hoped was lust all wrapped up in a single syllable.
"So, listen. I think we established I'm not good at this flirting thing, and I really don't want to give you a chance to rethink your yes, so I'm going to ask you a few questions, you give me your gut instinct answers. We can save up the rest of our awkward conversation for the actual date. Okay?"
Her sister, no competition for Meryl Streep's acting awards, clutched her chest with both hands and feigned an exaggerated faint, sprawling across the sofa cushions and sporting a rapturous smile. Monica didn't need a mirror to know she wore a matching one. She wished she'd beat Melody to the full-body flop.
Settling for a semi-swoon against the arm of the sofa, she closed her eyes and envisioned him propped up against the tree trunk. "Okay."
"Do you like spicy food? Like Mexican-type stuff?"
Picturing the swanky restaurant specializing in Korean-Mexican fusion she'd read about last week, she sighed. This date was definitely meant to be. "Is there anyone who doesn't?"
"Do you want me to pick you up, or would you be more comfortable meeting me someplace?"
The thoughtfulness of the question jolted her from her fantasies about Dakgalbi tacos. No pick up meant no drop off, and maybe less opportunity for post-drop off activities. "Uh, well, it doesn't really matter."
"I didn't know what your babysitting situation would be," he explained.
"Oh, well, Emma will be at my sister's." She bit off a yelp of pain when said sister's heel connected with her ribs. "I can meet you."
"Great. I know I'm used to eating earlier these days, and I'm sure

you are, too. How about we meet outside the Starbucks at Clark and Belmont at about six?"

Monica stifled a snort. Six? She was usually at work at six. And she couldn't remember exactly where the fusion place was, but she was thinking more Near North or West Town. Of course, where they ate hardly mattered. What mattered was she had a date with the hottest Saturdaddy ever to hit the Armitage Park playground. "Sounds perfect."

"I'll see you then."

The smile in his voice rang through loud and clear, spawning one of her own. "See you."

The moment she ended the call, Melody pounced. Her sister snatched the phone from her hand. "Oh my God, he sounded so hot. I need to see his picture again." She scrambled up onto her knees and sat on her heels, a dreamy sigh escaping her as the squishy couch cushion forced her to topple sideways. "I didn't know guys like this roamed around out there."

"Like unicorns?"

"The kind of unicorns that only live on Calvin Klein's estate."

"Stop ogling my date." Monica plucked the phone from her sister's grasp. "You're a married lady."

"Married, not dead. You're right about his skin. Was it really pretty up close and personal?"

"Like the man should be in a Dove commercial."

"Irish," Melody said with a sigh. "Has to be, with a name like Colm Cleary."

"A green-eyed Irishman. Imagine," Monica said with a smug smirk.

"He sure fills the Henley out well." Mel held the phone close to her face, a pensive frown bisecting her brow. "Maybe I should get Jer a couple."

Feeling generous, Monica refrained from pointing out that her beloved brother-in-law was a good four inches shorter and forty pounds lighter than Colm. Not that she was trying to sell him…well, short. Jeremy was a handsome man in his own lean and studious way. In truth, he was more the type Monica usually went for, but it wasn't every day a woman stumbled across a beast of a hottie while on a play date with her niece.

"I posted him to my friend Sarah's blog."

"What? Already?" Melody scowled at the phone. "You haven't even figured out what to wear." She gasped. "What *are* you going to wear?"

Monica opened her mouth to answer, but her sister stopped her with the hand.

"No. Nothing black, gray, or whatever boring shade of neutral Armani has declared the new white. You need color. Real color. Vibrant color."

Monica scowled, annoyed by her sister's assessment of her wardrobe options. "I don't wear vibrant color. Bright flashy things spook the traders."

"What happened to the wrap blouse I bought you for Christmas?"

Avoiding her sister's gaze, she pretended to give the question due diligence. "It's in my closet." Not a lie. The sapphire-blue length of rayon blend was somewhere in the bag of castoffs at the rear of her closet. The one she'd planned to donate to a local women's shelter. She bit the inside of her cheek as she considered the garment in question. The blouse was a pretty color, even if a bit too bright. And with the right bra, the wrap style might give the illusion of cleavage. Warming to the idea, she turned to Melody. "With a pair of black pipe-stem pants?"

Mel blinked as if she couldn't believe what she was hearing. "Pants? I thought you wanted to get laid?"

"Oops. Too soon," they heard Jeremy say a tad too loud.

Their heads swiveled in the direction of the kitchen in time to see the door swing shut again.

"And the awkwardness begins," Monica said with a giggle.

"You need to wear a skirt. A short one," Melody pronounced.

"I don't own any short skirts."

Her sister rolled her eyes. "Of course you don't, Business Barbie." Shaking her head pityingly, she unfolded herself from the couch, snagging Monica's hand as she rose. "Come on. I'm sure I have something from the pre-pregnancy collection that'll work."

Monica stutter-stepped to match her sister's pace as she allowed herself to be dragged toward the apartment's spare bedroom. "Pre-pregnancy? But that was seven years ago."

Bypassing a weaving loom she hadn't so much as dusted in months, Mel made a beeline for the closet. With a flourish, she threw open the door to reveal an Ali Baba's cave of clothing. "You're lucky skimpy never goes out of style."

* * * *

He had to stop looking down her blouse. Well, not really down her blouse, *at* her blouse. The spot where the two sides crisscrossed. Right there. And if he didn't stop gawking, she was going to notice. And here he'd been so proud of himself for walking the block and a half to La Casita without falling at her feet. If he had, he probably would have taken the opportunity to peek up her skirt.

God, he was a dog. Had he always been this desperate? Maybe not always, he reasoned. But definitely lately. He was going to have to get a handle on himself.

When he'd turned the corner and saw her standing by the coffee shop doorway, he'd almost chocked on his own tongue. Her legs were long. Supermodel fantasy long. And she was wearing a very short skirt. For one crazy second, all he could think about was her skirt. The hemline would never have escaped the nuns at his grammar school. He sent up a quick prayer of heartfelt thanksgiving for that singularly inadequate piece of fabric. For a man who'd spent the last few years jacking off to the lingerie catalogs that kept coming to his house long after his wife had died, those legs and a short skirt were a dream come true.

He'd caught a flash of disappointment in her eyes when they stepped into the restaurant's garishly festive vestibule, but she recovered with a smile tinged with a hint of sheepishness. As if she knew she'd been caught out being a little snobby. She had the good grace to be sorry, too. The tiny restaurant was packed, but he knew the owners, so they'd been seated right away. And while the table spared him the sight of those mile-long legs, the vee neck put the shallow valley of her cleavage right at eye level.

Monica glanced up from the menu. "I don't recognize some of the dishes listed here. What kind of fusion is this?"

"Fusion?" He looked at the laminated parchment as if he might cop a clue from the entrées section.

"I thought maybe there'd be an Asian influence. I hear the whole Korean-Mexican fusion thing is supposed to be awesome."

"Oh. No. Nothing fused." He flashed an apologetic smile. "It's Colombian. Authentic Colombian," he added, desperate to make the cramped restaurant seem somewhat more hip and cool.

"Oh." Color rose in her cheeks as she turned her attention to the selections again. "I assumed...You said like Mexican...I'll shut up."

Colm chuckled, charmed by her strange mix of brash and bashful. "Well, like Mexican in some ways, but a little different."

"Was Aiden's mother Hispanic?"

He should have expected the question. Not a difficult conclusion, given his son's coloring, and absolutely correct. "Yes." But he didn't want to talk about her. Or Aiden. Or anything remotely relating to Princess Clarissa and her cartoon cohorts. Leaning in close, he held her gaze. "I'd like to make a couple of rules for the evening, if you're game."

"I think I might be game." She gave him a coy half-smile. "What kind of rules did you have in mind?"

He watched in rapt fascination as she ran her finger around the rim of her glass. "No kid talk," he blurted. Colm grimaced when he saw her flinch the slightest bit. "I mean, they're great, and Aiden is the most important person in the world to me, as I'm sure Emma is for you," he continued in a rush. "But you have no idea how long it's been since I've had an adult night out. And I have to admit, even longer since I've had one with a woman." He cringed a little when her eyebrows shot upward. "I mean, like I said at the park, a date. With a woman. Not a guy. Not that there's anything wrong with that." He added the line with a nervous chuckle, and at last she cracked.

Her laugh rang out, clear and unchecked. The sound held the barest hint of rasp, but every hair on his arms rose in response. "Okay. I'm with you. No kid talk."

Relieved, he set his menu aside and reached for the IPA Especial he'd ordered. The beer was cold and crisp but did little to quench the thirst building inside of him.

"Listen, I don't want to…Like I said, it's been a long time. And I know I said I don't want to talk about the kids—and I don't—but I feel like I should be straight with you."

Monica lowered her menu but raised an eyebrow. "Okay. Be straight."

He winced at the implication but didn't take the bait. "I don't know how…involved I can get. I don't have time to catch up on laundry, much less dating, and I'd hate—"

She held up one hand to stop him. "Colm."

"Yes?"

"It's fine. Let's just…see how things go."

He exhaled loudly and turned loose a relieved smile. "Sounds good."

Returning her attention to the menu, she murmured, "As long as *you* are straight."

"Oh, I am," he assured her.

Wrapping his hand around the beer bottle, he gave her time to peruse the choices at her leisure as the familiar scents and sounds enfolded him like a warm blanket. Up until he finally gave the go-ahead on the overnights with his parents, he and Aiden had come here every Saturday night.

For the first three years of Aiden's life, Pablo and Carita had been the only family he and his son had. His own parents lived a mere thirty miles away, but disapproved of his marriage. His late wife shared no blood connection with the couple, but family ties hadn't mattered. They were the ones who'd been there for him through thick and thin. Bad and worse. Secrets and lies.

Monica placed her menu on top of his and reached for her sangria. "I think I'll let you order for me."

A rush of pure masculine pleasure pulsed through him. Leaning forward, he tapped his fingertips against the menus. "Any restrictions?"

"None whatsoever," she answered, her gaze unwavering.

Heat exploded inside him. He was on fire. Like the time Carmen teased him into biting into a habanero, but this time every inch of him burned. Particularly the inches that hadn't had the attention of a good woman in way too long. "Here we are, us grown-ups, trying our best not to humiliate ourselves." He drew his finger through the condensation on his beer bottle. "I doubt I'll pull it off."

"The evening is young," she intoned gravely, cracking herself up.

He tried not to gape like a schoolboy at the way her high, small breasts made the slinky top she wore shimmer. The bright blue color made him picture waves of water cascading over her. He could see the scene so clearly, droplets sliding down her throat and pooling at the hollow in the center. His mouth on her. Licking, sipping, tasting each tantalizing stretch of skin. His hands on her long, lithe body. Her hands on the tile walls of his shower stall. A fast-running current of water rushing along the curve of her spine. His fingers gripping her hips. Lifting. Tilting. Sinking—

"Well, if I had any doubts you were straight, you've certainly put them to rest."

The erection he'd been trying to hold at bay went from half-mast to battering ram in the blink of an eye. He jerked his head up. Frank blue eyes bore into him. He pushed the sleeves of his sweater up a little, hoping to release some of the heat building inside him, but there was no escaping. He knew she could read his every thought. And the smile curving her lips told him she liked what she saw. Thank Christ.

"I'm sorry." The words came automatically, even if the shame he expected to accompany them didn't. Parenthood made a guy a master of insincere apology.

"Part of me wants to demand you to tell me exactly what you were thinking, but the look on your face says your thoughts aren't fit for public consumption."

Every muscle in his body tensed. The tips of his ears felt like someone was taking a blowtorch to them. He reached for his beer, knowing the glass couldn't hold the fluid ounces he'd need to rehydrate his parched mouth. He gulped down a few anyway. He'd need juice to ask the questions pulsing through him. "And the other part?"

This time, Monica leaned in close, offering him a couple extra millimeters of skin. As if he needed incentive. "The other part wants you to show *and* tell."

"Oh, holy hell," he whispered. She gave him a smug smile. The struck stupid had to be showing on his face, but he was too far gone to care. "How hungry are you?"

"For food?" she countered.

Colm was waving to get the waitress's attention when the kitchen door burst open and Pablo charged out. The older man was short and almost as round as he was tall. His ever-present white apron was so stained and splattered with sauces they could have stretched the coated cotton over a frame and hung the apron in any modern art museum. The edges of his mustache drooped even as he beamed at them. He approached the table with his arms spread wide, and as Colm rose to his feet, he knew any chance he had at escape was gone.

"Co-lum, Co-lum," Pablo crowed as he wrapped him up in a bear hug, oblivious to the food spatters he was transferring to Colm's clothes. "Too long. Carita is so angry you've stayed away, she won't even come kiss you," he announced, waving the wooden spoon clutched in his hand. The exuberant man proceeded to plant a smacking kiss on each of Colm's cheeks.

The warmth and welcome he saw in his old friend's eyes trumped the urge to wipe the kisses away. Aiden could get away with refusing the show of affection, no problem, but Colm valued Pablo's friendship too much to risk insulting the man. "Pablo, this is my, uh, friend, Monica Rayburn."

Like a laser-guided missile, Pablo homed in on his date. "Mees Mon-i-ca."

Colm snorted at the man's exaggerated accent, but kept an eagle eye on the old goat. If the stories he told were only half-true, Pablo had cut quite a swath in his day.

"I ham so honored."

"You are a ham," Colm murmured.

The widening of his friend's smile told him Pablo heard and acknowledged the hit, but insults weren't about to stop him. "Why would such a bee-u-ti-ful woman waste time with this pasty, er, how you say? Galoot?"

Colm was about to point out that Pablo had lived in the States for over thirty years and knew exactly how to say everything he needed to say. Without another word, the sneaky bastard tossed his wooden spoon onto the table as if he never intended to stir a pot again and extended a hand to help Monica from her chair. "Come, I will show you. Latino men really are hot-blooded. We know how to pleasure a woman."

Clearly mesmerized by Pablo's dog and pony show, Monica placed her hand in his and rose from her seat. In her short skirt and high heels, she towered over the rotund chef, but old Pablo didn't seem to mind at all. The sneaky little bastard had a straight shot at the spot Colm had been ogling minutes ago.

"Wait a minute," Colm protested.

Pablo drew Monica's hand to his lips, then tucked her fingers securely into the crook of his arm, beaming up at her the entire time. "Come with

Pablo, sweet lady. You're too good for this potato farmer."

"Hey!" They were halfway to the kitchen door. Pablo was actually making off with his date. "Hang on a second!"

He dodged a waitress shouldering a loaded tray and ducked into the steaming kitchen in time to see Carita turn away from the counter. Plates of food in varying stages of assembly stood arrayed in front of her, the apron tied at her trim waist miraculously white.

"Look what your feckless Irishman has brought us, Carita."

The lines in Carita's work-worn face smoothed into a blank slate. They slowly reformed as brackets around her red-painted lips and a delicate fan of crinkles at the corners of her eyes. "Ah, so this is why the worthless boy has forsaken me," she said with a fatalistic shrug.

Rushing out from behind the counter, she tugged Monica's hand from Pablo's grasp and clasped her palm in both of hers. "Now I understand." Carita looked past Monica to seek him out. Their gazes met and held, and he saw all he needed to see. Affection, acceptance, understanding, and forgiveness. "But know if I were but ten years younger, he'd choose me."

He couldn't fight both of them off, so he gave in and stepped forward. Surrendering to their bullying didn't mean he was giving up his date, though. Placing a hand at the small of Monica's back, he moved in close at her side. She jolted at the contact, but didn't pull away. Instead, a delicate shiver ran through her. Colm bit the inside of his cheek as his blood began to sizzle. There'd be no early escape. They were stuck in this kitchen until they were stuffed to the gills.

Bending at the waist, he kissed Carita's cheeks with every bit as much affection as Pablo had shown him, but with more restraint and, he hoped, less slobber. "If you'd even looked at me twice, Carita, I'd choose you."

"Oh, go on." Giving him a swat with the edge of her apron, she nodded to a scarred wooden table in the corner of the kitchen. "You go sit." Shooing them along, she snapped her fingers and Pablo jumped to attention. "Get them a bottle of the Chilean chardonnay."

Knowing the effort was useless, Colm put up a token resistance. "Uh, I was drinking beer and Monica had sangria."

Carita shook her head adamantly. "No red wine. No beer." She tapped her temple, nudging them closer to the table. "I knew today would be special. As I lay in my bed last night, a thought came to me...I needed to make my Mamita's *lechona* today. Now I know I make *lechona* for you."

Shooting him a half-amused but mostly bewildered glance, Monica slid into one of the hard slat-back chairs. "Maybe we could eat in the dining room?" Colm suggested, nodding toward the swinging door. "We don't want to be in your hair."

"Ay, my hair!" Carita patted the messy knot of silver-streaked ebony piled atop her head. "You sit here. If I take my Mamita's *lechona* out there, they will stampede my kitchen."

"*Lechona*?" Monica asked, her bright eyes eager and inquisitive.

Carita clapped her hands. "Very special. Must cook all day." She nodded to the brick oven in the wall. "I put it in at four o'clock this morning, and now I serve to you."

She fired off a barrage of orders in Spanish so fast Colm could only pick out a word or two, then bustled to her ovens.

Reaching across the battered table where he'd eaten so many meals, he touched Monica's hand to get her attention. "I'm sorry. I wanted to take you someplace special, and I don't go to too many restaurants that don't give a toy with your meal." He frowned as he took in their anything-but-romantic surroundings. "I should have known they'd take over."

"This is amazing," she said, her gaze darting from point to point as she soaked up the frenzy of activity. She flipped her hand over and wrapped her fingers around his, giving them a gentle squeeze. "I gather you've known them a long time?"

"Years. They used to have a place over on the west side. I worked the neighborhood when I was fresh out of the academy." He tugged at his collar, wishing he'd opted for a shirt instead of the sweater. Between his nerves and the heat of the kitchen, he'd end up nothing but a puddle by dessert. Eager to distract her from his growing agitation, he forged ahead with his story. "Some of the gangbangers over there decided they wanted to target the non-Mexican Latinos."

"Wow. I had no idea there were such tensions between the Hispanic communities."

"Because most white people hear someone speaking Spanish and lump them all together. At least, I did." He glanced up as Pablo approached with a chilled bottle of wine and two glasses in hand. "I was nothing but a pasty Irish kid from the south side. Everyone who speaks Spanish is Mexican, right, Pablo?"

His friend set the glasses in front of them and poured the golden wine. Sets of flatware rolled in linen napkins appeared on the table. Colm turned to thank him, and was smacked upside the head. Hard. He shifted to Monica, his mustache pushed to the limits as he turned on the charm. "Run away with me, pretty lady. You deserve much better than this ignorant mick."

Colm smirked as he took a cautious sip of the wine. "Hey, I think you left some of your accent out in the dining room, a-meeee-go."

"Hush, both of you," Carita hissed, bumping her husband aside with her hip. "The poor girl is going to think she's visiting the lunatic asylum." She served them beautifully arranged plates. Rice and pork spilled out of triangles of crispy golden crust. Wedges of lime, seared tortillas, and whole red potatoes occupied the rest of the space, but the mouthwatering scent of garlic, onion, and spice made it clear they were mere supporting characters.

"Mm, Carita mia," Pablo groaned as he caught a whiff of the bounty she'd placed in front of them. Drawing his wife to his side, he lowered his eyelids and gave her a long, smoldering look. "Tell me you saved a bit for your Pablo."

Giggling like a girl, she shoved him away. "Get to work, Don Juan," she chided. "We'll leave these two to enjoy and perhaps you'll get yours later."

Monica looked up from her plate. The gleam in her bright blue eyes told him she was thinking exactly what he was thinking.

Swallowing the lump of nerves and desire knotting his throat, he raised his wine glass. "To getting bossed around."

Her eyes twinkled with mischief when she lifted her glass to touch his. She smiled sweetly as she murmured, "And here I thought you'd want to drink to getting yours later."

Chapter 3

The rest of dinner flowed as easy as the wine. Monica wondered briefly if she could order a vat of the yummy Chilean chardonnay with a spigot. Colm was as funny as he was gruff. Self-effacing, but most certainly assured. Mixed with the wine and the succulent meal, a potent combination. She had a hard time holding onto her balance as they said their goodbyes to Pablo and Carita.

The hand Colm planted to guide her made her feel both wobbly and utterly secure. The heat of his gaze made her skin prickle. As they wound their way from the kitchen to the exit, her eyes darted toward the doorway leading to the restrooms. She could grab him. Take him. Clasp his big, strong hand, yank him into the ladies' room, and press him up against the wall. Tension wafted off him like summer heat. He wanted her every bit as much as she wanted him. He was hers for the taking.

"I'll see you home."

Though the words drifted past her ear on a low, throaty whisper, she almost jumped out of her skin. His hand slid down to her hip to hold her close as he reached past her to open the restaurant door. Wetting her lips, she glanced over her shoulder as she stepped out into the crisp, clean night air. "I was hoping you would."

His warm palm landed in the small of her back again. "Did you drive?"

She wanted to do a wiggle dance to see if she could work his hand a bit lower but resisted the temptation. They'd get there soon. She had a rock solid knot of certainty balled in her gut. The same one she got when she knew the perfect time to buy or sell. This was going to happen. And they would be good together.

"I took a cab." She glanced down at the killer stilettos on her feet. "These shoes are not made for walking."

"No, but I can tell you exactly what they're made for," he murmured as he steered her toward the closest corner.

Tickled by his blunt assessment and preening a little, Monica decided to play against type and try coy on for size. "Oh? What are they made for?"

Colm huffed a laugh as he scanned the busy cross street for an available taxi. "I'd rather show than tell."

Leaning away, she smiled as his muscles tensed and automatically braced to absorb her weight. She inhaled a hit of his aftershave. Liking what she smelled, she upped the ante. "I like a little of both."

His arm snaked around her waist, holding her firmly against him as he hailed an available cab with the other. Monica wrapped her hand around his forearm. The corded muscles hidden beneath his sleeve were taut and oh-so-tempting. Dark hair. All night, she'd been catching glimpses of the silky dark hair peeking out from his cuffs. She wanted to stroke his forearm. She petted the pesky sleeve instead, eyes narrowing with smug satisfaction when the battered car coasted to a stop beside them.

Colm released her long enough to usher her into the cab and climbed in after her. She rattled off her address, and he pulled the door closed. Relaxing her head against the seat, she let her neck roll until she faced him. Lit only by the passing streetlights, he looked even more appealing than he had in dappled sunlight. Contrast suited him to a tee. Dark and light. Fierce versus fair. Predatory. Protective. Provocative. Perilous. Perfect.

She blinked, stunned by her precipitous and perplexing penchant for alliteration. Good God! What did they put in the *lechona*? He tore his gaze from the driver's identification framed in the Plexiglas partition and caught her staring. *Huh. Plexiglas partition. Score two more.*

"P words are funny, aren't they?" she blurted. A hiccup escaped. Eyes wide, she covered her mouth. "Oops." She grimaced through ineffectual fingertips. "Excuse me."

"I think maybe we've had too much…"

"No!"

Launching herself across the cracked vinyl seat, she framed his face in her hands, her fingers sinking into the luxuriant dark waves at his temples. His hair was every bit as thick and soft as she'd imagined while she'd been snapping his photograph. No way in hell was she going to let this evening be derailed by an excess of Chilean grapes and an attack of misplaced chivalry. She brushed her lips across his. More a shot across the bow than a kiss. An uncharacteristically timid opening gambit from a woman who was used to going for broke. But this time…This time she didn't want to be the pursuer. She wanted to be the one someone chased after.

"Don't," she whispered against his mouth. "Don't be sensible or chivalrous or even politically correct. Just be."

An oddly hippie-dippy sentiment. Definitely something more likely to be found in Melody's repertoire than hers, but she meant what she said. For once in her life, she didn't want to weigh risk and reward. All thoughts of strategy, angles, and outcomes went flying out the cab driver's half-open window. They rocked against the seat as the driver punched the accelerator. She caught a glimpse of a yellow light winking red and a very rude gesture made on behalf of the cross traffic. A horn blared. Colm's mouth claimed hers, and the two of them fell across the seat in a tangle of limbs.

He kissed her long and deep, letting her know their suddenly supine positioning was anything but an accident. When he pulled away at last, an arrogant smile curved his lips. He stared down at her, those eerily light eyes boring into her, pinning her to the duct tape-festooned seat. "You okay?"

"More than okay." She licked her lips, delighted to find the taste of him lingering there. She tried to peer through the window, but it was no use. She couldn't fix on a single landmark. "Should only be a couple more blocks."

"We should make the most of them."

He kissed her again, but this time the contact was slow and achingly sweet. Her body bowed, every nerve ending reaching for him, every impulse surrendering to the siren song of this unexpected tenderness. He brushed the underside of her jaw with his knuckles, his lips clinging to hers as he shifted to press his forehead to hers. "Sorry," he said gruffly.

"For what?"

He pulled back to stare down at her, but his fingers fanned across her cheek. Monica would swear she could feel each whorl of his fingertips as he mapped the slope from her temple to her cheekbone. He traced the edge of her ear, sending a shiver down her spine. "I'd forgotten how soft a woman's skin is," he whispered, almost to himself. "You smell so good. Fresh and flowery. Not like socks, gummy candy, and sour milk."

She laughed. "Thank you."

He winced, pushing himself into a sitting position as the cab started to slow. Ever the gentleman, he pulled her up, then made a valiant effort to erase the evidence of their backseat tumble by tugging ineffectually at her skirt and taking a brusque swipe at the front of her blouse. She jerked at the ungainly contact, and he yanked his hand away as if he'd been scalded. "Wow. I…" He pressed the heel of his hand to one eyebrow and blew out a breath. "You have no idea how close you came to getting a spit bath."

She shuddered at the thought. How many times had she watched Melody try to fix Emma's appearance with a few swipes, tugs, and licks? "Actually,

I have a good idea."

But his grim frown and creased forehead told her ribbing him about his paternal impulses wouldn't be the smartest tactic if she had any hopes of swapping more spit with him. The driver swerved closer to the line of cars parked in front of her brownstone, and she took the opportunity to scoot closer to Colm. Placing her hand on his chest, she noted the agitated rise and fall of his ribcage and pressed the center of her palm over his thrumming heart.

The cab jerked to a stop, but she stared straight into his eyes. "Pay the man," she said in a voice little more than a husky rasp, "so we can go upstairs, and I can show you exactly how I like mine done."

Colm dispatched the cab with heartening efficiency as she headed for her door. Keys dangling from the retractable latch, she watched as he climbed the stone steps, his hands tucked in his pockets, his gaze taking in the building's narrow facade.

"Nice place."

"Buying was a good investment." She twisted the key and bumped the solid mahogany door open with her hip.

He quirked an eyebrow as he stepped into the entry, taking in the refinished parquet floors and gleaming woodwork. "You get it as a fixer-upper?"

She laughed at his supposition. "Do I look like the fixer-upper type?"

Colm let out a low whistle of appreciation as he ran his hand over the scrollwork at the foot of the banister. "Hog heads must pay well."

Monica tossed her purse onto the entry table and added a little extra sway to her step as she sauntered past him. His gaze dropped to the hand she placed on the rail. She climbed three steps, trailing her fingers along the polished wood he'd found so impressive, then pivoted to face him.

"I think you'll find what you really want to see up here."

He followed. Of course he followed. He was a man and she was a woman wearing a short skirt and nose-bleed heels. The promised land lay at the top of those stairs, and she'd be damned if she was up for playing tour guide. She wanted to be staring up at the crown molding, not discussing it. Five steps from the top. She tugged at the bow tied at her side and the slick satin panels of her blouse swung open.

Though Colm was behind her, she heard his sharp intake of breath and made a mental note to thank Melody again for the shirt. The second she reached the top step, she shrugged and the slippery fabric slithered from her shoulders. Dropping her gaze, she sneaked a quick peek to be sure the ridiculously expensive excuse for a bra she wore was doing its job. The tiny marvel of engineering had the girls pushed up and plumped like pillows. The pale blue lace edging the demi-cups barely concealed her nipples, but didn't seem to be as much of an issue at the moment. They were hard and aching, practically begging to be released from their borderline inadequate confines.

Glancing over her shoulder, she found Colm staring at the puddle of vibrant blue draped across his shoes. He exhaled a semi-reverent "Jaysus" which wiped away any lingering doubts she might have had about getting down and dirty with this delicious daddy.

Tonight they'd both get exactly what they needed, and tomorrow they'd return to their lives, both a little better for the release. A feline smile spread across her face as she bent an arm to unhook the clasp on the bra, but his warm hand covered hers. She waited, expecting a request to slow down, or speed up, or maybe even leave the damn thing on, but nothing came. Nothing but heat.

Her blouse slid down a couple of steps. His chest was pressed against her nearly bare back. The sweater he wore was thin and soft, but made her skin itch anyway. To be touched. For the friction of his body rubbing against hers. The thought of feeling the maddening lace covering her nipples scrape the hair on his chest almost turned her knees to jelly. She started to spin toward him, but Colm planted his hands on her waist to stop her.

"Don't."

The gruff command was softly spoken but effective. She let her arm fall to her side and waited, relishing the delicious anticipation stirred by his warm breath moving her hair. His fingers curled around the curve of her hipbone as he nuzzled her shoulder. There shouldn't have been anything mind-blowing about the tender kiss he placed on her shoulder blade, but this man with his hot, moist breath and impossibly soft lips knew things. Things she didn't even know. Like the fact that a single fingertip trailing along the crevice of her thigh packed the power to make her mewl like a kitten. Things she was more than happy to learn.

He released his hold on her hip and hooked a finger under the clasp of her bra, pulling her to the edge of the stair. He slipped his other arm around her waist and pulled her tighter against him. The stairs offset the difference in their heights. The hard ridge of his erection pressed against her ass. He rested his cheek on her shoulder and exhaled long and slow.

"I haven't slept with a woman in four years."

Instantly, her brain started making calculations. Aiden was five. Four years. There'd been someone since his late wife, but not anyone who'd stuck. Good. The last thing they needed to do was get stuck. But four years? What kind of guy went so long between...bouts? Was this celibacy purposeful? Circumstance? The result of some kind of vitamin deficiency?

"I, uh, I didn't want the complications," he said, cutting into her thoughts. "And, you know, when you have a kid, everything is a complication."

"Right." She blurted the word as if she had a clue, but truly she was more focused on the relief his explanation unleashed. No complications she could do. "Yeah. Me either. I don't want"—she sucked in a breath when he released the catch on her bra—"complications."

"I can stay for a while tonight, but I'll have to leave. I always pick Aiden up early."

Okay. He was laying ground rules. Ground rules were good. She tried for cool as her bra straps started a slow slide over her shoulders and down her arms. "That's fine."

There. That should do the trick. We can go for the wham-bam and call it a night, or we can go a little more. No pressure. No expectations. Well, almost no expectations. She was fairly sure she'd explode if he didn't touch her soon. Colm slipped both hands up under her loosened bra to cup her breasts. She was tempted to make a crack about how he could probably handle the job one-handed, but his thumbs grazed her pebble-hard nipples, and she was off like a shot.

"Hey!" He grasped at air as she started down the hall toward her bedroom.

She shook the bra from her arms and reached for the side zip on her skirt. "Hurry. You just told me we didn't have all night."

Colm caught up to her in the bedroom doorway, his hand closing around her elbow as she struggled with the recalcitrant zipper. "Hey," he repeated, his voice gentler. "I didn't mean we had to rush."

Finally, the plastic teeth gave way and she yanked the tab down. "You're not the only one who's been on hiatus," she said, wriggling the snug skirt down and hoping he'd be too distracted by the lacy panties to notice the shimmy of her thighs. "Been a while for me, too." Kicking the skirt aside, Monica forced herself to stand up straight and tall. After all, she wanted this man here in her bedroom, and now she had him. This was not the time to show even a shred of weakness. Forcing a confident smile, she reached for the hem of his sweater. "But one of us is wearing way too many clothes."

Colm sprang into action—toeing off his shoes, tugging the sweater over his head as she pushed up from the bottom, and fumbling with his belt as he teetered from side to side, temporarily blinded but gratifyingly enthusiastic. Monica took a moment to run her hands over his shoulders. His skin was smooth as cream and stretched taut over surprisingly well-developed muscles. A smattering of golden freckles marked days spent in the sun. Black hair curled between his pecs and smoothed into a streak of silk. The line disappeared into his waistband. She ran her thumb around one flat brown nipple, smiling as the skin puckered and his stomach muscles rippled. She planned to follow the trail of hair to the very source.

He'd opened his belt and the top button on his jeans but stopped there. His hands landed on her hips again. He pulled her close and slid one down over her ass. "I feel like I ought to apologize. This is already so much better than pay-cable-induced self-flagellation. I don't know how long I'll be able to hold out."

Monica laughed, hopefully chasing some of his oh-so-earnest tension away. "Pay-cable-induced self-flagellation?"

"My friend James came up with the terminology."

Pressing her palm to his cheek, she smiled up at him. "Okay. Well, I bought a whole box of condoms. We can keep practicing until we get the hang of things again."

* * * *

Colm swooped in and kissed her. Hard and deep. Slow and thorough. The way he'd been imagining kissing her all day. He had abso-friggin-lutely no idea what he'd done to deserve the luck he was having, but he wasn't about to look a gift horse in the mouth.

Oh God, her mouth. Her mouth was incredible. Salty and sassy. Quick to smile and so fucking kissable he'd thought about little else since they'd squared off on the playground. He'd spent half of breakfast imagining he was swirling his tongue around hers like he swirled his pancakes through their pool of syrup. Why did she taste so sweet when everything they'd eaten had been spicy?

Needing desperately to get to the rest of her, he broke the kiss with a groan. He nibbled his way across her cheek and nuzzled her ear. She sighed, and he ducked his head, on a mission to find the pulse he'd spotted throbbing away beneath her jaw. He'd watched that spot all through dinner, fascinated by the tiny vulnerability. Her breasts flattened against his chest. They were small, yes, but he'd never been the type to chase after the overly-endowed girls. He left those for guys like James, who were fixated on a woman's cup size. Monica's breasts were pale and upturned, her nipples unapologetically pink and hard as cherry pits. He couldn't wait to sink his teeth into them. But first things first.

He found the pulse in her throat with unerring precision. Her breathing stuttered when he ran his tongue over the spot, and he couldn't help but smile. Her heart pounded against his chest, but he preferred the feel of that tiny thrum on his tongue. Savoring the taste of her heartbeat, he drew gently on the skin, half-tempted to leave his mark there. Instinct seized him by the throat. He wanted to mark her. Claim her. Make her his, even if only for this one night and nothing more.

The lace of her panties scratched against his palms. Cupping her spectacular ass in both hands, he bent his knees and lifted her off her feet. Their mouths met and fused. Their tongues tangled and swirled as she wrapped her long, long legs around his hips. The thin barrier of lace did little to contain the heat of her arousal. The crotch of her panties was wet. He felt the heat of her above the open buckle of his belt and called himself a thousand names for not having the balls to strip down further. He staggered toward the bed centered on the far wall, alternately cursing and blessing every step depending on which parts rubbed against what as they went. At last, his knees hit the edge of the mattress and they collapsed in a tangled heap.

"Sorry," he huffed, easing some of his weight off her.

"No. No sorries." She grabbed his upper arms and pulled him down again. "God, you feel good on me." She wriggled beneath him. "Lose the jeans. Lose everything."

For a guy used to issuing orders, Colm was surprised to find he was more than happy to follow hers. Leveraging himself off the bed, he peeled off his jeans and briefs in one motion, stooping only to make sure he slid his socks off with the rest. When he straightened, he found she'd pushed onto the bed and was laying with one knee propped. She slid her fingertips teasingly along the top of her panties.

"I have a thong. Matches the bra," she said with a sly smile. "This was so…impromptu. I didn't have time to do much in the way of…prep work." She dragged the center of the low-slung panties down to show a hint of curling brown hair. The elasticized lace snapped into place. "I hope you don't mind the natural look."

There was no containing his growl. Years of pain, anger, loneliness, and yes, self-flagellation, erupted from him like a burst of rock and lava shooting from the mouth of a long-dormant volcano. Colm was worried the force of his desire might blow the top of his head off. A simple crook of her finger obliterated every reasonably non-Neanderthal thought from his brain.

Sliding one arm under her leg as he dove for her, he hauled her knee up and planted his face in that sweet, damp triangle of baby-blue lace. He heard her gasp, but nothing on heaven or earth could or would stop him from getting a taste of her. Not now. Not when she was wiggling beneath him, her fingers threaded in his hair and her hips rising up off the bed. He dragged his tongue along the seam of her panties, every fiber of his being attuned to her breathy gasps and pants. She whispered his name and his dick grew harder. Inhaling deeply, he drank in the unmistakable perfume of a woman profoundly turned on. Thankful he didn't seem to be the only one riding the knife's edge, he pressed his aching erection into the mattress and his tongue to the sweet spot beneath the thatch of *au natural* she'd worried might offend him. He proceeded to devour her, kiss by kiss and lick by lick.

"Off," she panted, planting her heels on the mattress and arching up to meet each stroke of his tongue. "Take them off."

He caught a bit of the thoroughly-wet lace between his teeth and gave a playful tug. "No."

Monica moaned, her fingers tightening in his hair until he feared she might tear it out from the roots. Pleasure. Pain. His scalp prickled. His dick throbbed. Actually throbbed. He'd probably end up with some kind of contact burn from humping her sheets, but he couldn't stop. Wouldn't. Not until he made her come at least once. He had to get there before he allowed himself to do anything else, or he'd pop off like a teenager. And the second those panties were gone, he was going to be inside her. Deep inside her. So deep. His self-control slipping with each passing thought, he hooked a finger in the leg of her panties and yanked them aside. Damp light-brown curls glistened with her arousal. She spread her legs wider in the kind of bold, blatant invitation a man would have to be dead to resist. And he had a helluva lot of life left in him.

He drove her up fast and furious, each kiss, lick, and nip calculated to push her straight over the edge. He slipped a finger into her hot, tight wetness and groaned as she closed around him. Using the single digit to ground him, he focused all his attention on her clit. Flying high on her moans and whispers, he drew the sensitive flesh into his mouth, alternately swirling and sucking until, at last, she spasmed around him.

He opened his eyes and lifted his head, not wanting to miss a moment of watching cool, confident Monica Rayburn's unraveling. She rode his hand hard, taking him in short, swift strokes, matching the staccato pace of her breathing. Christ, she was incredible. Every bit of her. Peachy-pink skin. Summer-blue eyes. Tumbled brown hair. Her pretty panties were twisted obscenely to the side. He could see where the tension caused the waistband to cut cruelly into her hip and stomach, but she seemed oblivious. Thank God. He didn't want to do anything to detract from her absolute pleasure. The second her jerky movements slowed, he pulled his hand away.

She whimpered gratifyingly, then hissed a breath of relief when he stripped the mangled panties down her legs. Sitting on his heels, he took two long, hopefully steadying breaths. He ran his hand through his hair, massaging the tender spots on his scalp. He gazed down at her sprawled on the bed, all loose-limbed and flushed.

"I got a little carried away," he confessed, his voice so husky he barely recognized himself. He drew her underwear down her legs and tossed them aside. "But I'm not sorry."

A feline smile spread across her face as she shook her head from side to side. The gesture was a lazy nope and a shrug all wrapped up in one beautifully satiated package. Pride hit him square in the chest and exploded, flowing through him like the contents of some kind of sexual water balloon. He'd done this to her. He was the guy who turned this poised, purposeful woman into a rag doll.

"Not sorry, either," she murmured. "Do some more."

He crawled up over her long, lithe body, keenly aware of how perfectly they matched up. His shin slid along hers. Smooth, pliant thighs pressed against his, urging him to settle in the spot he wanted to be more than he wanted his next breath. But one of them had to be sensible. He planted his hands on either side of her head and pushed up even as she tried to drag him down. His dick grazed the soft, wet curls between her legs. The minimal contact was all he needed. The red-hot flow of lust her order unleashed swept away the last vestiges of his control.

"Condom," he managed to grunt.

Monica jerked her pointy little chin toward the nightstand and shot him a sly smile. "Drawer."

He lunged for the handle, ignoring the tickle of her fingernails running down his spine. Her hands closed over his ass as he located his quarry. She squeezed, and he tore the box nearly in two. With a combination of fumbling fingers, sheer determination, and the help of his teeth, he managed to separate a package from the string and tore the wrapper open. The condom landed with a soft *thunk* on Monica's collarbone.

"Talented man," she cooed, recovering the coveted ring of latex. "Need some help with this?"

He plucked the condom from her fingers. "No!" Squeezing his eyes shut, he inhaled through his nose. He had to blink twice to bring her into focus. "I can't. I'm so…if you touch me—"

Monica interrupted him by lifting off the pillows and kissing him square on the mouth. "Let's bust your cherry again and get it over with."

"My cherry?" he asked, mortified.

She fixed him with a grave stare. "If you were a woman, we'd call you born again." When he failed to come up with any kind of response, she laughed and kissed him once more. "Stop worrying so much. We'll take this one as a mulligan, and you can impress me with your skills again later."

Wetting his parched lips, he searched those clear blue eyes for signs of mockery. "Really?"

Her smile softened. "Really." Relaxing into the nest of pillows, she sighed as she ran her hand down the center of his chest. "Trust me, I'm not nearly through with what I want to do with you."

Biting down on his bottom lip, he looked anywhere but at her as he stroked the condom into place. Eyes locked on one of the spindles on the headboard, he settled into the cradle of her hips with a long exhale. Monica trailed her fingers from his ass to the nape of his neck, cradling the back of his head in her palm. Finally, she reached between them to guide him home. She lined him up at the entrance to her slick, sweet channel, then drew her hand aside, leaving the next move entirely up to him.

He claimed her hand, lacing his fingers through hers, and pressing them into the pillow beside her head. Bracing his weight on his elbows, he dredged up the courage to meet her eyes as he pressed into her.

"Jesus, Monica," he whispered when the heat of her enveloped him.

He managed to sink the rest of the way without completely losing his shit. Seated deep inside her, he took a moment to draw a shuddering breath, but pausing did no good. Her muscles tightened around him, and he was shredded. Toast. A mindless machine stuck on full speed ahead. She raked her nails down his back, and he almost howled. Or maybe he did. He made some sort of noise when his balls drew up tight, but he wasn't exactly sure how the groan came out. In his head it was more of a roar, but he'd lost all connection with reality the moment she squeezed his ass and pulled him in deeper.

"Oh, Christ, I'm coming." He ground the words out from between clenched teeth, half-hoping he could hold off, but knowing he couldn't. His climax hit him like a freight train. He started to come, and kept on coming. So hard it almost hurt.

Almost.

It felt so incredibly good to be fucking an actual honest-to-god woman instead of his fist. The orgasm packed a punch. Almost over the edge into punishment. But pain was impossible to quantify when he was buried so deep inside her. Monica. The woman who didn't bat an eyelash over his son playing with a doll. One who drank Chilean chardonnay and flirted outrageously with plump little chefs.

And she was a mom, so she knew exactly how hard an evening with no kid talk could be on a parent. A mom who understood why he wouldn't be staying for breakfast. He'd found possibly the only woman in the world with no expectations beyond one incredible night where they could both be unencumbered, unfettered, uninhibited adults. Best of all, she'd kissed him sweetly and promised him a mulligan, because she bought a whole box of condoms and wasn't nearly done with him yet.

This had to be the luckiest day of his life.

Chapter 4

Monica blinked up at the ceiling. Her cleaning service was getting lazy about dusting the corners. The room was covered in cobwebs.
"Are you okay?"
Jolted by the deep voice coming from the pillows beside her. She blinked once. Twice. Huh. What do you know? Her ceiling was clean as a whistle.
Turning her newly sharpened focus on Colm, she let a lazy smile curve her lips. "Oh, yeah. I'm fine."
He chuckled and turned onto his side facing her, one big hand splayed across her belly. She glanced down at his fingers, startled by both the intimacy of the gesture and how very right the caress felt. The heel of his hand rested in the hollow of her hipbone. The very tip of his middle finger traced the line opposite. His palm was warm and soothing.
Meeting his eyes again, she lifted a lazy brow. "You?"
He collapsed as if she'd left him boneless. "Couldn't be better."
She stared at him, feeling more than a little smug about the sheer masculine beauty stretched out beside her. His cheek pressed against the impossibly pale skin inside his bicep. She almost growled with territorial jealousy when he wrapped his forearm over his head and buried his fingers in his own hair. She'd mussed his hair until it reached this level of rumpled perfection. Monica batted his hand toward the headboard and performed a minor contortion to claim the thick, dark waves again. "Oh, I bet you could," she murmured, finger-combing those waves until they rippled over his ear.
A crease appeared between those inky black brows. "Bet I could what?"
His frown gave her the strength to overpower the part of her brain mired in post-coital stupor.
"Be better." Lifting one shoulder in a shrug, she fixed him with a pointed stare. "You said you couldn't."

This time, he laughed. Not a chuckle or rumble, or even a chortle. This was a full-on belly laugh. She loved hearing him let loose. Even more, she loved the way his contentment inspired him to trace slow, sensuous little circles over her own belly.

"I realize you made a massive investment in latex, but give a guy five minutes."

He flipped onto his back, taking his deliciously warm hand with him. The bastard.

"I'm only making sure you're prepared to live up to your…promises."

She must have struck a sore spot because he turned to look at her, his green eyes clear and his expression sober.

"I always keep my promises."

Carefully treading into what appeared to be a touchy area, Monica decided to keep things light by being a bit touchier in her own way. Without breaking eye contact, she marshaled the power of her yoga-pilate'd core and rolled up onto him. "I like that in a man."

Colm sucked in a sharp breath. "I, uh, I need to take care of old business before we can move on to a new round."

One hand planted beside his head, she swooped in and stole a soft, sucking kiss. "Hurry."

She struck what she hoped was a semi-alluring pose as he walked away. The second the bathroom door closed behind him, she stole a glance in the mirror above her bureau and groaned long and low. Unless the guy had a fetish for Medusa-haired chicks who got their make-up tips from copying old pictures of Courtney Love, the chances of pulling off either sensual or alluring were somewhere between slim and none.

She gave her hair a quick rake and ran a dampened fingertip under her eyes, hoping to wipe away the worst of the mascara smudges. The sound of water running in the sink caught her attention. This was her house. Her bathroom. A few feet away, she had every weapon a woman needed to repair even the worst ravages. Casting a longing glance at the closed door, she ran her tongue over her teeth and cringed. She needed to move fast and decisively.

The second the door swung open, she sprang from the bed. "Back in a sec," she murmured, hiding behind her hair as she ducked past him. Three minutes later, she emerged—hair combed, teeth brushed, and make-up smudges removed.

The second she slid into the bed, Colm hooked one arm around her waist and hauled her flush against him. "I appreciate the effort, but I really liked the way you looked."

Giving her lashes an innocent flutter, she asked, "How's that?"

He dipped his head and captured her mouth. The kiss started slow and sweet but ended so mind-bendingly hot, she wondered how she'd ever thought the word "sweet" could apply. He gave her a half-second to catch her breath, but no more. This time, his tongue swept into her mouth. Demanding its due. When he relinquished her at last, her breath came in short, soft puffs. They bounced off him and washed over her, tantalizing her damp lips.

"You looked like you'd been fucked," he whispered against her damp lips. "But that's okay." He trailed hot, open-mouthed kisses down her throat. When he reached the base, he nuzzled the little notch between her clavicles and dipped his tongue into the hollow. Her breath caught and held as he lifted his head to look her straight in the eye. "This time, I'll make sure you look like you've been well and truly fucked."

His crude language both shocked and thrilled her. Fisting her hands in his hair, she pulled him to her mouth once more. Lips, teeth, tongues. Within seconds, her entire body was inflamed. She ground against every hard bit of him, and there were a lot of those. Thighs. Hips. The rock-solid ridge of his cock. There might also have been a moment when she humped his arm, but neither of them felt the need to acknowledge the act of desperation.

His hands were everywhere. Big and strong, gentle but coaxing. He covered every bit of her body, stroking, shaping, and testing. Ticklish spots were noted. The ones that made her moan and writhe exploited. And where his hands led, his mouth followed. By the time he wedged his wide shoulders between her thighs, she was already a quivering mess of do-me-now-damn-it, but, Lord, there was no way she was about to tell him to stop. Not when he was nuzzling and kissing her. He was the type of man who appreciated women even in those messy, undignified, not-so-perfectly groomed moments. Exactly her type. He brushed the tip of his tongue over her clit as she cried out.

"Yes?"

The husky question struck a chord deep inside her. The simplicity reverberated through her. Yes. God, yes, she wanted this. Wanted him. Couldn't conceive of a world where "no" might be an option. But she could barely muster a grunt, much less a definitive answer. He flicked the sensitive flesh with his tongue again. He looked up at her, hitting her full force with his glass-green gaze.

"Say yes, Monica, because I don't plan to stop until I make you come again."

She wet parched lips. "Then I can have my turn again?"

"Greedy?"

Was there anything hotter than being challenged by a hot man? Hell no.

And like the gambler she was, Monica had every intention of getting the most out of the winning hand she'd been dealt. Smiling, she groped through the tangle of sheets until she unearthed the string of foil-wrapped condoms crackling beneath them. "I'm in an overstock situation."

He snatched the string from her grasp. "I think I can help with reduction, but I can't promise an inventory blowout."

"I could promise a blow out," she suggested.

Colm groaned and lowered his head. Warm lips grazed tender skin. He traced the crease of her thigh with a long, lazy stroke of his tongue. "Promises like that won't help your overstock issue."

Wrapping her hands around his biceps, she gave an ineffectual tug. "Perhaps we can combine the warm-up activities."

Almost immediately, his level of resistance dropped. "Yeah?"

"Yeah." She flashed a saucy smile as inducement to surrender to the tug. He needed a little more encouragement. Opportunist that she was, Monica ran her hands over every rippling muscle she could reach as he levered himself over her. She pressed her fingertips to his flat nipples, running her hands down his ribcage. The contrast between the crisp hair on his chest and the unspeakably smooth skin stretching down his sides and around his back was mesmerizing.

"What did you have in mind?"

His voice was thick and more than a little raspy. Knowing she could turn him on like this intoxicated her. Emboldened, she slid one hand down to encircle the stiff length of his cock. His stare was intense. Desire wafted off them like waves of heat rising from summer-scorched pavement. She licked her lips. Slowly. Deliberately. Unabashedly proud of the way his eyes darkened and grew heavy-lidded. She bushed a kiss over the dusting of golden freckles on his collarbone, then gave his shoulders an I-mean-business shove.

"On your back, big guy."

The moment he complied, she shimmied up to the head of the bed and swung a leg over. His long-drawn groan of appreciation only added fuel to her fire. He grasped her hips, trying to pull her down to his mouth, but she resisted. She mustered every ounce of womanly pride she had, and gave herself a little pep talk. She was on top. This was her show, and she was going to enjoy every second of this interlude. And to her way of thinking, she definitely won out in terms of the better view.

His torso was lean and hard, his hips narrow. His cock jutted from a nest of inky-black curls. The man was a study in contrasts. Diamond-cut planes covered in soft, supple skin the color of fresh cream. Black hair, white skin. Big, masculine beyond a doubt, and a little rough around the edges, but unflinching in his defense of his little boy's right to love a doll.

He was also funny, modest, quick-witted, and gave off an air of competence that made a woman want to curl up in his lap and let him handle all the pesky details of life. All in all, he was dangerous. Very dangerous. Because Colm was the kind of man any woman with half a brain would fall for hard and fast. If she was the type to fall at all. Plus, she had a whole brain and a big, fat lie of omission hanging over her head.

"For the love of God, you're killing me," he said, jerking her out of her thoughts by giving her hips another, more forceful, tug.

"Oh. Sorry," she said, a nervous laugh escaping her. Her cheeks flamed as she ran her hands down his chest, over his hips, and gripped the taut muscle of his thighs. "I was admiring the view."

"I'm enjoying it myself," he said gruffly. "But something's gotta give. Do I need to count down from three or something?"

Laughing, she took hold of his bobbing erection and lowered herself until she was poised with her mouth over him, but her butt was stuck safely up in the air. She stroked him once. Twice. Her heart fluttered with anticipation when she spotted the pearl of moisture gathering at the swollen tip of him. Striking quick and sure, she treated him to the same kind of glancing swipe of the tongue he'd used to tease her. His hips bucked and his fingers tightened on her, their blunt tips pressing into the hollow of her hipbones. He used his broad palms to spread the cheeks of her ass.

Not bothering to draw breath, she took him deep with the first stroke. He retaliated by running his thumbs along the crevice of her bottom and thrust his tongue into her pussy. Her control snapped. She drew her knees apart and allowed him to pull her down onto his mouth. He greeted her with hot, hungry swipes of his tongue. Those wicked fingers played along her ass and his tongue slid through her wetness, parting her wider, opening her up for the taking. Monica tried to give as good as she got, but the man had talent. Concentrating proved difficult when he was tormenting her with maddening flicks of his tongue, pushing her higher with bold, brash strokes, pausing to hear her whimper. And whimper she did. Those teasing fingertips tested her boundaries. Thank God her mouth was full. Otherwise she might have confessed she had no boundaries. She might have said she was his for the taking. Anything. Everything.

She came hard, the orgasm slamming into her so fast she almost screamed. But she couldn't. All she could do was pant and puff, groaning her pleasure as he continued to take his. She was saved from total embarrassment by the silken smoothness of his thick, hard cock. The man felt so incredible, and the pleasure he unleashed in her only redoubled her determination to push him to the brink of madness. His muscles trembled with barely contained restraint. His flesh was hard and hot. She traced the thick vein down the length of him and moaned. When she felt the telltale ripple of his climax, she took him deeper.

Beneath her, Colm yanked her up. His cock sprang from her mouth with a damp pop. Gasping with shock and more than a little outrage, she lost her balance when he gripped her hips and pushed her toward the foot of the bed. She braced her hands seconds before she face-planted on the mattress. On her hands and knees, she twisted her head to glare at him.

Somehow, he'd wriggled out from under her and was on his knees. She wanted to complain about the abrupt transition, but the hard, hot length of him was pressed against the crease of her bottom. He felt so wickedly delicious, she lost all will to protest. The sound of ragged breathing and ripping foil told her everything she needed to know about his intentions. Closing her eyes, she lowered her cheek to the bed and tipped her hips up. She felt him fumbling to get the condom in place. Smiled when he cursed softly under his breath, and let loose with an unabashed moan when he ran the flat of his hand from the base of her spine to her nape, essentially holding her pinned to the bed. He pushed against her entrance and took complete control in one powerful thrust.

"Grab the rail."

Monica opened her eyes, but the order didn't quite compute. "Wha?"

He drew back and pushed into her with such force, she scooted a few inches toward the end of the bed. "Hang onto something," he ground out.

In a daze, she slid her hands out from under her cheek and pressed both palms to the footboard, bracing herself for another powerful thrust. Instead, he withdrew to the point where he was barely inside her, then reached around to cup her sex. "Okay?" he asked, his middle finger gliding over her super-sensitized flesh.

"God, yes."

"I'm not hurting you?"

"No. Please...."

The entreaty in her tone must have done the trick, because in the next moment he was driving into her, setting a relentless pace matched only by the skillful strokes of his fingertips. Her hands gripping the rail, she hung on as he pushed them both closer to the edge. And, finally, over into bliss.

Her hair spilled over her shoulder, curtaining her face as she stared down at the polished hardwood floor. She gasped and panted, each inhalation a desperate grab for air, every exhale a testament to the waves of pleasure he'd given her. They lay there, Colm draped over her like a blanket. He was heavy, and a little sweaty, but she didn't mind. She could feel the thrum of his heart beating against her shoulder blade. His breath cooled the imprint of his hand on her neck. He pressed a sweet kiss to the curve of her ear.

* * * *

Colm blinked, hoping a little clarity might kickstart his brain. No-go. Last night, he'd laid in his bed alone, a half-hearted erection in his hand, trying to decide if he had the energy to jack off. Thank God he hadn't, because tonight he'd had two of the most intense orgasms of his life.

A full minute passed. He tried the blinking thing again. A little dazzled, he told himself he was only caught up in the moment. When the haze cleared, he'd be able to lump this encounter in with others he'd had in the day.

Nope. His mind was officially blown.

He tried to remember the days when he didn't have to weigh the chance to get off against his energy level. The days when his dick rarely came off the loser. Scrambling through his memories, he tried to remember if there was a time when he felt this physically…in tune with anyone. Carmen? Any of the women he'd slept with before he met her?

For the life of him, he couldn't remember ever feeling this raw. This free. From the moment he first saw her at the playground, he'd been drawn to Monica. Throughout dinner, he'd tried to convince himself there was physical attraction and nothing more. He wasn't sure calling it a physical thing made the pull better or worse. He didn't want a one-time encounter with a complicated woman to be the yardstick he used to measure any future encounter he might have.

This attraction was more than physical. He liked her laugh. Loved her quick wit and curious nature. Wanted to know more about her. Why did she pile ten thousand pillows on her bed? Did she sleep with all those pillows, or one? Did Emma crawl in with her late at night? How did she feel about pancakes? Was she really cool with his son playing with dolls? Would he like her any less if she wasn't?

Colm shook himself from his stupor and pushed up on his hands, relieving her of some of his weight, and giving himself some much-needed distance. Thoughts like these weren't going to do either of them any good. They'd agreed on one night to be grown-ups. The last thing he wanted was added complications, and he knew better than anyone no one came with more built-in insanity than a single parent. He needed to stay present. Naked. Spent—for the time being. And grateful.

He dropped a soft kiss to the sharp angle of her shoulder blade. "Sorry. Got a little carried away."

"Don't apologize. Lay down."

Her bossy tone made him smile. If there was anything sexier than a woman who knew her own mind, he didn't know what. He gave her a little more of his weight, but not all. No sense in breaking her in half when they had ten unused condoms at their disposal. Grimacing, he remembered he needed to get rid of the one they'd used. He forced himself to pull away again. "I'll be right back. Don't move."

By the time he returned, she had moved. But not much. Monica lay with her head at the foot of the bed, but she was face-up and no longer hung suspended. The sheet was wound tight around one long leg. Torn condom wrappers littered the playing field, their unused compatriots trapped under her thigh. Her cheeks were pink from the head rush, her hair was a tangled mess. In short, she'd never looked more appealing. Sliding into the rumpled bed, he propped himself on his side and stared down at her, storing the image away for future use. She ran her toes up his shin. Colm stared at her foot, transfixed. It was like the rest of her—slim, polished, and deceptively delicate looking. He'd bet good money she could kick some major ass with one pale, slender foot.

"Do you like pancakes?" The question popped out. Why? Why did he ask her? Would she think his quest for knowledge was an invitation? Worse, an expectation? He held his breath, waiting for her answer and hoping for some indication on how to proceed.

She shrugged. "Are there people who don't?"

Her easy answer was exactly what he needed. He let his breath go in a whoosh, trying to ignore the niggling pang of disappointment tweaking his gut. "I'm sure there have to be."

"If there are, I don't know any." She shifted onto her side facing him and propped her head on her hand. "Why? Are you hungry? We've had a very…active evening. Do I need to refuel you?"

Thankful for the distraction, he rubbed his hand over his stomach. "Hm. I could probably use a snack." Cocking his head to the side, he cautiously asked, "Do you cook?"

She laughed outright, her blue eyes dancing with amusement and a glint of challenge. "Do I look like I *can't* cook?"

"I, uh…" He swallowed hard, pulled a pained face, and fell onto his back. "Boy, I stepped right into the trap, didn't I? Is there a correct answer?"

Laughing, Monica rolled onto him. Her cheek landed on his chest, her hand settling low on his belly. She rested there for a second. She seemed to have a knack for becoming perfectly still as she gathered her resources. Maybe her ability to bounce back was some kind of Jedi mom trick. Something women learn in order to get through those months of being kicked and punched from the inside out.

"I actually love to cook," she said simply. "I don't get a chance to do a real meal as often as I should."

He knew exactly what she meant. Most nights, it was all he could do to resist the lure of fast food. He'd spent years pushing his skills beyond dumping fish sticks onto a tray and praying they'd cook through before Aiden lost all interest in nourishment and went straight into overtired kid meltdown. A part of him was convinced he'd never known true love until the day Carita had given him a slow cooker and a recipe book.

Monica jolted him from his reverie by giving his stomach a couple of firm pats. "I can, however, handle pancakes. I think. I can't really remember the last time I shopped."

Horrified by the implication, he stared after her as she crawled off him and over the side of the bed. "I wasn't hinting."

She ran her hands through her hair, but there was no restoring order. "No? Sounded like a desperate plea to me."

He swung his legs off the mattress. "I swear, it wasn't."

Hips swaying and a sassy smile curving her lips, she sashayed toward the line of clothing strewn across her bedroom floor. She shot a glance over her shoulder, bent at the waist to snag his sweater from the trail of discards. The view was anything but coy. "Methinks the gentleman doth protest too much," she murmured as she slipped her arms into too-long sleeves.

Christ, she was incredible. Backlit in the spill of light from the hall, the extra cashmere did little to mask the subtle curves beneath. The V-neck barely dipped below his collarbone, but proved to be far more tantalizing on her. He liked the way she looked in his clothes. He liked the way she looked in his arms. He liked her. A lot. Too much.

Forcing himself to tear his gaze away, he searched the wreckage for his jeans. Spotting them wrapped around the bedpost, he reached for them, only to jump when the knot of denim began to buzz insistently. "Oh, crap. Sorry," he said, shooting her a sheepish look as he pried the phone from a pocket. "I had it on vibe—" The words died in his throat when he saw the same telephone number he'd memorized when he was Aiden's age splashed across the screen. Swiping his thumb over the display, he pressed the cell to his ear. "Ma? Is everything okay?"

"Daddy?"

His heart sank the second the tear-soaked syllables registered. Dropping onto the bed, he sent Monica an apologetic glance. A hot flush prickled his neck as he angled his body away from her. "Hey, buddy. What's up?"

"Can you come get me?"

Closing his eyes, Colm inhaled deeply through his nose. He hadn't had a call like this in weeks. Of course, Aiden had to pick tonight, of all nights, to relapse. Disgusted by the flash of resentment he felt toward his own kid, he balled up his impatience and selfishness and swallowed them whole. He yanked his boxer briefs from the legs of his jeans and shook them out. One thing to try to talk to your five-year-old when naked, totally another to do so in front of an audience. One who was probably fifty times better at defusing difficult kid situations than he was. One who hadn't had a single sobbing phone call from her kid all night. Feeling as helpless as he had the day they first placed his infant son in his hands, and knowing he was fighting a lost cause, he made a futile attempt to salvage the first adult sleepover he'd had in years.

"It's really late, Squirt. What's the matter? You have a bad dream?" Snapping the waistband of his briefs into place, he started to unravel his jeans. "Turtles again? I told Grandma not to let you watch the turtle movie."

"But I like the turtles," Aiden sobbed.

Of course he did. Aiden loved the smart-mouthed little sewer thugs in the daytime. The problem was at night, when those freak-show reptiles haunted his little man's dreams. Any wonder the boy preferred the company of Princess Clarissa and her sparkly annoying songs? He shoved his legs into his jeans and jumped to his feet, bouncing to hike the waistband into place.

"Maybe Grandma can make you some cocoa."

"I *had* cocoa. Di'nt helllp."

Colm dropped to the edge of the bed and curled his shoulders in, his son's plaintive wail wringing the last drop of hope from him. Breathing deeply, he willed the vise gripping his heart to ease up. Though he knew exactly what he had to do, he didn't want to.

For the first time in five years, he wished he wasn't Aiden's father, mother, and protector. A few hours where he didn't have to be everything to someone. One selfish, reckless night where he could just be a guy. A man. Not a dad.

The guilt came hard and fast, a tidal wave of remorse washed away any tiny seedling of self actually taking root inside him. He scanned the floor for the remainder of his clothing. Socks, shoes, undershirt—they all lay scattered at his feet. Everything but his sweater. It was wrapped around the woman he'd been banging while his kid was having a nightmare.

"You really want me to come get you?"

The question was largely rhetorical. A way of making it clear he was going to need his sweater without having to meet Monica's questioning gaze. Surely she'd understand. There wasn't a parent in the world who hadn't gotten a "come get me" phone call at least once. She was lucky Emma was so comfortable staying with her aunt. But of course she was. Monica was the epitome of calm, cool, and collected. Why wouldn't her kid be, too? Plus, Monica's sister probably had a relationship with Emma from the day she was born. Too bad his parents couldn't say the same. Tucking the phone under his chin, he pinched his socks with his toes and bent his knee until they were within reach. Aiden's gut-twisting sobs slowed to stuttering hiccups as he pulled them on.

"You're okay, buddy. Hang in there. I'm coming," he said with a resigned sigh. He'd liked the sound of those words so much better a few minutes earlier. Which, of course, made him the worst freakin' dad in the world. Shoving his toes into a shoe, he rose from the bed. "Lemme talk to Grandma for a minute."

There were most certainly more dignified ways to slip out of a lady's bedroom than doing the shoes-half-on scuff, but Colm figured whatever cool he might have convinced Monica he had was blown. He ducked his head through the neck of his undershirt and turned his back on his hostess. This way, he could pretend the woman who'd made him see God minutes ago wasn't listening to his conversation. Wasn't getting a fairly accurate glimpse into his everyday life.

"I thought I told you not to let him watch that movie," he growled the minute his mother came on the line. He pulled the phone away from his ear as she launched into a litany of excuses and explanations, all of which he ignored. "Yeah, I know he says he likes the movie, but Ma, I told you it gives him bad dreams."

He ran a frustrated hand through his hair and took all three of the deep breaths the parenting books recommended in one big gulp. Colm was starting to think training his already lackluster parents to be decent grandparents might be harder than keeping one scrawny boy alive. "Going to take me about forty minutes," he warned his mother. He paused for a second, mentally adding in extra time to find the right words to tell Monica their date was over and ask for his sweater. "Maybe closer to an hour."

A fall of pale green wool appeared in front of his eyes, and he heaved a heavy sigh of defeat. He turned to find Monica dangling the sweater by two fingers. A very sexy, very short silk robe patterned with big red flowers clung to the subtle curves he'd only begun to explore. Looking her square in the eye, he exhaled through his nose, relieved her of his sweater, and mouthed a grateful, "Thank you."

"Yeah, well, I know it's late and you're tired, but I'm not the one who lets a kid who's barely over three feet tall boss me around." Lie. A big, fat lie, but neither Monica nor his mother needed to know the extent to which Aiden ruled their roost. "I'll be there as soon as I can get there."

Ending the call, he tossed his phone onto the mattress and pulled his sweater over his head. "I'm so sorry," he said, grateful for the thin barrier of fabric between them. He was positive there was no masking how sorry he was, for so many reasons. He yanked the sweater down and yanked the sleeves to settle it into place. "Please tell me you understand."

Monica hit him with a rueful little smile and he felt one hundred percent better. "Oh, I understand."

Patting his pockets, he made certain his keys and wallet were in place. He paused as he bent to scoop his phone from the bed. One corner of the fitted sheet had slipped its moorings at some point in the proceedings. The string of unused condoms lay stretched across a pillow. Their pristine orderliness in the midst of the havoc they wreaked on her bed seemed almost like a taunt.

"Come on." Monica tugged on his hand and turned toward the door. "I'll walk you down."

Her hips swayed under the slinky, silky fabric. She paused at the top of the stairs, casting a sidelong smile over her shoulder as she stepped over her discarded bra and blouse. Midway down the stairs, he caught her arm, urging her to turn and face him. Staring into those cool blue eyes, he shook his head in helpless defeat. "You have no idea how sorry I am."

Monica pressed a fingertip to his lips. He kissed her knuckles tenderly, and she fell against the wall, her expression mirroring the smug, wistful thing he had going on inside. "Don't be sorry. We had a great date."

"Yes," he agreed gravely.

She grinned up at him, her eyes twinkling. "And you can't say the evening didn't go out with a bang."

He groaned, equally appalled and abashed by her quip, and moved closer, crowding her. She tipped her face up in clear invitation. One he had no intention of refusing. He kissed her firm and sweet, waiting until the magic moment when her lips went pliant beneath his. The second she surrendered, he poured his all into the kiss. If he was going to get cock-blocked by mutated turtles and the fallout from their shenanigans, he wanted to leave her with something to remember him by.

Monica heaved a gratifyingly tremulous sigh when he pulled away. He laced his fingers through hers and started down the stairs again. Neither of them spoke. What was there to say? They'd agreed to an evening without complications, and he'd proved he couldn't even manage that. Bad jokes about banging aside, Colm agreed with the sentiment. Better to have their grown-up kind of play date end on a high note.

Pausing inside the front door, he brushed a lock of tangled brown hair away from her cheek. "Thank you."

She gave him a slow, smug smile. "Thank *you*."

There were so many things poised on the tip of his tongue. Things like "You're incredible" and "I'd love to see you again" and "I'll call you," but any mention of the future seemed to go against the unwritten rules they'd been playing by all evening. In the end, he settled for another kiss, this one soft but lingering, and a simple, "Goodnight, Monica."

She ducked her head, a peachy blush coloring her cheeks as she twisted the locks and gave the heavy old door a no-nonsense yank. Slender fingers wrapped around the edge, she rested a cheek against the varnished wood and met his eyes with her disconcertingly direct gaze. "Goodnight, Colm. And wish Aiden sweet dreams."

He stepped out into the crisp, cool night. Regret rose in his throat like bile. He forced himself not to look back as he started down the stairs. The door closed with a solid *kerthunk*. He held his breath until he heard the locks click into place, ducked his head, and took off toward the corner at a brisk pace. Time to leave all thoughts of rumpled sheets and a certain sweet-smelling woman behind and get back to his real life. First, he needed to catch a cab to get to his car. Then, he'd break every speed limit posted between him and his scared, motherless little boy.

Chapter 5

Melody blinked up at her, the to-go cup of coffee poised millimeters from her lips. "And that was all? He left?"

Monica peered into the depths of the cardboard box in the center of the island and shrugged. "Well, yeah. What was he supposed to do?"

Her sister texted at ten on the dot, asking if the coast was clear. Given the affirmative, the doorbell rang mere minutes later, and the post mortem began. Monica had to admit she was having fun being the grill-ee for a change. When Mel was single, Monica was usually the one extracting bits of information in exchange for the caffeine and carbs.

Even on a normal day, the largest container of doughnut holes available didn't stand a chance against the Rayburn sisters…plus one. And this day, this weekend, was so far outside of the norm, Monica figured these delightful little morsels had about five minutes left to live. Tops.

Emma zipped through Monica's kitchen, high on hot chocolate and fried dough, singing a song about a sparkly castle on a glittery hill. She ran smack into Monica's leg mid-twirl, grinned up at her, completely oblivious to bits of flyaway brown hair adhered to her sticky cheeks, and held up one sugar-glazed hand in silent supplication. Monica obligingly dropped a ball of blueberry dough into her waiting palm. Emma stuffed the hapless doughnut hole into her mouth.

The little girl twirled off toward the television blaring in the living room, and Monica turned to her sister. "What would you have done?"

Melody took the delayed sip of her coffee, then heaved a dramatic sigh. "I suppose I would have gone."

Monica snorted. "You'd have been out the door like a shot."

"Yeah, but I would have at least said I'd call you or something."

Unable to contain her laughter, Monica balled up a paper napkin and tossed the wad at the big, stinking liar. "Bullshit. You were the queen of the one and done."

"I was not!"

"And the revisionist history begins," Monica intoned in her best documentary narrator voice. "I was practically a virgin the day Jeremy looked my way," she mocked in a high-pitched, annoyingly breathy tone.

They both laughed, knowing Melody had shed every technicality and moved onto technology by the time she'd graduated high school. In truth, Monica was jealous and sometimes intimidated by the way Mel embraced her own sexuality as if it was another one of her lovers. Three years older, Monica was a virgin at the time. She was more than a little shocked when she stumbled across what had to be the biggest, purplest vibrator on Earth while helping her baby sister move into her dorm room.

"Remember The Count?" she asked, a blush warming her cheeks.

Melody beamed and pressed a hand to her heart. "I can make you orgasm in one…two…three!"

Mimicking her sister's horrendous Transylvanian accent, Monica joined in on the bit they'd loved to use. "Six…seven…eight! Eight orgasms!"

"Oh, The Count." A wistful smile curved Mel's lips. "Best vibrator ever made."

"Whatever happened to him?"

Mel ducked her head and chuckled. "Well, you know, Monica, not all love affairs last," she began, her tone grave, her expression somber. "Some only last long enough for one…two…two orgasms, then run out the door." Straightening, she plucked a chocolate-glazed doughnut hole from the box and popped the morsel into her mouth. "Stop trying to change the subject," she mumbled as she chewed. "Why aren't you seeing him again?"

Ignoring the twist in her gut, Monica reached for her own coffee. "That was the deal. One night, no kid talk, no expectations."

"*Pffft.*" Melody sneered. "I bet the no kid talk was an easy one for you."

"Yeah, well, my lack of kid to talk about certainly makes the no expectations part easier."

Lifting her chin, Mel leaned in to scan the contents of the doughnut box. Using her thumb and forefinger, she extracted what had to be her dozenth toasted coconut with the daintiness of a duchess selecting a sandwich at high tea. She eyed the sphere with a considering frown, pinkie finger fully extended. She consumed the tidbit in one voracious bite. Once her victim was chewed and forced down, she licked the crumbs from her fingers. "You could tell him."

Wrinkling her nose, Monica circled the counter and claimed the stool beside her sister. "What would be the point? Even if I did come clean and he was okay with the fact that I let him think I was something I'm not, I'm not exactly the maternal type."

"Because you've never let yourself be," Mel countered.

"Let myself? How do you figure?" Shaking her head, Monica waved away her sister's argument. "I've never been the girl who gets all gooey over babies."

"You're a great aunt to Emma."

Though she appreciated the attempted compliment, they both knew the word great was a gross exaggeration and laughed.

"Okay, you're not a great aunt, but you're getting better as she gets older."

"Because she's more like a real person."

"She *is* a real person," Melody retorted, adding a glare for good measure.

"See? That. That right there is what I lack." Monica pointed a finger at the spot between her sister's eyes. "I don't have the killer-mommy protective instinct."

"Bullshit."

Their sisterly staring contest was interrupted by a whirling dervish with bat ears, a sugar jones, and a flare for the theatrical. "*Bullsheeet! Bullsheeeet!*" Emma sang as she twirled into the kitchen once more. "Some *bullsheeeeeeeeet*, please," she trilled, holding out her sticky hand, her eyes fixed on the pastry box.

"Hush." Melody waved her daughter's grasping little paw away, then pressed two fingers to Emma's glazed lips. "Don't say that word. It's a bad word."

"You said it."

Monica smiled. Apparently, her niece wasn't the type to be digitally edited.

"Mommy is a very bad girl," Melody said solemnly. She lowered her fingers, shooting a sidelong glance in Monica's direction. "Don't be like Mommy. Be like Aunt Monnie."

"Oh, I don't know about—" Monica began.

"She's smart and classy. Hardly ever says bad words. Aunt Monnie has a big-time job where she gets to boss lots of boys around, which you know must be fun." A saucy wink was added for emphasis. "She wears pretty clothes and has pretty brown hair like yours." Amazingly, she kept a straight face while prying loose the strands adhering to her daughter's sticky cheeks. "But, best of all, she's a really good big sister. She doesn't really realize, but most of the time, she was a better mommy to me than our own mommy."

Melody spoke the last softly, her nose wrinkling playfully, but her eyes were serious when she looked up. "She always took care of me. Always tried to help me, even if I didn't listen to her very often."

Emma blinked, stunned by these unexpected revelations. "Why di'ent you listen to her?"

"Because I was silly. And a little jealous of her," Mel whispered the last part into her daughter's ear, but clearly for Monica's benefit. "I wanted to be perfect like her—"

"And I wanted to be silly like your mommy," Monica chimed in.

Heedless of chocolate stains and perma-glaze, Mel pulled her daughter closer. "That's how sisters are. They always want what the other has, but I have to tell you, Monnie was much nicer about sharing things than I was." Wrapping her arms around the little girl, she hugged her tight but never looked away. "I want you to be more like your Aunt Monnie. That way, you'll be the most awesome big sister in the world."

Monica chuckled and waited for her stickler of a niece to remind Melody she had no younger sibling to shower all her awesomeness on. Then, she saw the sparkle in her sister's bright eyes.

"No way," Monica breathed. "Really?"

Mel covered her stomach with her hand, a beatific smile curling her lips. "We're hoping if this one is a boy, you'll raise him for us. Jeremy and I think you're the best male role model a kid could have."

Monica's eyes filled with tears, but the sentiment didn't stop her from giving her sister's shoulder a shove. "I want to call you a really bad word right now." Glancing at her niece, she assumed a pious expression. "But I won't. Someone has to set a good example for these poor kids."

"I love you, my Monnie." Emma cooed as she snatched another doughnut hole from the box. Her mother scowled as she twirled from the room once more.

"I don't know what I was thinking," Mel said, staring at the empty doorway.

"About having the kids or the doughnut holes?"

Melody shrugged. "The combination of the two can be lethal, but I was second-guessing the trip to the bakery." She turned, and Monica had to stifle the urge to shrink from the intensity in her sister's probing stare. "You really think you don't want any kids?"

Biting the inside of her cheek, Monica paused to consider the question. She'd thought about motherhood, or the possibility of passing on the chance, a thousand times. As far as she was concerned, she'd spent more than her fair share of time probing her psyche, taking her emotional temperature and shaking her biological clock to check for ticking. Every bout of self-examination returned the same result. No, she didn't think she was destined to be a mother. Maybe because she knew deep down she was too much like their father. But she'd never give the thought voice.

Besides, she didn't have to answer to others. This was her life, her decision, and she shouldn't have to explain herself to anyone.

She wasn't some kind of baby-hating monster. She loved her niece. The kid left her confused and exhausted after only a few minutes together, but Monica did love the kid and was coming to enjoy the time she and Emma spent together more and more. And if Melody managed to pop out a boy, she and Jeremy were right. She could teach the kid to catch and throw, pick the best stocks and the smokiest tasting scotch.

The image of Colm's gorgeous little Aiden clutching his beloved doll stopped her short of female chauvinist pig status.

Squaring her shoulders, she stared into her sister's expectant face and made a promise to herself and her unborn nephew. If the kid wanted to play with dolls, he could play with dolls. She'd buy him all the dolls he wanted. If Emma wanted to learn about stocks and scotch, Aunt Monnie would show her the ropes. She'd use the jujitsu skills she'd picked up at the gym to defend their choices if she had to. Because she was a good aunt, even if she lacked the mommy gene.

"No," she answered at last. "No, I don't think I do."

"Maybe you'll change your mind when you meet the right guy." Mel pinched a doughnut hole between her thumb and forefinger. "A guy like this Colm, maybe."

"Stop."

"What? You said it was really sexy to see how good he was with his son."

"It's demeaning to tell a woman the 'right man' will change her mind. I know *my* mind, and I'm telling you I am ninety-nine percent sure I don't want to have a baby. Respect that."

Melody looked instantly contrite. "You're right. I'm sorry." She widened her eyes, the picture of hopeful innocence. "But I feel compelled to warn you, nothing kicks the old hormones into overdrive like seeing a man with his child. I swear, I came home from yoga to find Jeremy sitting on the floor drinking invisible tea and passing a plate of contraband Oreos to the teddy bear beside him, and the next thing I know…" She popped the pastry into her mouth and gestured to her stomach like a fairy godmother waving her magic wand. "…Bada-bing, bada-baby. Here we are."

To be fair, both to herself and to her sister, Monica searched her memories of Colm's interaction with his little boy to see if they elicited even the tiniest pang. She came up with zilch. Nada. Her memories of the same man stripped down in her bedroom and devoting himself to her satisfaction?

Those set off five alarm bells, a couple of wailing sirens, and a handful of mental wolf whistles.

"I don't think so." She couldn't help feeling a tinge of regret, even though a one-and-done was what they agreed to. "I did have a good time last night, though."

"Good." Melody heaved a sigh and popped the lid on her to-go cup, and cast a baleful eye at the contents. "Probably just as well. We have a sad, sorry state of affairs when a woman is driven to drinking friggin' decaf and pretending to like it."

* * * *

"So you left?" Mike stared at him, a mixture of awe and incredulity written all over his face.

Colm smothered a bark of laughter. His best friend would never win any poker tournaments. Hell, the guy only won a single pot when he held cards so good he couldn't suppress his glee. In those rare instances, he or James nudged the ante before folding to make their buddy feel good. If Mike ever figured out he truly sucked at poker, they'd risk losing the only Friday night entertainment they'd seen in forever.

He'd managed to go an entire workweek without spilling the beans. One hand into the game, he cracked, blabbing like a teenage girl mooning over her first kiss. Moving the baby monitor parked on the card table aside, Colm extended the deck in James's direction. "You taking any?"

"Two." James selected the two cards he didn't want in his hand and plunked them down on the table. "You're missing the point, Mikey boy. He had every man's dream date. Dinner, sex, and a clean getaway."

Colm huffed and tossed two cards in James's direction. All action stilled when a muffled squawk came through the walkie-talkie-shaped monitor. The three men stared at the speaker, each sending up their own silent pleas to Benny Binion and the gods of poker the noise was simply a minor disturbance in the force. All five kids were bedded down in Aiden's room. If Chrissie got fussy and woke the twins, it would be game over for everyone. When a full minute passed without any indication of activity, Colm turned to Mike. Despite the lack of two-way communication, he pitched his voice low. "Cards?"

Mike quickly shuffled three losers from his hand and placed them on the table. "Three, please."

He doled out two for himself and reclaimed his cards. A long moment passed. He picked up a package of fruit snacks and tossed it into the center of the table. "I open with Spidey Snacks."

Both Mike and James tossed a bag of compressed fruit morsels into the pile. James upped the ante. "See and raise you two string cheeses."

"I'm out," Mike said without a moment's pause.

Colm stared down at his cards as if he might have the power to telepathically transform the nine of clubs into the queen of hearts. He gave his head a shake. There'd be no queen magically appearing in his hand. His luck with women was as crappy as ever. Tossing his cards toward the center of the table, he propped his elbows on the surface and planted his face in his hands. The stubble on his cheeks and chin scraped like sandpaper. He wondered if he'd left patches of red on Monica's smooth skin, if she felt the burn of the heat sizzling between them, if she'd even spared him one second of thought since he'd walked out her door six days ago.

"Yeah, I left," he said, lifting his face from his hands to gauge his friends' reactions. "And I'm an idiot."

James sprawled in his seat, hooking one arm over the back of his chair as he poked one of the packages of string cheese he'd managed to retain at Colm. "I don't know what you're complaining about. You got yours, she got hers. Everyone went to sleep happy."

He acknowledged the veracity of the statement with a nod but refused verbal confirmation. "I liked her."

"I bet you did. I bet she liked you too." James ripped open the packaging on the cheese, and spit the wrapper out. "Leave good enough alone."

Mike wrinkled his nose in distaste and turned his attention to Colm. "Did you tell her you'd call?"

"Nope."

"Has she called you?" Mike persisted. Colm shook his head and his friend's brows shot up. "Texted? Emailed?"

"Leave your pet bunny boiling on your stove?" James chimed in helpfully.

Colm rolled his eyes. "No, I haven't heard from her. That was kind of the deal."

James gnawed through the little log of cheese like a beaver on a mission. "Why can't I ever get that kind of deal?" He waved the cheese stump at Colm. "I'd love a deal."

"Sure you would," Colm muttered.

"You *had* a deal once," Mike reminded him. "You got a bonus set of twins, remember?"

"I meant the no strings thing." James' cocky smirk disappeared and a shudder shook his long frame. "Man, if I gave those twins a ball of string, you'd find me tied to the railroad tracks like in those old cartoons."

Colm could only chuckle. "I remember the first time someone told me to dose Aiden with cough medicine. I was so pissed I wanted to call child protective services on her. Now, I wish I could send her a thank you note."

"I understand why my parents drank so much," Mike said, hoisting his beer bottle. "If Chrissie turns out anything like Megan, I should have a decent case of cirrhosis by the time I'm forty."

They all paused, paying the appropriate homage to the force of nature known as Mike's sister Megan—the twins' absentee mother—and to the near-certain demise of Mike's liver.

"Was she hot?" James asked, breaking the silence. Colm's head jerked up when he caught the wistful note in the question. His buddy blustered on. "I saw she was built like a board, but was walking the plank a good time?"

Narrowing his eyes, Colm zeroed in on his friend. "You're an ass."

James shrugged. "Just got the memo?"

Colm stowed his annoyance and took a good, hard look at his friend. Weariness etched the lines around his eyes and mouth a little deeper. His skin was pale but pastier than usual beneath the copper stubble. And despite his callous words, a soft gleam of longing burned steady in his eyes.

Drawing a deep breath, Colm tried to form words into a sentence. "She was..."

He started and stopped. Hot wasn't the word. Monica had been a tour de force. Whip-smart and funny. Friendly and warm. Oddly easy to be with. How could he explain the nights he'd lain awake thinking about calling her, but always talking himself down? Contrary to their agreement, easy-going didn't strike him as her style. The woman was clearly wound tighter than a spool of the string James was so hip to avoid. If he tugged, he might end up tangled up in her. Then what? She'd been burned, like him. Obviously. He was fairly certain Emma's father wasn't on the scene. No evidence of a man at her house. What if she was too scared to take a chance? Was he? Could he risk Aiden getting attached to her? What if he fell as hard for the daughter as he did the mother?

"She was hot, or, were you looking for another word?" James prodded.

Colm looked up to find both men watching him expectantly. Though the descriptor hardly did her justice, he went with the adjective for the sake of closing out the topic. "She was hot."

Grunting his disappointment, Mike reached to gather the cards. "Well, that commentary was hardly worth the build-up."

"What? You want the details?" He glanced from one man to another, and when neither demurred, he scoffed. "No. Sorry, girls, I'm not dishing the dirty."

James watched Mike shuffle the deck. "You were earlier."

"I was venting, not dishing." Colm cut the deck Mike set in front of him neatly in half. "I just…It's been a long time since I've dealt with any of this. Longer than you guys." He shook his head as Mike started firing off cards like a professional dealer. The guy had no poker face, but he could deal like he'd been born in Vegas. "I don't know why I thought you'd be any help."

"Mistake number one. There isn't a guy at this table qualified to give dating advice." Mike nodded as he gathered his hand. "Remember that."

"Two," James said, leaning in. "Might've been a long time since you've been involved with someone, but I know it hasn't been as long since you got laid."

Colm blinked. Time was a matter of perspective. The last time had been less than a year after Carmen died, which, when viewed in the context of the sleep-deprived haze of Aiden's first three years of life, wasn't so long ago. He'd had a couple near misses in the time since a sassy-but-sweet dispatch officer he used to work with popped his pathetic widower cherry, but he hadn't been the least bit interested in seeing any of those women again. Which is why this week had been so disturbing. Built like a plank or not, Monica Rayburn was stuck in his head.

Maybe he only needed to get a bigger dose of her. Surely he'd get sick of a bossy woman like her. Right? And the kid complications on both sides would likely get old fast. He'd sport her a couple bonus orgasms and work her out of his system so he could get back to living his life. Rearranging his hand of cards, he pulled a random heart out of what was shaping up to be a dandy collection of clubs and placed the card face down on the table. "I just need one."

"More than one wouldn't hurt you, though." Mike lounged in his chair, a smirk twisting his lips as he discarded two. "You've got her number, in more ways than one," he added with a leer. "A second night isn't a lifetime commitment."

"I thought you guys were all for leaving things as they were. The perfect date and all." Colm shot James a sneer.

"I'm only playing devil's advocate. You don't seem to be done with her, so why not milk the…arrangement for all it's worth?"

"An attractive picture you paint," Mike muttered.

James picked up the cards Mike tossed at him and scowled as he studied them. "Been a long time since anyone's had anything worth talking about at this table." He plucked a couple of mini packs of Teddy Grahams from the pile in front of them and flung them into the pot. "Cheer up. If Mikey wins his dick back in the divorce settlement, we could be talking about him next."

Protectiveness surged in Colm's chest. When Carmen died and the web of lies she'd used to tie him down began to unravel, Mike stood solidly by his side. James came later, and though he appreciated the guy's caustic humor most of the time, there were moments when the undercurrent between the quasi-brothers-in-law took him by surprise. He never particularly cared for James razzing Mike about his never-ending divorce proceedings. "What about you? Your dick fall off or something?"

"I'm sticking to self-abuse," James replied without pause or even a hint of humor. "Each minute I spend trying to keep up with those red-headed hellions, I'm more convinced celibacy is the only safe answer." He looked up, his freckled face open and optimistic. "Hey, you think I'm too far gone to become a priest? I mean, they have to be desperate for applicants these days, right? I could dump Heckle and Jeckle off at the convent and boom! Free as a bird."

"Priests aren't supposed to take matters into their own hands, either," Mike reminded him, unstirred by their partner's hyperbole.

Colm chuckled. They heard some version of the same escape fantasy at least once a week. Entertained a few of their own, too. But no matter how much James or any of the rest of them complained, they were all talk. Smirky jerk that he was, James was almost always as amused by the twins' antics as he was annoyed. And he adored them. Unabashedly.

Tossing his Teddy Grahams into the pot, Colm waited for Mike to follow suit. "Call," he prompted when no one upped the bet.

The three of them laid their hands on the table. His flush took Mike's three sevens and James's pair of deuces. He smiled, pleased with his haul. Teddy Grahams were Aiden's favorite. He was going to be a happy boy when he opened his lunch box this week.

"You should call," Mike said quietly.

Colm's head jerked up and he stopped sorting his winnings. "What?"

"Obviously you want to," his friend continued. "What's the worst she could say? No?"

He blinked, taken aback by the quiet vehemence in Mike's voice. James tossed a little fuel on the fire. "A simple 'no' is easy to take." Ginger eyebrows shot up as he fixed Colm with a pointed stare. "The worst thing she can say is 'I'm pregnant.'"

A choked silence filled the room. All three of them had heard those words when they'd least expected them. Though the relationships hadn't turned out great, those two little words were the precursor to the best things to ever happen to any of them. Two of them had done what they thought was the right thing and married. Mike and his soon-to-be-ex had been dating two years at the time, so the marriage and baby thing seemed like the next step. At least to him. Colm found himself exchanging vows with a woman he'd known for three months, but hadn't known at all.

Even James, who managed to side-step the altar altogether, hadn't emerged unscathed. There was no way any man could prepare for the whiplash whims of a woman like Mike's willful little sister. Megan had been the ultimate earth mother throughout her pregnancy, then the day of her six-week postpartum checkup, she took off for parts unknown. No one heard a peep from or about her until she showed up at the twins' first birthday party.

She stayed for less than half an hour.

Though Mike often complained about his sister's behavior, James liked to pretend he was okay with Megan's free-to-be-me lifestyle. But underneath his bluff and bluster, the guy was as conventional as the rest of them in terms of parenting.

Colm never expected to raise Aiden without a mother. Mike certainly never planned for his ex to walk out on her kids, completely ignoring her offspring until she discovered they were handy bargaining chips in her attempts to squeeze every last dime out of him in the divorce. And James, never the most reliable guy in the world, wasn't exactly a prime candidate to be anyone's be-all, end-all. Now he had small people who looked to him for everything, and Colm could honestly say he'd never seen the man let his children down.

None of them signed on for this, but as much as they complained, not one of them would trade fatherhood for anything. Not even an endless buffet of stringless women. They were the ones with the strings. And with five kids five and under between them, the last thing any of them needed was another mess to clean up. He had all these reasons and more to leave the thing with Monica alone. They'd had a nice night. Pleasant. Exciting. Sexy. Beat the shit out of watching Princess Clarissa trill and twirl and smile all the time.

As if he'd conjured her, the princess herself appeared in his lap. He looked down to find Aiden staring up at him, big brown eyes droopy with sleep. "Hey, buddy, what's going on?"

Without waiting for an invitation, Aiden ducked under his arm and clambered into Colm's lap. One elbow jabbed straight into his ribs, and a bony knee nearly erased the possibility of ever finishing the job with Monica Rayburn or any other woman ever again.

Pushing his chair away from the table, he squirmed in his seat as Aiden wiggled in his lap, seeking the comfy spot they both knew was there. The scents of bubble gum toothpaste and tear-free shampoo filled Colm's lungs.

Pressing his cheek to the crown of his little boy's head, he took another hit. "Thirsty?"

Never chatty when he first awakened, Aiden shook his head.

"Bad dream?"

"Huh-uh."

Too tired to let the guessing game play out, Colm grabbed the doll from between them and handed her to his son. Aiden wrapped his arms around the doll and hugged her to his narrow chest. Heaving a sigh of resignation, he shifted into interrogation mode. "Why are you out of bed?"

"Jamie peed."

James rose and scooped his pile of snack packs into a crumpled grocery bag. "And there's my cue."

Colm closed his eyes. The twins, Jamie and Jeff, and Mike's son, Tyler, had all been sleeping curled up like kittens on Aiden's new twin-sized bed, while Chrissie slept on the old toddler mattress nearby. Sighing into Aiden's hair, he resigned himself to having company in his bed while he let the newly christened mattress air out.

"Got some cleaner?" James asked, the tips of his ears glowing pink and his mouth set in a grim line.

Feeling bad for the guy, Colm waved him off. "Don't worry, I'll take care of it."

"Sorry, man," James mumbled, then took off to claim his kids.

"You want help?" Mike asked, gathering his take into a Hello Kitty diaper bag.

The bag gave both him and James ample opportunity to question their friend's masculinity, but he claimed the moon-faced kitten was a chick magnet. The first time he'd brought the bag to the park, they'd literally cringed at the sight. Mike manfully shouldered the bag and carried his daughter over to one of the picnic tables for a quick change. A bevy of helpful mommies and nannies swarmed within seconds, and when Mike and Chrissie emerged, they were both beaming.

"Nah. Gather your crew."

Aiden wriggled, his bony little butt slicing into the top of Colm's thighs as he twisted to look up at him. He held up a package of teddy bear-shaped crackers, his dark eyes suddenly sharp with avarice. "Are these for me?"

Without missing a beat, Colm divested his son of the purloined snack and rose from the table, dumping the boy over his shoulder like a squirming sack of potatoes. "Those are for lunches."

"I know where you hide them," Aiden gasped between giggles.

Colm's lips twisted into an appreciative smirk. "Not anymore you won't."

He paused at the end of the hall, watching as his buddies ushered their drowsy offspring toward the door. Jamie wore a pair of familiar-looking superhero pajama bottoms. As they approached, James followed his gaze and shrugged. "I'll wash 'em and bring 'em next week."

Waving the offer away, Colm shook his head. "Keep them. They're too small for sonny-long-legs." He swung Aiden up and held on tight, hardly caring about Princess Clarissa's attempt to implant herself in his ear when his little boy wound his spindly arms around his neck. "Night, guys."

"Night, guys," Aiden echoed.

The second the door closed behind their guests, Colm swung around and stalked down the hall. He paused outside the bathroom. "You need to go?"

Aiden shook his head no, but his father wasn't easily put off.

"I think you should try."

"I don' hafta," Aiden whined, holding on tighter.

"You wet my bed, and I'm making Princess Clarissa sleep in the puddle."

"Eww." Aiden pulled away, his tiny face puckering.

Knowing he'd won this round, Colm set his son down. With a playful swat on the bottom, he propelled the boy toward the master bedroom. "Go."

Five minutes later, Aiden was tucked into Colm's big, empty bed. As he watched his boy snuggle in, he had to admit he was relieved. Sleeping alone sucked. If a kick or two in the kidney was the price he had to pay for some company, he'd endure. Even if admitting his loneliness did make him more than a little pathetic.

Laughing at himself, he pulled the door partially closed. A peek into Aiden's room showed James had stripped the sheets and mattress pad from the bed and piled them at the foot of the bed. A spot roughly the size of Lake Superior darkened the middle of the mattress. He took a step into the room and paid the ultimate price—a Lego, dead center in the arch of his foot. The colorful string of curses he uttered as he hopped around on one foot played at full volume through the baby monitor on the kitchen table. Gritting his teeth, he hopped to the relative safety of the hall, hit the wall, and slid down like a glob of ectoplasmic ooze.

Letting his skull thud against the wall, he stared at the ceiling. The following night, he could regroup. Aiden would go to his grandparents' again. The condo would be clean. He wouldn't risk impaling himself on a building block. There'd be no one to kick him in the kidney. Nothing but the sound of his own breathing. And the memory of how sweet Monica Rayburn tasted and how hot those noises she made in her throat made him.

No big deal to call and see if she was free, right? They'd pick up where they left off. Same rules. Same expectations. Or lack of expectations. Two nights wouldn't mean there were strings. They simply had unfinished business. Shifting his weight, he freed his phone from his pocket and tapped the screen to bring up her contact info. Steeling his nerve, he opened a text window, ignored the throbbing in the sole of his foot, and began to type.

Chapter 6

She had every intention of sticking to her guns. Keeping her word. Respecting the boundaries they had drawn. He was the one who texted first. And he was the one to reestablish the rules.

Monica's breath had caught as she read the magic words: *I didn't get enough of you last weekend.* Seconds later, another message popped up. *No kid talk. No pressure. I want to see you again. Free tomorrow?*

She'd responded in an instant. Her thumb moved over the Y, E, and S keys without a single thought for the plans she already had in place. The hottest revival to come out of Broadway was in town for three nights only, but she didn't think twice about ditching the sort-of date she'd arranged with a fellow broker. There was no way she was missing out on a revival of the Colm Cleary bedroom floorshow.

She hadn't been able to stop thinking about him all week. His hands. His magical mouth. The feel of his broad, strong body braced over hers. This was the only encore she wanted, and, for the life of her, she couldn't remember why she'd thought meeting him at the bar where she arranged to hand off the tickets would get him into her bed any faster. She should have met him at her place. They could be halfway naked by now. But no. She had to try to get the upper hand. And why? All she wanted was to be under him again.

When he talked like that, any thoughts she had of calling the shots flew right out of her head. When he looked at her like he was, heat prickled her skin and the tips of her ears burned. No games. No dances. When she looked into those startlingly clear eyes, she saw only pure, naked want.

He wanted her and nothing else.

Monica shifted on the tall stool but purposefully did not look at her phone again. Or her watch. Or the clock behind the bar. The last time she checked, he was five minutes late, and that had been at least five minutes ago. Was this tardiness some kind of karmic payback? Would he show at all? Why would he bother asking her out again if all he was planning to do was stand her up?

"I'm so sorry."

The rushed apology came complete with a broad, strong chest heaving—actually heaving—with exertion.

"I couldn't find parking, so I had to use a deck a couple blocks over..."

He moved in closer, his magnetic gaze locked on her and lines of sincere concern bracketing his handsome mouth. God, she couldn't wait to have his mouth on her again.

"...Apparently there's something going on down here. I think I got the last spot on the top level, and it was marked for a compact car."

Monica smiled, delighted by his befuddlement. "Theater district." His expression melted from perplexed concern to utter blankness. "This is the theater district. Parking is tight this time of night." Cocking her head, she watched in awed wonder as her explanation bounced right off him. "Curtains go up in about an hour."

"Oh." He slid onto the stool beside hers but didn't signal for the bartender.

Her smile widened. Usually she dated men who felt the need to draw attention to themselves, but Colm seemed utterly unconcerned about his surroundings. His attention was focused solely on her. A sensation she recognized from their previous encounter and welcomed like an old friend. He smiled and her insides melted. She'd forgotten about the dimple. And the way his eyes crinkled with laugh lines. Until she saw him live and in person again, she didn't know it was possible to miss the twinkle in someone's eyes. But she had. Everything about this guy called to her without any extra effort on his part.

Animal attraction. Had to be the answer. The reason why she almost purred when his hand brushed hers. He slid the pad of his thumb across her knuckles and she wanted to pounce. A low hum of approval rattled in her chest when he pulled her hand to his mouth and marked her with a lingering kiss. She could feel the imprint of his smile on her skin after he let her go.

He was a man with a mission, and she was ready, willing, and chomping at the bit to be conquered.

Swallowing a sigh, she gestured toward the backlit bar. There was a dance to be done, and this time she was going to lead. "Do you want a drink?"

He stared straight at her. "There's only one thing I want, but if you want another drink, we can stay."

"No."

He smiled a smile so wide and happy and boyishly charming it almost knocked her off the stool. All pretense of playing cool was gone. They were absolutely on the same page, even if she'd hesitated when he messaged to see if she could be free for drinks or "something" that evening.

Afraid she'd combust on the spot if she didn't look away, she fumbled for her purse. By the time she managed to extract some cash from her wallet, Colm had snagged the bartender's attention and slid a twenty into the bar's gutter to cover her tab. He wrapped his hand around hers, crushing the money into her palm as he rose, pulling her off her stool and straight into him. The bills crinkled, the creased paper biting into soft flesh as his grip tightened.

"I've thought about you all week. I swear I could *taste* you all week."

The rough rasp of his confession twisted her insides into knots and woke every chill-bump on her body. Wetting her lips, she gazed up into those mesmerizing eyes. "I've thought about you, too."

"I know we said one night, but we didn't have a whole night, so I'm calling this one on a technicality."

"Okay by me."

They stared at one another, paralyzed by the inevitability of what was about to happen. There'd be no charming dinner tucked away in a bustling kitchen. No more getting-to-know-you conversation. This would simply be a continuation of their first night. The same rules applied. She wouldn't be guilty of a fresh lie of omission; she'd just be letting the original one ride. Though she felt a twinge of guilt, Monica found the justification shockingly easy to live with. God, she wanted this man. She wanted him bad.

"We're either going to have to get out of here, or run the risk of getting arrested for indecent exposure," she whispered.

Without another word, he turned on his heel and stalked toward the door, pulling her along behind him like a caveman dragging his conquest to his cave. Though she knew she should have found the thought offensive, she didn't. In fact, his take-charge attitude was incredibly arousing. She'd made her choice, and he was going to make sure she saw the night through. Was there anything sexier than a man with a plan?

Out on the sidewalk, she trotted to keep up as he wove his way through the knots of people snagging a pre-curtain smoke. Wrinkling her nose as they passed a particularly prolific group of puffers, she grabbed the hem of his sweater to capture his attention. "Colm?"

He pushed through to the corner. "You okay?"

"I just…" She gave her hand an experimental tug, but his grip remained firm as ever. "I need my hand for a second."

"Oh!" Eyes widening, he released her immediately. "Sorry."

Forcing herself to smile rather than wince, she uncurled her fingers to reveal the wad of cash balled in the center. Colm took one look at the lines cut into her palm and groaned.

"Crap. I'm sorry." He reclaimed her hand the second she tucked the money away, but this time his hold on her fingers was infinitely more gentle. He pressed his lips to the center, his mouth soft and tender, and released her with another gruff, "I'm sorry."

Instead of letting her hand fall to her side, she cupped his cheek with stiff fingers. "I appreciate your enthusiasm."

His lips twisted into a wry smile. "Well, if you think that was enthusiastic, you're gonna love the rest of the evening."

Her breath caught as the possibilities sifted through her mind. "We could get to my place faster if we took a cab."

Colm turned his head toward the grimy parking garages lining the block. "I can't leave my car here. What if Aiden—"

She cut him off with a finger pressed to his lips. "Right. You're right." Taking his hand again, she gave it a tug when the light turned green and the walk signal appeared. "Which garage?"

"Another block."

Glad she'd chosen to wear her cute ballet flats with her skinny jeans, Monica took off at a determined clip. "Come on, big guy. We've got places to go and things to do."

Monica had to admit, there was a lot to be said for delayed gratification. And for being courted a little bit. She liked the protective warmth of his hand on her back. And the urgency in his long strides. Opening the passenger door of his SUV was probably more a matter of expedience than gallantry, but the hand he offered as she stepped up into the vehicle unleashed a flutter of girly anticipation low in her belly. She also liked the way he glanced over to make sure she was buckled in. Probably some kind of dad instinct, but the spot check played well in other contexts as well.

The man even drove sexy. She spent the entire trip to her brownstone torn between staring at the fingers wrapped tight around the steering wheel and the hot hand planted high on her thigh. He stared straight ahead the entire time, his focus homed in on getting them to their goal, and she stared straight at him, drinking in the details of his chiseled profile.

"I wasn't going to call," she said, feeling the need to goad him into conversation.

"I know."

"I'm not surprised you did, though."

She got his attention. Slowing as they approached an intersection, he spared her a quick glance. "You're not?"

"Well, the way we left things...We were a little rushed."

His jaw tightened. The muscle there ticked off a couple of beats.

"I don't blame you," she said in a rush.

His Adam's apple dipped, but he didn't take his eyes off the road again. "To be honest, I felt bad."

"Did you?" The hand resting on her thigh slid higher. Her heart skipped a beat, then rushed to play catch-up with itself.

"Sure."

"Most guys would consider it the perfect escape." Covering his hand, she let her fingers slip between his. There she discovered the skin between each strong, masculine digit was indescribably soft. Vulnerable. A shiver ran through him as she stroked the newly uncovered pleasure point. She let the tips of her fingernails tease the tender skin with each pass. "I might have, if..." She coughed slightly to get his attention, sliding him a devilish look. "...we'd been at your place."

He laughed, and a heady rush of adrenaline pulsed through her. As if she'd cornered the market on the sound of happiness. Colm Cleary laughed out loud and that gorgeous sound was hers. All hers.

"Good to know." He slid her a sidelong smile as he turned onto her street. "What were you doing downtown?"

"I was dropping off some tickets for a friend to use."

His brow buckled slightly. "Tickets?"

"Theater tickets. I was going to see a show tonight, but a better offer came along."

The frown dropped into a full-out scowl as he made a beeline toward an open parking spot toward the end of her block. "A show? You were going to a show?"

"No big deal."

He whipped the SUV into the snug space in three jerky maneuvers. Jerking to a stop, he turned to look at her, his arm hooked over the steering wheel. "Was it a date?"

"Excuse me?"

"Were you going to the show alone, or did you have a date?"

"Why do you care? I'm here and not there, aren't I?"

"You're here with me, but were you planning to spend the evening with some other guy?"

She blinked, thrown by the mixture of arrogance and anger in his tone. Monica didn't care much for being off-balance. Clenching her abs like she was preparing to do one of those crazy stork-like yoga poses Melody loved so much, she closed her eyes and drew a deep breath. The second her heart rate started to slow, she opened her eyes and let her indignation go with the stale air. "Does it matter?"

Colm started to say something, then clammed up. His teeth clacked when he snapped his jaw shut. The muscle beneath his ear jumped again. Silence hung taut between them as he inhaled through his nose and touched the tip of his tongue to his upper lip.

"No," he said at last. "Doesn't matter."

Nodding her approval, she gave him a tentative smile. "It wasn't a date-date. Just a...I didn't think twice about changing plans." She raised both eyebrows as testament to the sincerity of her statement. "Not for one second."

"Poor guy."

She grinned, wrinkling her nose with pleasure at the implied compliment. "Not sure he cared much, either, but thank you." The keys dangled from the ignition. The engine purred right along with the tension humming between them. She tipped her head toward the window. "The sooner we get inside, the sooner we can work off a little of this awkwardness."

He rewarded her candor with another one of those deep, rumbling laughs. "God, I love the way you think."

* * * *

He did. He loved the way her mind worked. Colm was sure if he stared good and hard, he'd actually see gears turning. And since he was a guy, and therefore attracted to all things mechanical, he was every bit as attracted to her brain as he was her body. He wanted to kiss her into submission, take her apart with his hands, drive her to the very edge with his mouth, and then... then he wanted to have her. Bury himself inside her. Feel her fall to pieces all around him. After, he'd watch as she pulled herself together, because he found every bit of her fascinating. Even her control-freak tendencies.

When it was all said and done, he'd take her again.

By the time he crept out of her bed in the morning, he wanted there to be nothing left of the maddening ache he'd suffered all week. He'd use her and let her use him. They'd sweat this attraction out and get back to reality. Hamburger Helper and stain sticks. Pre-school musical programs and after-school snacks. Gold stars, frowny faces, and the occasional watercolor masterpiece. Parenting.

Colm released her hand to let her unlock the door to her brownstone and disarm the alarm. They stepped inside, and once again he was struck by the difference in her lifestyle and his own. Not the comparative real estate values, but the utter lack of chaos in her foyer. His own was a jumble of shoes and toys, discarded outerwear, and the occasional shopping bag tossed aside the moment he crossed the threshold. Monica had a coat rack, which held exactly one lightweight jacket and a hall table with a small stack of mail and a delicate-looking glass bowl.

"Would you like something to drink?"

He shook his head, unable to tear his eyes from the gleaming table. "No. Thank you."

As she locked the door behind them, he mentally sentenced the bowl to a three-minute lifespan in his house. The glass was too delicate, temptingly shiny, and practically screamed "Don't touch me!" In other words, decorative catnip to a five-year-old boy.

Hell, there wasn't even a speck of dust on the gleaming glass. Or the table. The woman had no clutter. He found the lack of dust was almost disturbing. How could a person raise a child in a clutter-free, dust-free environment? Her cleanliness was downright unnatural. Or supernatural. Maybe she was some kind of witch.

Taking in the sleek fall of light brown hair and creamy complexion, he dismissed the last thought. She was no witch. She was a woman in strict control of her life. Most likely her kid's life, too.

But, who was he to judge? Maybe she was as good a mother as she was an organizer. Maybe those skills made her the best mother ever. Probably awesome. Perhaps he was an extremely crappy dad. He grimaced as he scrawled one more item on his list of shortcomings—selfish bastard. He hadn't asked her who was watching Emma. Hadn't wanted to know. As if having intimate knowledge of the childcare arrangements she had at her disposal might change this into something different. Something more. Something he wasn't prepared for and not entirely sure he wanted. He couldn't exactly say he didn't want to learn more about the mysterious life of Monica Rayburn. When she turned to look at him, her eyebrows lifted and her gaze expectant, he blurted the safest question that came to mind.

"How do you keep your place so clean?"

She cocked her head, a smile lifting one corner of her mouth. "I have a service. They come on Fridays. Check me on a Thursday and see what you think."

Her crooked smile and an admission of slobbishness shattered the awkwardness. Hooking a hand around her waist, he pulled her to him. She came with the right amount of resistance. The kind that said, "I let you in the front door, buster, but you're going to have to work your way in from here." And if there was one thing he'd never been afraid to do, it was jump in and get dirty when he had to.

Anchoring her to him hip-to-hip, he gazed down into those vibrant eyes. "Makes me feel much better."

He slid his hand up her back and pressed her chest to his. The ends of her hair tickled his knuckles. Unable to resist, he slid his fingers into the silky strands. The base of her skull fit his palm to perfection. She wet her lips with the tip of her tongue. A blatant invitation—one he planned to take her up on—but he wanted to savor this a little first.

Given the abrupt end to their activities the previous week, there was a distinct possibility he'd regret slowing things down this time. He'd extracted Aiden's solemn vow to stay the whole night with his grandparents, but he knew the kid was a promise breaker when it came to things like cleaning his room, eating broccoli, and giving in to nightmares. And he also knew he'd be off like a shot if his boy called for him again.

But last weekend, he'd been too caught in the rush of discovery and the heat of lust to absorb the details of the time they spent together. Though he'd replayed their bedroom antics time and again over the past few days, he wanted to soak up the details this time.

"Are you going to kiss me?"

The question cut through his internal debate like a hot knife through butter. It also awakened a perverse need to keep her waiting a bit longer. Running his fingertips down her cheek, he took his time tracing her jaw. "Yeah, I'm gonna kiss you."

Her lashes fell and she bowed into him as he stroked the side of her neck. Her breath hitched and held when he pressed the pad of one finger to the pulse in her throat.

"Soon? Are you going to kiss me soon?" she asked without opening her eyes.

"Soon," he promised.

But instead of making good right away, he slicked her hair from her face, using both hands to gather the slippery strands. They escaped his grasp lock by sleek lock. As attractive as he found decisive, no-nonsense Monica, he found himself drawn to this side of her, too. She clung to him. Soft. Pliant. The slightest bit needy, but only in a physical way. This woman wasn't in the market for a rescuer. He wasn't here because she thought he'd be the answer to her troubles. Monica invited him into her home because she wanted him in the barest, most basic of ways.

Her style of raw, unspoken honesty turned him on.

His own breathing grew shallow when she tipped her face up, offering herself up to him. She wore gloss on her lips. A pinkish-red color that looked like it might taste like strawberries. He hoped it did. Mesmerized, he slid his thumb over her lips, smearing the sticky lipstick onto her cheek. The streak of pink sparkled on her creamy skin. He leaned in and pressed his lips to the corner of her mouth. A groan caught in his throat. He'd been wrong. So wrong. The gloss tasted like raspberries, and Colm knew he'd been a fool to hope for anything else.

She turned her head in an attempt to steal a real kiss. He chuckled at her head in his palm. He let her take what she wanted, controlling the kiss by giving her the lead. If only for a moment. Monica parted her lips and he didn't hesitate to take her up on the invitation. The kiss was hot, sticky, and sweet, flavored with fake fruit and fevered woman. Her tongue swirled around his, demanding a response he was all too happy to give. She slid her hands into his hair. He loved it when she dragged her nails along his scalp. The way she stroked his nape. She was a cocky woman, and she thought she could tame him. Hard not to admire her confidence. He gave her a minute more to taste, test, and tease. He could afford to be generous for a little longer.

But not much longer. His dick was so hard he ached. He slipped one hand between their bodies and made a quick adjustment. The new positioning both alleviated the ache and provided an alignment far more pleasurable for both of them, if he interpreted Monica's throaty moan correctly. He moved against her, letting her kiss him as hot and deep as she wanted, but leaving absolutely no doubt where this encounter would end.

At last, she broke the kiss. "Upstairs."

Colm gave the change in locale all the consideration he could muster, but it wasn't much. He'd thought he could savor her. For those few blurry moments when their mouths first met, he thought he had this in hand. All he wanted was Monica pinned against the wall. Or on the table. And his dick inside her.

He glanced at the staircase, and down at her, shaking his head all the while. He'd been waiting too long, thinking too much about her, to give any plan that didn't involve burying himself balls-deep in her as soon as humanly possible the old heave-ho.

"No? You don't want to come upstairs?"

Confusion puckered her brow. He pressed his lips to the crease between them and peeled his body from hers, needing a bit of space to regain his powers of speech. He watched as a hectic red flush crept up her throat. Color stained her cheeks a pretty peach and set the tips of her ears aglow. He was so enthralled he didn't realize Monica was twisting her shoulders, trying to wrest herself from his hold.

Desperate to make his intentions clear, he held fast as he swept the nearly empty foyer with an assessing glance. The only furniture was the table holding her mail and the pretty glass bowl. Sliding a hand into her hair, he gathered the silky locks in his fist and gave a tug. She stopped squirming, which was both a relief and a disappointment. He'd liked when her chest and hips brushed against his, enjoyed the feel of long, lean muscles tensed for flight, and relished the way she surrendered a chunk of her pride to have what she wanted. She wanted him, and he didn't want to wait one minute longer.

"How much do you like that bowl?" He practically growled the question, giving her hair another tug to draw her attention as he nodded toward the table.

She wet her lips. The gloss was long gone, but they were red with raspberry stain and swollen from his kisses. "I like it a lot. I bought it in Italy." Her voice was warm and rough-edged, like she'd been doing shots of whisky all night. Her blue eyes gleamed with speculation as she surveyed the table. "Maybe we could just…" She twisted away from him, and this time he let her go.

Heart lodged at the base of this throat, he watched as she stepped over to the table, slid both hands under the delicate piece of glass, and carried her treasure into the first room off the foyer. Leaning to his left, Colm craned his neck to catch a peek through the open doorway, but spotted only a wall of built-in shelving. Living room? Dining room? Hard to tell. Some of the shelves were fronted with glass. Most of them held one or more pieces of china, glass, or pottery. His brain assessed the potential for wreckage. By his calculations, collateral damage could be significant. She reappeared, a smug smile curving her well-kissed lips.

"There." Flashing a brilliant smile, she grasped the hem of her sweater and whisked the soft knit up over her head. She used the ball of expensive wool to sweep the stack of mail to the floor, give the already gleaming table a polish, then tossed the sweater aside like a rag. Leaning against it wearing nothing but a lacy black bra and jeans barely shy of painted on, she lifted a challenging brow. "Better?"

Colm appreciated the sentiment almost as much as the view. "Much." Taking a step closer, he hooked a finger under the top button of her jeans. "Take off your shoes."

Monica continued to smile her sunny smile as she stepped out of the flats she wore. "Is that all you want me to take off?"

Her nipples pressed against the nearly sheer fabric of her bra. Hard. They'd be so hard. But soft. Lowering his head, he cupped the slight curve of her breast as he captured one taut point between his teeth. The fabric was rough against his tongue, but he caught hints of the silken sweetness of the skin beneath. Yes, her breasts were small, but God, they were sensitive. Monica writhed, her long, sinuous body moving to some spellbinding tune only she could hear. He sucked her deep into his mouth, drawing a moan straight from the very core of her. The button on her jeans gave way under pressure from his fingertips. The rasp of her zipper matched their ragged breathing.

"Right here." He punctuated the words with a graceless tug on her jeans.

Thankfully, Monica wasn't the type of woman who shrank from a challenge. Pressing the tips of her fingers to the center of his chest, she looked him dead in the eye as she pushed him off. Those blue eyes remained locked on him as she shimmied out of her jeans. Colm swallowed hard, dying to peek, but reluctant to break the connection between them. He could almost see the bolts of electricity arcing through the air. Hear them sizzle and pop. Feel the voltage pulsing through his veins. His whole body jerked when she looked away. He glanced down in time to see her jeans slide across the polished floor, a scrap of black lace tangled in the wad of denim. When he looked up, she was reaching for the clasp on her bra.

"No. Leave it."

Monica blinked, clearly surprised by the urgency in his tone. "Leave it?"

The flicker of uncertainty in her eyes gave him all the confidence he needed to take hold of the situation again. He also took hold of his belt buckle. "I'm gonna use it."

Interest flared hot and bright in her eyes. "Use it?"

He held her gaze as he opened his jeans. "Makes you crazy when I tease you, doesn't it? The lacy stuff rubbing your nipples. Drives you nuts when my mouth is on you, but not really on you. Doesn't it?"

"Yes."

He loved the way she answered without hesitation or shame. Loved the smile she wore as she bent at the waist, completely unself-conscious about her nudity. But for the life of him, he couldn't figure out why she needed her purse. Now, of all times.

Pausing with his thumbs hooked in the waistband of his briefs, he stared at her, incredulous. "Please tell me you're not checking with the sitter. I'd hate to have to punish you for breaking the rules."

"Nope." She pulled something out of her bag, but it wasn't her cell phone. "Doing my part to ensure our mutual safety," she said, a smug smile curving her lips as she held up a foil-wrapped condom.

In one shove, he pushed his jeans and briefs down to his thighs. "You are one hell of a woman."

Monica propped her hips on the edge of the table and braced her long legs wide as she tore the wrapper. "Don't you forget it."

He stared at her as she rolled the condom over him, breathless as a teenager getting his first grope. A lump of red-hot need burned low in his gut. He rested his hands on the subtle flare of her hips and stepped closer. "I haven't been able to think about anything else all week."

His confession seemed to fluster her. Colm liked flustering her. As much as he admired her confidence, the unexpected flashes of vulnerability were what kept him hooked. "I'm going to make this so good you forget to count."

She gave a short laugh. "I never lose count." Her hair curtained her face as she glanced down. "I'm not sure this will work."

Colm followed her gaze, noted the height disparity between him and the mirror-like surface of the table, and set his jaw. There was no way in hell he was going one step further without having her first. Slipping his hands to her thighs, he pressed them wider. She moaned, and he slid his palms under her.

"I'll have to make it work."

His arms quivered with exertion as he lifted her off the table, but she was quick. Thank God she was quick. And nimble. And every bit as needy as he was. In the space of a heartbeat, she'd wrapped her long legs around his back, pressed her palms into his shoulders, and surged up until she hovered above him. The sleek smooth strands of her hair cascaded over her shoulders as she slid down. The tip of his cock nudged the hot crease of her sex. He bit off a groan as he shifted his hips to find her sweet spot. He let the sound loose when she sank onto him.

Her head bumped the mirror mounted above the table. Colm met his own heavy-lidded gaze in the reflection. Monica's thighs flexed and her nails bit into his shoulders as she pushed up again. He could only see from mid-chest up, but the visual worked for him. Not only was he inside her again, but he could watch as he fucked her. The thought almost drove him straight over the edge.

"Christ." He gripped her by the nape and pushed her down hard, burying himself so deep inside her he could feel the thrum of her heart. Or maybe because she was wrapped around him like a monkey on a tree. The sight of her slim, pale back shouldn't have been so mind-blowing. Hell, he was only looking at her back. Not even her ass. Certainly not the good parts. But the sight made him hot. She curled around him. Holding him buried deep in her molten heat.

"Go fast," she whispered in his ear. "I'm close."

Moving his hand down to grip the soft globes of her ass, he spread her wide, letting his fingertips play along the crevice, knowing the tease would push her further faster. He thrust fast and shallow at first, letting the slick shaft of his cock drag over her clit. But the second he felt her tighten around him, all bets were off. Desperate, he turned and braced her against the wall, plunging into her, driving hard as she came apart in his arms. Soon she was reduced to nothing but panting moans and delicious spasms. He let her ride him, losing himself in the wild bucking of her hips against his.

She said his name.

It was barely more than a whisper, but the creak in her voice broke him. His knees buckled and legs folded under him. He lost his grip, his hands sliding to her thighs, grappling for some purchase as she slid down the wall. He braced his feet wide, grateful he hadn't taken his shoes off. Finding traction again, he pistoned his hips, hell-bent on getting off.

Monica was determined to do her part as well. Hitching her legs up, she dug her heels into his ass and plunged a hand into his hair. He yelped when she yanked, pulling his hair until she could look him in the eye.

"Come."

One word and the woman completely unraveled him. Biting his lip, he closed his eyes and emptied every bit of loneliness and longing built up over the week into her. But even after the initial rush passed, he couldn't stop. Her thighs felt like satin sliding against his hips. Her toes tickled the backs of his calves. Moving inside her, he bowed and yanked the straps of her bra down her arms, trapping them there. He claimed one breast and gently abraded the distended nipple with the lacy barrier.

Pressing his forehead to hers, he exhaled long and loud. "We'd better find someplace more comfortable, because I plan on doing this all night long."

Monica tipped her face up and their lips met and held for a moment. "Bed. Now."

He grinned, grimaced, and slowly disengaged. "Yes, ma'am."

Chapter 7

Colm Cleary was a man of his word.
The second time around, he made her come and come so hard she almost screamed. Almost, but not quite. The guy really was an expert at dishing out the most exquisite kind of torment. He was talented, but not too cocky about his prowess. Strong, but secure enough to surrender the lead. And giving. So, so giving.
Monica couldn't remember the last time she slept with a man so utterly selfless about getting her off. Oh, he liked to get his, no mistake. But she had a feeling he got as much of a charge out of pushing her limits as he did in ringing his own bell. She'd had one lover who'd made a point of keeping tabs on how many times he got her across the finish line. Not because he demanded quid pro quo, but as a matter of pride. He'd wanted bragging rights to her orgasms, and Monica wasn't sure she wanted to give him full marks. After all, there was more than a little effort on her part involved.
She could understand a man wanting tit for tinglers, too. She had a competitive nature and wouldn't allow the scales to tip too far out of balance in order to satisfy her own sense of fair play. But Colm's generosity sprung from something more. Something fueled by passion, not ego.
He liked getting her there. She'd actually felt him get harder when the grips of her climax coincided with her grip on him. And his passion…his dedication to achieving excellence in fucking. Well, she was on the verge of ordering him a plaque.
She jerked when Colm's fingers stopped their lazy slide through her hair, caught up by a snarl. He managed to work them free with a minimum of fuss and no loss of follicle. Something she considered a minor miracle. In her experience, most guys tugged, yanked, pushed, or shoved at obstacles. Not Colm. He was the type to work through every roadblock he encountered

thoughtfully. Methodically. And most arousing—logically.

He didn't get worked up or give in. Whether he was facing babysitting logistics, parking hurdles, or the fact her hair turned into a friggin' bird's nest during sex, he remained unfazed. His brand of patience must come with the parental territory, because she sure didn't have a supply of her own.

He didn't hurry. Sure, they went at each other fast and furious a couple times, but they weren't rushing to glory. Their frenzies were more along the lines of not being able to hold their horses. Either way, he never skimped on the kissing, licking, stroking, or squeezing. His diligence alone showed a level of appreciation that put him a notch above many of the men she'd known. Nothing worse than a man who claimed to be a connoisseur but tried to skip courses. She was a firm believer in people living up to their full potential. And, so far, Colm had exceeded her expectations in most every way.

Maybe she *should* order a plaque after all. Or maybe a trophy. A nice dick-shaped trophy with a little engraved plate lauding him for knowing what to do with his.

"You okay?"

Oh, yes. The pillow talk. Colm had mastered basking in the afterglow without smothering. He asked simple questions. The kind she could answer with a yes, a no, or something more expository if her mood allowed. Monica appreciated his flexibility. He also had a gruff, grumbly thing going as they basked in the wreckage. Like he'd swallowed a bag of rocks and had to work each and every word out from cracks between them. Sexy as hell.

"I'm perfect," she replied, punctuating the sentiment with a feline stretch. "You?"

"I think you're perfect, too."

She chuckled and rubbed her nose in the patch of curling hair surrounding one flat nipple. "Someone's going for a triple-header tonight." She pressed a chaste kiss to the circlet of pale brown flesh. "I love a man with ambition."

No sound came out when he laughed, but his chest shook. "Ambition and limited free time."

"Ladies and gentlemen, we have a contender." Shooting him a flirty look, she kissed her way down his ribcage.

He pushed his hand into her hair and urged her head up. "I'm highly motivated, but I have to confess, I think I need a little down time."

She grinned and planted a lingering kiss on his hip bone. "Something cold to drink?"

"Please." He sighed as she disentangled herself from him. "Maybe a snack?"

Monica answered with a short laugh. "Unless you're into yogurt, I'm not going to have much to offer."

"That's right, you don't cook." He made the statement in a matter of fact tone. No judgement. Maybe even a hint of envy in there.

She watched as he ran his hand over his stomach, lazily roughing the line of hair she found so tempting. "No, I love to cook. I don't grocery shop, remember?"

"Ah, yes." He flashed a half-smile. "You got eggs?"

"Possibly." She shrugged as she tried to recall the last time she actually inspected the contents of her fridge. "I think I have crackers."

He snorted, turned over, and practically flung himself over the side of the bed. "Come on, let me see what's lurking in your cabinets."

"Has to be the weirdest proposition I've ever heard."

But, she followed. When a man with an ass so fine walks by completely naked, a woman would have to be a fool not to. She wasn't as comfortable with running around in the buff as she wanted to believe she was. Snagging his shirt and boxer briefs from the tangle of clothes, she followed him out the bedroom door.

He strode into her kitchen like he owned the place and started pawing through her cabinets. A hot flush of embarrassment prickled her skin as he opened door after door only to find a whole housewares department worth of plates, glasses and utensils, but very little to put on or in them.

To cover his discomfiture, she slipped her arms into his shirt and buttoned a single button in the middle. He turned and she dangled his underwear from the tips of her fingers. "Want these?"

He shrugged as if he weren't the least bit worried about strutting around with his dangly bits hanging out, but took the briefs and stepped into them.

Heading for the refrigerator, Monica yanked on the handle. A quick scan of the barren shelves told her she couldn't even offer the man the aforementioned yogurt. She stood there for a moment, letting the chilled air rush over her hot cheeks. Food. Making a mental note to remember to pick up at least some basics, Monica zoomed in on what she did have. Water. Bottles and bottles of water. And a few assorted odds and ends. Nothing any reasonable person would consider a decent snack, much less a meal.

"Can I offer you water, or water?"

Stepping in close behind her, he huffed as he took in the empty shelves. "Um, I think I'll have water, please." He accepted a bottle with a little laugh of exasperation, but promptly uncapped it and drained half in two gulps.

"Thirsty work," she commented, enjoying the methodical bob of his Adam's apple.

"Not an easy customer to keep up with," he tossed over his shoulder as he nudged her aside and returned to the hunt. From the depths of the fridge, he extracted a package of bread she'd worked nearly down to the heels and a bag of shredded cheese she had no recollection of purchasing.

Placing a pan atop the stove, Colm went to the fridge and frowned as he scanned the contents of the door. "Butter?"

She shook her head. "I usually use olive oil on bread."

He cocked an eyebrow. "Seriously? And Emma eats that?"

Monica froze for a moment. She'd forgotten the kid factor. Any person with a kid would have food in the house. Not bottled water and shredded cheese "I'm, uh, leaving on a business trip," she stammered. Uncertain where to go from there, she deflected. "Was Aiden's mom a good cook?"

Colm tensed, but quickly recovered. "I didn't think we were talking about kid stuff."

"I'm not clear on what's covered under the 'no kid talk' rule." She eyed him challengingly, though her heart hammered. "Do you want to?"

"Let's not."

"Okay."

A strange mixture of annoyance and relief swirled in her belly as she hauled herself up onto the counter. The sharp bite of cold granite on warm skin made her suck in air. He shot her a disapproving glance.

"Can't be sanitary," he said, pointing a spatula at the spot where she perched.

"Don't tip off the health inspector. He might shut down this kitchen."

He smiled indulgently. "Where is this alleged olive oil kept?"

She countered his tone with exaggerated patience. "Above the stove, of course." The view as he reached for the bottle was nothing short of spectacular. She traced every line with her eyes, smiling when he made a show of curling his bicep on the way down. "Very impressive."

"I aim to please."

"And you do," she purred. Leaning her head against a cabinet, she felt her eyelids grow heavy as she watched him drizzle oil into the pan, then toss a slice of bread in.

"You hungry?" he asked as he topped the bread with an even layer of shredded cheese.

She gave her head a lazy shake. "I'll have a bite of yours."

"You don't even have ketchup. Or macaroni and cheese," he mused, topping the cheese with the heel from the loaf.

"Don't like ketchup, prefer my mac and cheese with truffle oil."

"Right, but Em—" He caught himself and turned his full attention to flattening the sandwich with the spatula. "I'd say no wonder you're so thin, but I've seen you put some food away."

"Love eating, don't see the point in making a mess."

He tapped the corner of the spatula against the edge of the pan. An outward sign of nerves. His fidgeting made her insides feel squishy. Colm was nervous. She liked making him twitchy. Knowing that, she didn't have to feel weird that he could make her unspool so easily once they were between the sheets.

"How do you not like ketchup?"

The question came out in a grumble. She smiled and shrugged. "You mean 'cover-up juice'? I put ketchup in the same category as steak sauce."

Colm's brow furrowed. He pressed on the sandwich again, then flipped the bread with an expert flick of his wrist. "What's wrong with steak sauce?"

She swallowed the urge to smile, carefully keeping her features appropriately somber as she replied. "If you have a good cut of meat cooked correctly, smothering it in steak sauce would be an insult."

His snort spoke volumes. "I guess I've never met a piece of beef that couldn't use a little extra something."

Giving up the pretense, she grinned and gave his bicep an enthusiastic squeeze. "I think you're perfect just as you are."

He shook his head as he opened the cabinet to the right of the stove and pulled down a salad plate. Monica tried not to make too much out of his unerring ability to sense where she stored her plates. Most likely some fluke of unwritten kitchen arrangement code. Instead, she focused on the sandwich he was bisecting with the tip of the spatula. Each move he made was quick, efficient, and decisive. She liked watching him. This was a man who knew what he was doing. At least, as far as women and grilled cheese sandwiches were concerned.

He offered her the plate, and she eyed his creation with the narrowed squint of a cooking contest judge. The bread, though squashed and misshapen, was cooked to a delectable golden brown. The edges were nicely crisped, and the shallows glistened with golden olive oil. The cheese was perfectly melted and pooled slightly between the toasted bread. Her mouth watered with anticipation. She met Colm's steady gaze and he nodded encouragement.

"Ladies first."

She slid her fingers under the triangular wedge. Strings of melted cheese clung to the plate and to Colm's half. She wound the wayward strands around her finger and snapped them off. Colm swooped in and captured the digit.

His mouth was hot. His tongue velvet soft but nonetheless commanding. Scraping the edge of his teeth from first knuckle to the tip, he drew the swirls of the cheese from her skin, his piercing eyes never straying from hers.

"You're a...dangerous man," she said, a trifle breathless.

He flashed a crooked smile and withdrew, taking the plate and any extra spoils with him until he bumped against the opposite counter. "I think the word you're looking for is talented." Cocking an eyebrow at her, he turned his attention to his half of the sandwich. A self-satisfied smile tugged at his lips as he pried the cheesy bread from the plate. "Multi-talented," he amended, taking a bite.

The other brow rose as he chewed. She liked the way he owned the things he did and did well. No false modesty, no playing things down as if she needed his assistance to catch up with his accomplishments.

"I make a mean grilled cheese," he boasted, taking another huge bite. "If you don't want—" He let the offer-slash-insinuation dangle between them.

She took a bite to rival his. "No, I need the fuel."

Colm pushed away from the counter and stepped right up to her. She opened her knees a little to give him room. He shifted his hips to take even more space. Gripping her ass, he dragged her to the edge of the counter, steadily polishing off his half of the sandwich the whole time. Monica smiled. She loved to win when in business, but when it came to these playful power struggles, there was nothing she enjoyed more than the battles where they both won.

Her heart rate sped up when he gave each of his fingers an appreciative lick. His gaze slid to the bit of grilled cheese in her hand, and she popped the rest into her mouth. His lips kicked up in a half-smile, he brought her hand to his mouth as she chewed.

Monica gulped, afraid she wouldn't be able to get the food down if she didn't hurry. He sucked her index finger into his mouth, and she gasped.

"You're a bad man."

"We've only got a few hours of freedom left," he murmured, straightening her middle finger and grazing the tip with his lips. "I want to make 'em all count." He released her hand in favor of filling his. The pads of his fingers pressed into her thighs. He nuzzled the base of her throat. "I could eat you in three big bites."

She ran her hands through his thick hair, over his shoulders and the bunched muscles of his upper back. She loved the contrasts of his skin— rough here, soft there, the crisp rasp of hair, the patches so silky smooth she wanted to lap him up like soft serve ice cream. But there was nothing soft about Colm's body. Only his spirit. And she needed to be careful. So careful. The last thing she wanted to do was hurt this beautiful man.

Swallowing the thought, she tried to make her voice light and airy as she asked, "Still hungry, huh?" But she came off sounding like a horny Minnie Mouse desperately in need of a hit of pure oxygen.

"Always." He murmured the word into the side of her neck. His kisses were wet, his breath hot. She shivered when he worked the collar of his shirt entirely off one shoulder. "I like the way you wear this."

Giving herself up to the sensation of his lips gliding over her skin, she let her head loll to the side. "Well, I'd never have thought to go with one-shouldered tops, but if this works for you—"

"It does," he whispered directly into her ear.

"—works for me."

Monica closed her eyes as he pressed his mouth to the pulse thrumming in her neck. She loved the way he absorbed each sensation. His kisses were never hurried, no matter how hot he was. He didn't simply taste her, he savored. Like he was taking the time to appreciate her texture as well as the flavor. As if they had all the time in the world, rather than a few stolen hours here and there.

Planting one hand behind her, she arched, allowing him better access as he kissed his way down the gaping front of his shirt. The single button she'd fastened sprang open. She heard the plastic disc ping along the ceramic tile. Monica let loose with a husky chuckle.

"What?"

She gave her head a shake. The ends of her hair tickled her neck and shoulders. She reveled in the shivers racing down her spine. "Nothing. Just…poor button didn't stand a chance."

He smiled as he tilted his head to press his mouth to the hollow of her throat. "How are your sewing skills?"

"Not as good as my cooking," she replied, panting softly as he worked his way lower.

"Alleged cooking." He nudged the shirt open wide and affixed his mouth to one beaded nipple. "Cleaning?" he asked on a gasp as he released her.

She inhaled sharply when he pinched the taut, damp point between his thumb and forefinger and twisted a little. "I have a service, remember?"

"You have to have some other skills." He nuzzled, kissed and licked his way from one breast to the other. "Can you do my taxes? Balance a checkbook?"

She grinned. "I can make it so you don't have to worry about balancing your checkbook ever again."

"Because you spent all my money?"

This time, she laughed out loud. "Exactly." She pressed at soft kiss to his smooth shoulder. "I can make it so you don't have to worry about money."

He looked up at her, pure devilry lighting his eyes. "So, you're more the decorative type?"

"About as useful around the house as a blow-up doll," she said with an unapologetic shrug. "But without the plastic-y smell."

"You do smell incredible."

Without warning, he yanked her off the counter and up against his chest. Monica wrapped her arms and legs around him instinctively. "Where are we going?"

"Back to bed. I want to show you how handy a good blow-up doll can be."

* * * *

Monica stared at the window, waiting for the inky black sky to lighten to the grays and pinks of dawn. She needed the new day to come. She needed the man beside her to leave. Soon. She gave in and snuggled deeper into the warmth of his big body.

His heavy hand on her hip was making her crazy. She liked the way he rubbed his foot against hers, stroking her even as he slept. Liked it too much. Because she liked him too much.

Turning her head, she took full advantage of his unguarded state. Good gracious, he was handsome. But he wasn't handsome in the polished, superficial sort of way as most of the men she dated. Colm was the kind of handsome that ran bone-deep. His looks were more than the sharp angle of his jaw or those striking pale green eyes. No, this man's appeal lay in his slightly crooked nose and the wave in his hair he couldn't quite tame. And highlighted by the clumsy moments he didn't try to gloss over and set in stone every time he took complete and total possession of her body.

He snorted in his sleep but sank deeper into the pillow with his next exhale. He looked so calm in his sleep. Serene. Not at all boyish, though she could clearly see Aiden in him, but more…like a warrior with his weapons down. Rolling her eyes at her own fanciful observations, she balled her hand into a fist to keep from plowing her fingers into his hair. This night, and their first night, were blips. He wasn't hers. She'd lied to him from the start. She couldn't keep him even if he could forgive her. And for some reason, she didn't think he would. Colm was a man of integrity and not a little pride. He wouldn't take being fooled well.

"What time is it?"

The question jolted her from her scrutiny. Cheeks burning, she turned toward her nightstand. The display on the docking station read 5:36. On a weekday, she'd be sipping her first cup of coffee by now, but on the weekend she usually managed to sleep in to six-thirty or seven. "A little after five-thirty," she whispered, settling on her pillow.

He snaked an arm around her waist and pulled her closer to him. Satisfied he had her where he wanted her, he slid his hand up to cover one of her breasts. She tried so hard not to go gooey inside when he hummed his approval into her ear. He nestled his crotch against her ass. He was fully erect, and not the least bit shy about letting her know he was up for another round. His breath stirred her hair, but the gravel in his voice gave her the shivers.

"I want you, Monica."

"We have to stop." Ignited by his touch and fueled by panic, the words shot out of her mouth like a missile. He pushed against her, tempting, teasing, and tormenting her with what she could have—his body—and what she couldn't. Him. "I won't be able to walk."

He pinched her nipple, and she squeaked. Squeaked. Like she was some kind of toy for him to play with. But she had a hard time feeling indignant when the man was covering her shoulder in kisses so sweet and tender they complemented the sharp tug of his fingers to perfection.

"I can't stop. There's something about you," he whispered into her ear. "I can't stop thinking about you. Even when I'm with you."

The confession set alarm bells ringing in her head, but wasn't what brought her to her senses. It was his raw honesty. She believed him. Believed he couldn't get her out of his mind any easier than she'd be able to eradicate him.

"This is bad," she whispered aloud. Pressing her leg back, she bowed her body away from his, startling him into releasing her. In a move worthy of a ninja, Monica flipped off the side of bed and landed on her feet. She pushed her tangled hair from her face and tried to ignore the fact that she wasn't wearing anything but his beard burn as she tapped into the reserve of cool calculation she used when she needed an extra boost to make a risky trade. "We can't keep doing this halfway thing, and I don't think either of us is ready to go all in."

"I don't know, I really…" He pushed a hand through his hair. "I like you more than I want to."

"Well, there's a rousing endorsement." Drawing a deep breath, she let her gaze travel over the gorgeous man tangled up in her sex-decimated sheets without allowing herself to linger on any part she might find too enticing to resist. She settled on a patch of skin in front of his right ear, and brushed her lips over the prickly stubble poking through. "Colm, we both agreed. Keep things simple. No strings."

No need to come clean, she clarified mentally.

He propped himself on his elbow, but she didn't dare anything more than a quick glance at his face. She knew if she let herself look down, the incredulity she saw in his eyes would be well-justified. She had to be a crazy woman for not taking him for at least one more tumble. But she couldn't. He'd spent the previous night giving her everything a woman could want in terms of filling a carnal need, but the last time—that sweet, sleepy coupling where they were both too spent to do much more than rock together, but too crazed to resist—she knew this was more than a tumble. She was about to take a fall, and her gut said it would be a hard one.

He ran his hand over his face. "My marriage wasn't exactly what I thought it was."

"We don't have to do this," she interjected in a rush. "We can leave well enough alone."

His eyebrows shot up. "Do you think this is well enough?"

Panic welled up inside her. "I think maybe this is all it needs to be."

Impatience flashed across his face. "Come back to bed."

He held out a hand, gesturing for her to rejoin him, but she couldn't. Curling up against him was too risky.

"Let's talk about this."

In an instant, the impatience was gone. Something hard and bitter lodged in her throat. This wasn't fair. He wasn't playing fair. There was nothing worse than someone trying to change the rules in the middle of the game. Crossing her arms over her chest, Monica hated herself for ever getting drawn in to this whole mess. She should never have gone there. He could have stayed nothing more than a hot guy in a world full of hot guys. She should have taken her niece to the park and delivered her straight home. She should not have passed Go, flirted with a handsome stranger, and walked away letting him think she was something she wasn't. "I don't think we need to talk."

A look of stunned hurt flashed across his face. A deep red flush of fury quickly followed. "I do."

She needed to end this. Their affair would only get messier. She was ashamed to have let things go this far. She might've had a sharply honed killer instinct in business, but she'd never been deceitful. Until she met him, she went straight after what she wanted, no bullshit, no games.

"Listen, we've had a good time, but let's not make more out of this than a fling." Cold? Maybe, but effective.

"A fling?" he repeated slowly.

"I had a really great time, but neither of us want the complications—"

His jaw locked and suddenly his handsome face looked to be carved out of granite by someone using a jackhammer. "Fine." Kicking away the sheet, he growled at the wad of hapless cotton when the fabric dared to cling to his foot. "You're right. Who needs the complications?"

But the edge in his tone said he wasn't entirely opposed to having complications with her, and the knowledge cut deep because she wouldn't have minded sharing a few with him.

If only they'd started out on the right foot.

But she couldn't tell him. Certainly not when he was already pissed off. Hoping to end things on a better note, she grabbed a short robe from her closet and slipped her arms into the sleeves. Knotting the sash at her waist, she turned in time to see him extricating his boxer briefs from the leg of his pants. A wave of nostalgia hit her hard. She'd watched him do the same thing last week. She should have come clean with him. By perpetuating the myth to have one more night, she'd managed to mess up any possibility they might have had for more. She knew she was on thin ice when she'd agreed to meet up with him again, but was more than happy to hide behind the ridiculous terms she'd agreed to without giving him the benefit of full disclosure. The least she could do was make certain he left on better terms than this.

"Colm, wait—"

He shook his head, the very picture of wounded male pride. "No, you're right. I need to get going. I always pick Aiden up early, anyway, so it's no big deal."

"But I'll go get us coffee." She opened her hands, hopeful he'd accept this small peace offering. When he shoved one leg into his jeans without bothering to reply, she sweetened the deal. "And I owe you pancakes."

He visibly tensed. He looked over his shoulder at her, disbelief etched into the lines of his face. "Pancakes? You don't even have flour. I can't believe Emma hasn't wasted away to nothing."

"I could...We can go out."

"No, I'm good, thanks."

"Colm, I..." She trailed off, her hands fluttering in helpless futility. "I like you. I do. Probably too much. I don't want you to leave here thinking this was just..."

"What? Sex?" He stood, pulling his jeans up onto his hips, not bothering to fasten. "But it was. I get it." He bent to snatch his shirt from the floor and strode from the room.

"Colm, wait," she called as he flew down the stairs.

"Really. We're cool." He checked his pockets for everything he never had time to unload. "I enjoyed it, too. The sex. Thanks."

But his choppy assertions made his discomfort crystal clear. He wasn't cool. There was nothing she could do to make things right. They had to end this sooner or later. Might as well be sooner, because if saying goodbye hurt this much now, she didn't want to even consider later. She tucked her hands into the pockets of the robe as he fiddled with the locks.

"See ya," he said as he yanked the door open. "Take care."

A cool blast of early morning air ruffled his hair as he stepped outside. She grabbed the edge of the door and held on, watching his fine ass as he walked away. "I'll, um…I'll call you," she said, desperate to salvage something from the situation.

"Yeah." He tossed an angry glance over his shoulder and hooked a sharp right on the sidewalk.

If she wasn't mistaken, Monica thought she heard him say something along the lines of "I'll hold my breath" as she closed the door.

Monica didn't bother working up a response. What was the point? He was right. She wasn't going to call. The very thought of placing the call and having him reject her loomed too large. Trudging up the steps, she realized she'd made a mistake. A big one. She went and let herself develop feelings for a man. She wasn't scared, she was terrified.

She liked him. Truly liked him as a person, not a plaything. Given half a chance, she might more than like him, but there was no point in going down the path of what-ifs. She'd blown any chance they had from the get-go. There'd be no salvaging anything.

Stepping into her bedroom, the truth of what she was facing struck her full-force. A few short weeks ago, she would have described her bedroom as her sanctuary. Memories of Colm permeated every corner now. The scent of sex hung heavy in the air. She flung herself onto the well-rumpled bed and grabbed the pillow he'd used. Clutching it to her chest like a lovesick girl, she inhaled deeply. His scent surrounded her. Tears seeped from the corners of her eyes, but she didn't bother wiping them away.

Too much work.

She'd think about moving on and all that entailed later. She'd have to strip the bed at the very least. Would clean sheets do the trick? She could delete his contact info from her phone. Might keep her from making an even bigger fool of herself. Oh, God. She'd better. What if she had one too many margaritas one night and ended up drunk dialing him? How mortifying would that be? And what would she say if she did? I miss you? Come back? My bed smells like you?

Pathetic.

Panic seized her, making her chest tighten and forcing a sob to rise up into her throat. But she couldn't let loose. A few tears were one thing, but she couldn't let go entirely. She didn't deserve a big, sloppy cry. There was no one to blame but herself for her predicament.

A single simple sentence uttered at the start. "I'm her aunt," she whispered to the ceiling. Or maybe two sentences. "Oh, Emma is my sister's kid. We're having one of our days at the park." But playing like she took Emma out regularly would have been kind of a lie, too. It made her sound like a doting aunt, rather than the crappy one she'd been so far. At least she had a chance at fixing that bit.

How easily those little lies and bits of spin popped into her head these days. She'd never been one to care overmuch about what other people thought of her. But she cared about what Colm thought. How could she not? Here was a man who'd stepped up and shouldered responsibility. And she, apparently, had become a woman who wallowed around in her sexed-up bed cooking up more lies to feed him.

He deserved better. Aside from the fact that she wasn't at all what he thought she was, this wasn't the woman she chose to be. She wanted her pre-Colm life again. The one she knew and understood. Where she was the old Monica. The woman who set goals and charged straight at them. Not this weepy, wussy fool who'd gone and done the unthinkable—fallen in love with a man she'd been lying to from the start.

Chapter 8

She called exactly three days later. Colm wasn't surprised. Not that he thought he was so irresistible, or they left things on such a high note, but because she was stubborn and determined. She was also clearly used to getting her way. And he was weak. He wanted to see her. Desperately. So he let the call slide to voicemail.

Then, there were the text messages. He responded, but with only the briefest answers. He'd put her off for a week, but he was going to have to either man up and end their relationship once and for all, or give in and let her have her way.

And, Lord, did he want to let her have her way. Colm would gladly let her have her way with him all she wanted. He couldn't let her have her way with them. Because he couldn't shake the feeling if he left everything up to Monica, they'd meet for a few hot sweaty hours once a week…period.

And he wanted more.

He liked her. Despite her inherent bossiness and the weird, clutter-less life. Or maybe because of those two mind-boggling traits. Hard to say. The reasons for his attraction to her were variable. Depending on the moment. And right this very minute, he was in a mood to be stubborn and a bit bossy himself. Gripping the phone, he cleared his throat and cut right to the chase.

"Listen, I'm in the pickup line and I don't have a lot of time. What can I do for you, Monica?"

"Oh, the list is long and inventive," she replied, her tone as husky and playful as his was brisk.

He wasn't buying. "Sorry, no fun and games this weekend. I don't have a sitter."

"Oh."

Somehow, she managed to infuse a metric ton of disappointment into a single syllable. Colm found himself weakening. What man wouldn't when a beautiful woman called? Or when he heard and recognized the want in her voice. He'd been living with the same dull ache since he walked out her door. He hated the way they left things. Cringed every time he thought too hard about how he practically stomped out her door, as pissy as a toddler told he couldn't keep the awesome toy he'd found.

He didn't want to be that guy any more than he wanted to be her sometime piece of ass. Clearing his throat, he made an attempt at exploring new territory. A real date. The kind without invisible boundaries and topics marked off limits. Not some adults-only fantasy land, but one which incorporated the most essential pieces of their real lives. If there was any chance of them moving forward, one of them had to take the first step.

"I'd like to see you out of bed."

"Colm, I—"

He waited. And waited.

At last, she sighed, "There are things I need to tell you."

"So tell me."

Again, a long pause. "I don't know how."

Sighing, he conceded a little ground. "How about the four of us have a play date?"

"What?"

"I can bring Aiden by when you get home from work. We'll bring pizza, since I suspect poor Emma is smuggling snacks out of aftercare to keep her strength up."

"Oh, I, uh…"

She paused, and he almost relented. He, more than anyone, understood the risks of getting the kids involved. But he wanted to see her. Wanted to watch how she interacted with Emma, and yes, Aiden, too. And he could be every bit as dictatorial as she could. Without giving her any more time to think through the pros and cons, he closed negotiations.

"The kids can play and we can talk."

"I don't know if—"

But a weird self-preservational instinct made him cut her off. "I'll be by at about six-thirty. Does Emma have any food allergies?"

The question seemed to catch her off-guard. She stammered and stuttered for a moment. "Uh, um…No. Not that I know of."

"Lucky. There's a kid in Aiden's class with a nasty tree nut allergy and another with Celiac disease. Birthday parties are a nightmare."

"Right. Yes. I mean, no, Emma isn't allergic," she said, sounding slightly dazed.

He couldn't blame her. A woman as undomesticated as Monica would have a hard time adapting to the demands of a specialized diet. Emma probably lived off a combination of truffle mac and cheese and chicken nuggets. Poor kid.

"Great. We'll see you at six-thirty." He let off the brake to creep forward a couple feet. He wanted to end the call before she could come up with an excuse, so he told a bald-faced lie. Staring at the eight cars ahead of him, he said, "Gotta go, I'm next in line. See ya later."

He barely gave her time to say goodbye as he ended the call and blew out of a gusty breath. Bringing Aiden into things was a ballsy step, but he had a niggling suspicion that pursuing any kind of real relationship with Monica Rayburn was going to call for drastic measures.

The phone rang a moment later. Her name flashed onto the screen. The temptation to answer was strong. Nearly overwhelming. He didn't give in, though. She'd had a couple minutes to let the prospect of mingling their worlds sink in. She'd either have to ante up or call it a bad bet. Colm's gut instinct said she was calling to bet off, and he wasn't in the mood to make doing so easy for her. She wanted sex; he wanted a date. This was an impasse. She had two choices—leave a voicemail with some lame excuse, or play out the hand he'd dealt.

He wasn't too worried about getting a message. Backing down was not her style. Monica charged at life like a bull. He eyed the phone he'd tossed into the console tray warily, watching with trepidation for a flicker of life. Waiting for an electronic chime to tell him he'd read her all wrong. None came.

Colm smiled to himself as he inched closer to the pick-up area. He spotted his son in the crowd of students easily. The *Teenage Mutant Ninja Turtles* pack strapped to his back was nearly as big as his boy. Princess Clarissa's tangled hair gleamed dully in the afternoon sunlight. Aiden danced from one foot to the other, craning his neck to keep the truck in sight. As if he might simply poof himself out of this never-ending line.

With a sigh, he drummed the steering wheel, silently acknowledging his friend Mike may have been right about Aiden being too young for them to start on the *Harry Potter* series. Even though they talked about each chapter they read, and Colm painstakingly explained which phenomena were real and which were fictional, there were a few concepts Aiden clung to believing. Like the fact that parents weren't guaranteed to be a permanent fixture in a boy's life.

He glanced down at the console again. The phone didn't buzz or chirp to indicate a message. Mouth set in a grim line, Colm gripped the wheel tight and inched forward on the tail of the minivan ahead of him. They'd stop at the library rather than the grocery store tonight. After all, there was pizza on the menu. They could make through the next day without squeezable yogurt.

Minutes later, the door flew open and Aiden scrambled up into the seat, enormous backpack humped over his neck like the turtle shell.

"Shell off, seatbelt on," Colm ordered, not taking his foot off the brake until he was sure Aiden complied. "How was your day?"

Aiden kicked the seat a few times—revenge for making him remove his shell, no doubt—and made him wait for an answer. "Okay. Billy Morton had a huge booger hanging out of his nose, and Miss Marci didn't see for the longest time."

Colm finally had the fatherhood experience to give the appropriate response. "Awesome."

"She made him blow his nose and all this green stuff came out."

"Wow."

"So cool."

"I bet." Colm smiled into the rear-view mirror. "Hey, I was thinking we'd run by the library, then pick up a pizza."

"Cool." Pleased by the evening's agenda, he started bopping in his seat and singing, "Pizza, pizza, pizza. Pizza, pizza, pizza."

Colm chuckled. In the past few weeks, Aiden had pared his vocabulary down to a handful of words: Cool, ew, nope, okay, why, and a noncommittal uh-nuh seemed to fit multiple occasions. Conversations went a lot faster these days.

"So, uh, you remember that girl Emma we met in the park a few weeks ago? The one who helped find Princess Clarissa?" He might have been enlightened enough to let his boy tote a cartoon princess around with him, but he wasn't about to refer to her as a doll. He glanced up at the mirror. Aiden was knotting his fingers in the strap of his backpack and staring out the window, his mind a million miles away. "Hey, bud?" he called, tossing a glance over the seat. "You remember?"

"Huh?"

"The girl from the park a couple weeks ago? Emma?"

"Uh-nuh."

"We're going to go hang out with her and her mom tonight. Cool, huh?"

He glanced up to find Aiden staring at the mirror. The moment their eyes met, his son scowled at him. "Why?"

Colm saw the intense gleam of suspicion in his kid's eyes and knew his only recourse under such scrutiny was to deflect and defuse. "Why? Why not?"

Aiden blinked once. "She's a girl."

Lips twitching, Colm refocused on the road ahead of them. "Yes. They both are."

"So why?"

Stifling a sigh, Colm turned on his blinker, hoping they'd reach their branch of the library before Aiden could launch a full interrogation. "They were nice, right?" He shrugged as if he suggested play dates with girls every day. But they both knew he didn't. "Hey, I'm thinking we need some different books to read. I can't take any more of the creepy-crawly stuff Harry has to deal with." He gave an exaggerated shudder. "I'm having nightmares."

He glanced up to find Aiden studying him intently. At last, his son let one scrawny shoulder rise and fall. "You can sleep with me."

Colm smiled, but held it together. At least, on the outside. If anybody ever knew how easily his kid could turn him into mush, he'd not only be forced to relinquish his Man Card, but maybe the equipment, too. And he couldn't risk that happening. Not now. Not when said equipment was finally proving itself useful again.

"Hey, thanks, buddy," he said, masking the rasp in his voice with a growl.

Wheeling the SUV into the minute parking area beside the library, he surveyed his options. He could either take the chance of blocking a fellow patron in for a few minutes, or double-park in the street. He was weighing the relative merits of pissed off citizen versus exorbitant parking ticket when Aiden's train of thought circled around.

"Why do we hafta have pizza with girls?"

Colm chose put-out patron over meter maid and wedged the car into a space behind a battered compact with a dozen pro-reading stickers on the back window. With a little luck, the car would be Miss Carol's, the super-friendly librarian who ran the children's reading room and not Miss Rachel's, the stern-faced battle-axe who ran the circulation desk like a field battalion.

"Because Emma was nice and found Princess Clarissa and gave her back." He yanked the keys from the ignition and popped the latch on his seatbelt. "We need to thank her." Hoping to cut the question and answer session short, he bailed from the car.

By the time he opened the rear passenger door, Aiden had already freed himself from his restraint. "But that was a long time ago. Three Saturdays."

Crap. The kid had done the math. He was some kind of genius. An evil genius with mad deductive skills. Colm had no one to blame but himself. The two of them had been playing detective since the boy could say, "Just the facts, ma'am."

"I know, but we've been busy and they've been busy," he said as he ushered Aiden toward the doors. The sooner he got him inside, the sooner he could shush him. "So, I talked to Emma's mommy and we decided tonight was a good night."

Okay, technically, he decided tonight was good and forced the issue. But if he wanted Monica to get over her aversion to mixing their so-called real lives, he was going to have to push her limits. No one knew wary as well as he did. He appreciated her caution. But the other night he realized they were fooling themselves with the oh-so-casual sex thing. The way he saw it, they owed themselves a chance to at least test-drive the idea. In order to get behind the wheel, he needed to get his kid somewhat on board. No one knew better than Colm how fast a sulky five-year-old could run an entire day off the rails. He had no doubt in his son's ability to deep-six what would at best be a couple hours of dinner and play time in a matter of minutes.

He reached the double doors and opened one to allow a mother and her two squabbling daughters to leave. A ripple of pride shot through him when Aiden stood courteously aside and let them pass without charging ahead. The kid was learning. Manners and so many other things. And while it puffed Colm up a bit, the evidence of Aiden's maturity also dinged his heart. It was all happening so fast. Too fast. He'd blink, and the kid would be asking for the car keys.

These moments wrung his heart like an old, wet washrag. He wanted to stop time. Savor every minute. Share them with someone. A person who would understand the muddled mix of triumph and terror called parenthood. He knew without a doubt he and Monica were combustible when left alone. He wanted to see if their kids might get along. Was it too much to ask? And if so, who knew how things might develop?

He waved the boy into the lobby, smiling as he caught him goggling over a poster featuring a superhero holding books. When they reached the inner door, Colm whispered, "I'm hearing good things about a guy made out of stinky cheese. Should we ask Miss Carol about him?"

To his relief, Aiden giggled and ducked under his outstretched arm and raced toward the children's section. All objections forgotten the moment Colm uttered the magic word—stinky.

* * * *

"You can't do this to me," Monica hissed into the phone.

Melody snorted. "Do what? Deny you the use of my daughter as a prop in your sex games?"

Scowling at the supplies she'd chosen in a frenzy at the corner market, she shuddered. "Okay, that was too weird to even count as sarcasm."

"But essentially, that's what you're doing." Her sister's words came out in puffs indicating some intense activity of her own. "If you had asked me if your baby beard was available tonight, I would have reminded you for the third time she has a dance recital and is expecting you to have your skinny butt in one of the seats."

Pressing the heel of her hand to her forehead, Monica closed her eyes and counted down from five. When she opened them, she hadn't found a shred of serenity, but she did have the nervous munchies. Snatching a package of string cheese from the fridge shelf, she fell against the counter as the door swung shut. She had to have looked like a crazy woman zooming through the mini-market, trying to remember every sort of snack Melody had ever jammed into Emma's tote.

"Maybe I can tell him she's got the flu or something and meet you there," she speculated as she pried open the package.

A strong huff of breath nearly burst her eardrum.

"Do you even hear yourself?"

Monica straightened, prepared to go on the defensive. "What?"

"You're turning into quite the liar."

She blinked, a strip of string cheese dangling from her fingers. "What?"

Melody sighed, but for the first time since she answered the phone, Monica stopped to give the conversation her full attention.

"All you've done since meeting this man is lie to him."

Monica managed a syllable of protest, but her sister continued.

"Lies of omission are lies all the same, Monica."

Monica dropped the cheese into her mouth and chomped, disgruntled by her sister's bluntness. "Since when did you become a nun?"

"I'm not judging, I'm stating a fact."

Monica heard a shuffle and a click, and the background noise of her sister's life cut out. Her eyes narrowed with suspicion. "Did you take me into the bathroom with you?"

"I need a minute," Melody replied unapologetically. "I was up until three sewing scales on Emma's leotard."

"Scales?"

"Sequins that look like scales," she explained in a dismissive rush. "She's a mermaid, remember? She only told you sixteen times."

"I remember," Monica insisted, though she hadn't.

"Wow, the lies keep coming."

Setting her teeth, she tossed the string cheese aside. Melody was right, of course. And truthfully, the lying was keeping her up at night. In the beginning, letting him believe that one little thing had all seemed harmless.

He kept his illusions. She got in his pants. They'd had a little fun. Nothing more. But life got complicated. Colm turned out to be more than a hot guy or a sexy single dad. So much more.

"I like him," she said in a whisper.

The silence on the other end of the call spoke volumes. At last, Melody drew a shaky breath. "I know you do, Monnie. You can't go on letting him think you're something you're not."

"I know." The words came out small and squeaky. "I'm not ready to…" She bit her lip. "I like him."

"Tell him," Melody advised. "Just tell him it was a mix-up, things went too far, and you didn't know how to tell him. Everyone's gotten stuck sometime. He'll understand."

"I know, I know." Swallowing the burning lump in her throat, she couldn't resist taking one last shot. "So…you're sure Emma can't come over?"

"You're a train wreck."

"Tell me something I don't know," Monica muttered.

"We'll save you a seat. If you manage to get loose from the tangled web you've woven, the performance starts at seven."

Monica glared at the screen on her phone until the background faded to black. She slid the useless lifeline onto the counter with a murmured, "Thanks a lot, sis."

She tried to call Colm's cell again. Straight to voicemail.

Alone in her underused kitchen, Monica tried to quell the panic rising inside her. Everything Melody said was true. He might be a little pissed at first, but when he thought things through, when she explained how it all got so far out of hand, he'd understand. After all, he'd wanted all the same things she did in the beginning. Neither of them expected anything more.

She glanced at the clock on the microwave. Only twenty minutes until Colm and Aiden would arrive. She could do this. Colm was a reasonable man. And Melody was right; everyone stumbles into one of those "how do I get out of this?" situations at some point or another. She'd simply explain she hadn't believed they'd see each other after the first night. He hadn't expected anything from her, either, so he couldn't fault her.

When he came, she'd be straightforward and honest. He'd have to accept reality. Either they had a real chance or they didn't. If they had real feelings for each other, all the lies in the world wouldn't make a bit of difference. Pushing away from the counter, she steeled her spine and headed upstairs to ditch her suit in favor of something more casual.

By the time her doorbell rang, she wore a T-shirt, faded jeans, and an expression of grim resolve. Which crumbled the moment she spotted the dark-haired duo standing on her doorstep with an enormous pizza box. Colm smiled at her through the leaded glass, and every good intention she ever had melted. She ran a hand over her hair but couldn't make herself reach for the door.

The dark-eyed boy shuffled his feet and looked up at her with the kind of unconcealed impatience only kids under ten could get away with displaying. Colm's smile faltered a fraction as he cocked his head questioningly, but brightened when she took hold of the deadbolt toggle. She had to do something. Anything. But she hadn't the first clue how to begin. All she knew was she wasn't ready for this to end. There had to be some way to delay the inevitable.

She opened the door only a crack and pressed her face into the opening. Colm's smile disappeared the moment she whispered, "I'm sorry. We can't do this tonight."

"What's wrong?"

He craned his neck to look past her into the house, and instinctively, Monica turned to follow his gaze. But all she saw was the immaculate entryway. The lack of clutter should have been a dead giveaway for him. She'd seen Melody's place. She knew even at their cleanest, kids left an indelible mark on a home. He should have noticed. Maybe he had.

Monica squinted up at him, searching for signs of duplicity in his eyes. All she found was confusion. She'd been shining him on for a while, but he could be playing innocent, too. After all, in one giant leap they'd gone from a mutually agreeable kid-free arrangement to a pizza party for four, when in truth there were only three.

Was this his way of flushing her out and forcing her to own up? The very thought of being trapped raised her hackles. Her competitive streak kicked in with a vengeance. She wouldn't be boxed into a corner. No way in hell she was going to let him railroad her into a relationship without her consent. And, if he was going to try, he'd have to work harder to outmaneuver her.

"I tried to call." Truth. She had. Multiple times. In the end, he could split all the hairs he wanted, but she never outright lied to him. She simply let him believe what he wanted to believe. The same way he seemed to see only what he wanted to see. "I'm sorry, we can't have pizza tonight."

"Why not?" Colm asked.

"We already got the pizza," Aiden pointed out. "It's in the box."

She smiled down at him. The boy was adorable. And, oh, how her fingers itched to ruffle this wavy dark hair. He looked at her with wide brown eyes. Soft as they were, they seemed to cut right through her. Like he could see every lie swirling inside her head. Lies. Here she was, lying to this good man and his sweet boy. Her stomach twisted.

"I see, and I'm really sorry I can't have any." True. So true. She couldn't eat a bite if she tried. She pressed a hand to her belly to emphasize the point.

Colm stared at her for a long moment. At last, understanding lit his handsome face. "Are you sick?"

Monica grabbed hold of the excuse like a life preserver. "Yes. I'm sorry, things are, uh, out of control here." She waved an all-encompassing hand but was careful not to take her niece's name in vain as she threaded yet another lie through the web she'd started weaving the day she met him. "Came home feeling cra...cruddy. Don't want to expose you guys to the germs."

She watched Colm's face as he processed this information. His jaw was set at a stubborn angle, but he cut a worried glance at Aiden. Monica knew she had a winner. No parent in their right mind would risk exposing their kid to illness. Melody once grabbed Emma and bolted from Thanksgiving dinner when their cousin's kid went full-on projectile. She explained to Monica later the narrow escape was a matter of self-preservation as much as concern for her kid. Aside from being on full-time nursing duty, a sick kid meant mountains of laundry and an unending supply of puke, snot, or other bodily excretions to mop up.

Monica could almost see the wheels turning in Colm's head as he weighed risk versus reward, so she upped the ante. Pressing her hand to her forehead, she heaved a heavy sigh. "I'm...feeling wiped out."

"Can we take the pizza home?" Aiden asked, his voice plaintive but edging toward a whine. "I'm really hungry."

"Oh, yeah," Monica said, holding up a hand as if to hold the evil pizza at bay. "Please take it home. I can't..." She let her protest trail off, leaving the exact nature of the plague infesting the Rayburn household as vague as possible.

Colm shifted his weight as Aiden tugged on his belt loop urging him to go. But the man stayed planted, obviously torn. "Do you need anything?"

The genuine concern in his voice raised a lump in her throat. Another rush of heat engulfed her. Pressing her lips together, she forced herself to answer with a jerky shake of her head.

"Gatorade? Crackers? Soup?" he offered.

"Daddy," Aiden whined. "Come on."

Monica did her best not to smile at her unwitting ally. "Go on. If I need anything, I'll call my sister."

At last, Colm nodded his acceptance. "You two get some sleep if you can. Call me if there's anything I can do."

"I will."

Her smile felt shaky, but she kept it in place until he turned away. She closed the door and twisted the lock, pressing her hand to her lips when Colm looked up and nodded his approval at the sound of the bolt. He gave her a sad little smile. Melody was right. She couldn't go on lying to him. But her smarty-pants sister was wrong about one very important thing. Monica was sure Colm wasn't going to understand. No matter what she wanted to believe.

Monica walked up the polished hardwood stairs as if her feet were encased in blocks of cement. Her bedroom was dim, cool, and empty. Thanks to a couple restless nights, every surface gleamed sleek and polished. She'd changed the linens. No good. Everything smelled like Colm. A new duvet and pillows were the only answer.

She fell face-first onto the bed, not bothering to put her hands out to break her fall. The down comforter billowed around her. Not a single whiff of eau de Colm floated up to greet her. But he wasn't completely gone. She'd stuffed the old pillows and bedspread into the depths of the guest room closet, but they were far from forgotten. The impulse to open the door and take a hit had struck no less than a dozen times. So far, she'd resisted, but knew she couldn't hold out indefinitely. A woman only had so much strength, after all, and at the moment, she didn't have enough to hold her shit together.

Closing her eyes, she allowed her thoughts to drift until they settled on a more pleasant scenario. She and Colm seated on a vinyl-covered bench of a diner booth. Aiden on the other side, stuffing forkfuls of crisp golden waffle into his mouth. But something niggled at her. A piece of this picture wasn't right. Did she not fit in? Would Aiden hate sharing his time with his dad? No. She didn't think so. Sure, the boy looked a little put out when they stood on her doorstep, but he hadn't looked angry or resentful. Just confused. And she could hardly blame him. She was every bit as befuddled by the whole thing as he'd looked. Besides, in her little daydream he'd been smiling at her. At them. No, something else niggled her…something small…

Her butt buzzed, jolting her from her lame attempt at analysis. She groped for the pocket of her jeans and plucked her phone from its depths. The screen showed an incoming text from Colm. Sighing, she fell out on the bed, the phone above her face. She squinted until the message swam into focus, then sighed again. This time deeper, more pathetic.

Sorry you guys are sick. The pizza was bleh. Company not much better since i am the worst dad in the world bcuz i said no pokemon during dinner. Hope tomorrow better.

Biting her lip, she blinked three times fast as she let her arm fall to the bed. She wouldn't reply. Couldn't. What would she say?

Sorry I lied. Again. Sorry I keep lying. I can't seem to help myself whenever you're around.

She erased the type, tossed the phone onto her fluffy new pillow and pressed the side of her fist to her forehead. As if she could physically calm her swirling thoughts. She let her eyes drift shut.

Blanking her mind, she channeled what little energy she had to breathing in, and out. In, out. In...out.

She must have dozed, because the next thing she knew, Night Ranger was blaring *Sister Christian* at top volume. Gritting her teeth, she lunged for the pillow, hoping to quell the build up to motorin'.

"Hey," she breathed into the blessed silence.

"Hello. Are your pants no longer on fire?" Melody asked in a chipper tone. "If they are, we're talking in a good way."

"Kill me."

Mel's groan was low but heartfelt. "Sounds like I need to put the hit out on someone else. Was he a jerk? Should I make his death really slow and painful?"

"Not him, me. I didn't tell him."

"What?" Her sister's horrified gasp was sharp.

Monica pulled the phone away from her ear.

"How? What did you...How could you not tell him? Didn't he notice you were short one adorable kid?"

"I lied. Again." Her chest squeezed. "I told him I was sick."

"Oh, Monica."

The disappointment in Melody's tone sent a hot rush of tears to her eyes. Her phone vibrated to indicate an incoming text. Blinking furiously and curious to see if her sister had found a way to chastise her on multiple fronts, Monica looked at the screen. The message was from Colm and so sweet she could probably curl into a ball and die without any outside intervention.

You must be sleeping. Get some rest. I have a dentist appt in the AM. Will call after.

Her breath caught in her chest, and for the life of her, Monica couldn't remember exactly how the whole breathing sequence was supposed to go. With the last of what she had trapped in her lungs, she managed a tremulous, "Melly?"

"Yeah?"

"His little boy is so cute," she whispered, her voice breaking. "I—I like him so—" She bit her lip as the tears spilled over her lashes. "I think

I'm in trouble."

There was only a millisecond of silence on her sister's end of the call, then Melody's voice came through soft but firm. "Breathe, Monnie. In, and out. In and out," she chanted. Once Monica caught on to the cadence, Mel's tone shifted into brisk and no-nonsense. "Jeremy is getting Emma settled in. I'm picking up Ben and Jerry, and the three of us will be over in fifteen minutes."

"Mel, no—"

"Fifteen minutes. Hang in there, Monnie. Chunky Monkey is coming to the rescue."

Her preferred flavor for heartache was Coffee Toffee Crunch, but Melody hung up. Monica gave a moment's thought to calling her sister back to beg off, but she knew she wouldn't win. She'd have to make do with banana ice cream rather than the caffeinated kind. The switch up seemed only fitting. Her well-ordered life had somehow gone completely nuts.

Chapter 9

Colm was unspeakably relieved when Aiden showed no apparent signs or symptoms of illness while they were preparing to leave the house. Sure, they hadn't actually stepped foot into Monica's place, but you never knew with kids. They seemed to pick up and pass along viruses like relay racers with a baton. Swallowing his guilt, he dropped his well-rested kid off at daycare, and proceeded to his early morning dentist appointment without attempting to call and check on Monica and Emma. He hoped they were getting at least some sleep and didn't want to risk waking them.

He was at the door when Dr. Holt's hygienist, Andrea, arrived. "Wow. Someone's excited to get their X-rays."

Colm smiled and pushed away from the wall opposite the office door. "Yeah, well, what guy doesn't want a bat-wing of his own?"

"Hate to break this to you, champ, but they're called *bite*wing, not bat wing."

Affecting a scowl, Colm waited as she flipped on overhead lights. "Oh. In that case…"

She laughed and waved him in. "Nope. Shauna's not here yet, but I'll check you in and get you all shined up before Dr. Holt gets here."

He followed her into one of the patient cubicles and took his seat in the chair. Andrea handed him an ancient copy of *Field & Stream* and told him to keep himself entertained while she juiced up the coffee maker. Colm ruffled the pages of the magazine, but the pictures barely registered. He liked fishing and stuff but wasn't really up for reading up on the subject. Pulling his phone from his pocket, he tapped his way through his inbox and a handful of other notifications.

Nothing new from Monica yet. Unable to hold off a minute longer, he typed a quick message about hoping they felt better and promising to call after his appointment. The little whooshing noise made him feel slightly less guilty about getting a full night's sleep. He knew how miserable spending the whole night dumping puke pots and changing sheets could be.

"Ready to go?" Andrea asked, snapping the cuff on her latex glove.

"You love the snap, don't you?" he asked, eying her warily.

She grinned, then pulled her mask up over her nose and mouth. "Limited career options for born sadists," she said, her voice only slightly muffled by the covering. Her eyes twinkled as she slipped a pair of wrap-around safety glasses onto her nose. "My choices were dental hygienist or beauty aesthetician."

"Beauty aesthetician? What do they do?"

The corners of her eyes crinkled as she ripped open a pack of sanitized instruments and pressed the pedal to lower the chair into supine position. Looming over him, she raised her instruments. "They get to do bikini waxes and all the fun stuff." She tapped his chin with her pinkie finger. "Open wide."

Thirty minutes later, Andrea pronounced him sparkling clean. Mask crumpled around her neck, she patted his shoulder as she returned the chair to an upright position. "You were a good boy."

He smirked at her condescending tone. She said the same thing to Aiden when he was done, too. Except Aiden got his pick of toys when he was through, and Colm got stuck paying the bill. "Thanks. Do I get to visit the treasure chest?"

"We'll see what Dr. Holt says," she said in a sing-song voice. "I heard him come in. I'll send him on in."

Upright again, Colm worked his jaw back and forth as he took a moment to study the exam room. A picture Aiden had colored was pinned to a corkboard, surrounded by pictures of grinning patients. The countertops held anatomically correct models, a disturbing display on gum disease, and an oversized pair of plastic chattering teeth sat right in front of a framed photo of Dr. Holt and his family.

He'd been about to move on to an advertisement for whitening treatments when the hairs on his neck prickled. Turning to the photo, he skipped over the good doctor and squinted hard at the woman and child clustered close to him. Mrs. Holt was a pretty woman in an all-natural sort of way. Her wavy dirty-blond hair was carelessly styled and a little wispy. She had the wispy look of an artist or a gypsy. Or maybe the assumption was based solely on the patchwork skirt and floaty white blouse she wore. But there was something familiar about her. Maybe her eyes? Possibly the nose. Her smile. Yes, that was it. He'd seen her smile. Knew that smile. Intimately.

Swinging his legs over the side of the chair, he planted his feet on the ground, but his body seemed to be moving in slow motion. His gaze slipped from the mother to the daughter. The skinny brown-haired girl had the same smile as her mother.

His stomach twisted into a knot as he pushed the toy teeth aside and picked up the frame. He needed a closer look to be absolutely sure. But there was no denying what he was seeing. The little girl's grin confirmed she was standing exactly where she belonged.

"My wife, Melody, and my daughter, Emma."

Colm jumped and the frame almost slipped from his hand. He caught the picture with a grunt, pressing the glass into his stomach to be certain he'd secured it, then fumbled the photo back into place. "I was, uh..." He adjusted the angle on the counter and shoved the chattering teeth into place. "Nice picture."

"Thanks." Dr. Holt gestured for him to take a seat in the chair again. Once Colm complied, he immediately began to flatten and lower the chair. "My wife hates studio photography. She says it's stifling." His soft snort let Colm know he thought his wife was both wacky and wonderful. "My sister-in-law took that one last spring."

Colm managed to get a quick "Yeah?" out as the doctor motioned for him to open his mouth.

"Yeah. Melody likes candid stuff, has all this crazy expensive photography equipment." He craned his head to peer at Colm's molars. "Our place is littered with pictures of crumbling bridges and shacks. For family pictures, I have to rely on Monica and her cell phone."

Dread pooled cold and heavy in Colm's belly. He closed his eyes as if he might be able to block out the truth. But there was no point. He'd known the minute he saw the little girl in the photo. Emma wasn't Monica's daughter. Lies. Everything Monica had told him from the moment they met had been complete bullshit.

Exactly like Carmen.

The moment the connection was made, there was no way of unknowing. The dread he'd felt a moment ago congealed into a ball of icy anger. He said nothing. Couldn't with this guy probing around in his mouth. Taking deliberate breaths through his nose, he fixed his gaze on the muted television screen mounted on the ceiling. The news was covering the mayor's press conference. Colm narrowed his eyes as he watched the man dodge and duck the questions being lobbed at him. He didn't need to read the closed captioning to know the man was lying his ass off, too. The whole fucking world was filled with nothing but liars.

"Looking good." Dr. Holt sat back and pulled his mask down. "X-rays were clean. You're good to go for another six months unless there's something bothering you."

The chair hummed and vibrated beneath him. Colm stared at the dentist's open, inquisitive face, wondering if the guy knew. If he'd been in on the joke. Maybe they all thought Monica using their kid to meet guys was a hoot. Or, maybe old doc here was trying to offload the sister-in-law on some poor, unsuspecting schmuck.

"I think I've met your daughter," he said, jerking his chin toward the picture. "She was at the park with your sister-in-law. Monica," he added as if unequivocal confirmation was needed.

"You did?"

"Yeah." Rubbing a hand across his jaw, he licked his latex-dry lips. "Your Emma found my kid's toy for him. Nice girl."

"She's awesome." Dr. Holt beamed. "Best thing to happen to me ever. Don't tell Mel I said so, you'll only get me in trouble."

Colm couldn't help but return the man's smile. He knew that level of enthusiasm well. "Yeah, kids are great. They make you crazy, but they're great."

"Set him up for another six months, Andrea." As the hygienist pecked at the computer, Dr. Holt peeled off his gloves and nodded to the picture. "She and Aiden are probably about the same age."

Six months apart, Colm thought. But he couldn't say so, because Monica had told him how old Emma was, and for all he knew, that was another lie. Monica had lied to him. Lied over and over again. The implications were too much to absorb. The park. Her whole "let's not talk about the kids" bit. The convenient stomach bug she'd made up to keep him from crossing her threshold last night. Had she been sick, or was the stomach bug just one more lie? Like the cherry on top?

His gaze drifted to the photo again, but this time he zeroed in on the sister. Had she been in on the plot? Did Dr. Holt know his wife was letting his daughter be used as a prop to pick up guys in the park?

As if reading his thoughts, the doctor continued. "Funny, Emma looks and acts so much like Mel's sister. Emma's very no-nonsense like Monica. Melody swears the two of them gang up on her."

Colm swallowed hard. "Yeah, I guess I assumed they were mom and daughter when I saw them in the park."

The other man snorted. "Not hardly." When he caught Colm's startled stare, Dr. Holt shrugged. "Monica's not the maternal type. She's one of those high-powered career women who doesn't have time to date." Turning away, he tossed the balled up gloves into a container. "Don't get me wrong. She's a good aunt, but she's definitely more the hands-off type with kids."

"She is, huh?" Colm practically launched himself out of the space chair. He needed to get out of there. Turning to Andrea, he made a show of checking his watch. "Hey, I have to get going. Will you set me up for six months and send me a reminder?"

The hygienist seemed taken aback by his sudden rush. Muttering his goodbyes, he beat a path to the office door.

He was in front of Monica's brownstone in a matter of minutes. Of course, she wasn't home. He unclipped his phone from his belt as he jogged down the steps but didn't place the call. The thought of having this confrontation over the phone crawled all over him, but he couldn't imagine storming her office and trying to have it out with her in front of all her colleagues. Sitting in his truck, Colm stared down at the photo he'd attached to her contact information.

This was the Monica he knew. Tousled, sexed-up, and satiated. Until that moment, he hadn't realized he didn't have the first idea where her office was. He didn't know if she stopped for coffee on the way in to work at the crack of dawn, or if she was one of those freaks who didn't drink coffee. Rubbing the pad of his thumb idly across the screen, he searched his memory, trying to recall if he'd even spotted a coffee maker in her barely used kitchen. He knew nothing about her other than how to make her come.

Except, she was apparently a compulsive liar.

Jaw set, he tapped the option to place the call. She answered on the first ring, her tone crisp and business-like.

"Monica Rayburn."

He inhaled through his nose, but forced a civil tone. "How are you feeling today?"

"Oh, hi." Her voice softened like butter left too long in the microwave. "Hey."

"Fully recovered?" he persisted.

"Hm? Oh! Yeah. Must have been one of those overnight bugs."

"And Emma?"

She hesitated for a second. When she did, there was a note of caution in her voice. "She's fine."

Colm couldn't take the lies and half-truths any longer. "And you'd know this because you stopped by your sister's on the way in to work this morning?"

Silence. The question and all of its implications and accusations hung there. Her lack of response was like a bucket of sand tossed over the last smoldering coals of hope burning in his gut. Of course she wasn't going to deny it. To deny would be to confirm, and Monica was too sharp to fall for anything so obvious.

"I had a dentist appointment this morning. Guess who had a picture of a little girl I know named Emma? My dentist, Dr. Holt."

"Colm—"

"Imagine my surprise when he told me Emma was his little girl, and the woman in the photo with them was his wife. Emma's mother."

"I can explain—"

"Can you? You can explain how everything you told me was a lie?"

"Not everything."

She stopped talking. Of course she did. Monica was sharp. The nit-picking defense wasn't a great strategy to take at the moment, and she'd tuned into the volume of his silence. She was perceptive. He knew that much about her, even if he didn't know anything else.

"How do you take your coffee?" He couldn't stop himself from asking.

"Colm—"

"Where's your office?"

"Please listen—"

"No, I think I'm done listening to you." He couldn't deny himself the pleasure of prodding and pressing her. Even if it meant he had to subject himself to every ounce of pain her deception produced. After all, he deserved a good dose, too.

He was the idiot who'd been so gullible. Again.

He'd let himself believe. Again.

And look where he was—alone. Again.

"When were you going to tell me?" he demanded.

To her credit, she didn't lie this time. "Never."

"You were going to fuck me for a while, and what? Stop calling?"

The minute the words were out of his mouth, he wished they hadn't escaped. Because they had a deal. They'd agreed to exactly those terms when they started. The set-up he thought he wanted. And now he was pissed at her for sticking to the plan? Christ, he sounded like a needy teenager.

Covering his eyes with his hand, he pressed his temples with his thumb and middle finger. "Well, you can stop," he said, his voice flat and forbidding.

"Colm, don't," she said in a rush. "Let me explain."

"That you lied? You've been lying and planned to keep on lying?" He gave a short, mirthless laugh. "No need. I clued in all on my own."

"I didn't lie."

There was a knife's edge keenness in her tone. One that said she was adept at splitting hairs. Suddenly, he felt tired. So tired. Like he'd been the one up all night with a fake kid nursing the fake flu. There was no point in dissecting this. Whatever he thought their relationship was, or might have become, they obviously hadn't been on the same page.

Letting his breath go, he forced his shoulders to come down and stretched his neck forward to release the tension. There was really no need. They'd had a mutually satisfying physical relationship. If he'd developed unrealistic expectations about what was happening between them, the fallout was his problem and he'd deal. Alone.

"Good-bye, Monica."

He didn't wait to listen to whatever she had lined up behind the desperate-sounding "But—" she blurted.

With a single tap on the screen, he stopped the lies.

* * * *

Monica dropped into her desk chair like a stone. Her assistant came scurrying to her side. "What? What's wrong? Are you okay? Are you sick?" Nicole dropped to a knee beside Monica's chair and reached out as if to touch Monica's forehead. "Do I need to call 911?"

Monica batted the young woman's hand away. "What? Why? No!" She gripped the arms of her chair and forced herself to sit up ramrod straight. "I'm fine."

"But you're sitting," Nicole insisted, her forehead puckering in consternation. "You don't sit when there's trading."

Startled by the truth in the observation, Monica blinked. Her glass-walled office offered little privacy for either her or her staff. Usually, she liked it. As a matter of fact, in all the years since she'd become partner, she'd never once closed the sliding glass door to her office while the market was open. She wanted to see all. Hear all. Thrived on the chaos of business surrounding her.

Ironic. Now, her actual life was in chaos, and she didn't have the first idea what to do to fix things.

Needing a moment to gather herself, she forced a weak smile for her assistant. "Hey, would you grab a bottle of water for me?"

Nicole hopped to her feet. "Sure thing, boss."

Teeth set on edge, Monica continued to grip the armrests as she watched the younger woman scurry away. The warren of cubicles they called the bullpen was alive. An electronic board scrolled acronyms and numbers. Monica was proud of the team she'd assembled. Pleased by how far she'd come since she'd wormed her way into one of those cubicles. This was a man's world, but she'd conquered every obstacle put in her path to a corner office. Proved she had the chutzpah to make the boys shut up and listen. This was her queendom. This modern-day bedlam pulsing with shouts.

She lived her life to a soundtrack consisting of cries of either anguish or ecstasy. And for a long time, she'd thrived on the thrills and chills, but now she was stepping back from the melee.

Those glass walls allowed her to witness the mayhem but not actually take part. She handled trading for only a select handful of clients anymore. She staffed all the others out to the junior traders she'd trained and groomed herself. The business world called it "delegating," but Monica knew what her need for distance really was.

Cowardice.

She'd lost her edge years ago, but she wasn't about to admit as much. Not when she'd fought and crawled and clawed her way up the ladder. These days, she preferred to hand the reins and any resultant blame off to one of her subordinates. When anything did go wrong, she could step in, smooth the waters, and step back again without any personal loss of face.

Covering her face with her hands, she leaned forward until her elbows hit the desk. This was exactly the kind of self-analysis she'd spent most of her adult life avoiding. Melody was the one who loved soul-searching. Monica wasn't even entirely sure she had a soul, and, frankly, she was too scared to look. What if all she found was a big, gaping hole?

The worst part was she couldn't blame Colm for being pissed. He'd done everything right, and she'd been all wrong. From the very start, she wanted to indulge herself with Colm, but not really risk anything in the process. From the get-go, she had no intention of showing who she really was. Hell, it had been so many years since she even attempted to have a life, she wasn't certain she could tell him who she was outside of her career.

Worse, she hadn't even been able to tell him the most basic facts about herself. She was known among family and what few friends she kept in touch with for her glib comebacks and pithy asides. But with Colm, she fumbled the simplest truths. Even when those truths were nothing to be ashamed of. Certainly not worth hiding. How pathetic could one person be?

So she wasn't Emma's mom. There was no law stating only parents could take a child to a public park. And yes, she might have set the record straight on any number of occasions, but she hadn't sworn an oath upon accepting his dinner invitation.

"Boss? You okay?"

The quiet question undercut all the ambient noise coming from the bullpen and sliced clean through her line of justification. A low moan gurgled in her throat. She forced herself to raise her head, intending to whip out a standard "I'm fine" and send Nicole to her own desk, but her vision came up blurry. And though her brain screamed the words like a petulant child, no sound came out.

"Monica?"

The concern in Nicole's tone spurred her into action. Pressing her palm to her stomach, Monica did something she hadn't done since she was a junior trader.

She called off sick.

"No. I think I have to go." Gripping the edge of her desk, she made a feeble attempt to stand. When her knees failed, Nicole appeared at her side in a flash.

"Here." The younger woman thrust an ice-cold bottle of water into Monica's limp hand. "Uh, you're okay," she murmured unconvincingly. This was new territory for the both of them. "Sip this slow. I'll call down and tell Joe you need a cab." The moment the words were spoken, her uber-efficient assistant sprang into action. Snatching the handset of the desk phone from its cradle, she tucked the receiver between her shoulder and ear.

Ten minutes later, Monica had cleared the snarl of downtown traffic and was speeding toward home. This was a first. In so many ways. She couldn't remember a day when she ducked out of work prior to the close of trading. Definitely the first time she had ever ditched work because of a guy. She'd never let any man close enough to influence more than what she ate for dinner, much less ruin her entire day.

Her breath snarled in her chest. Monica pressed the side of her fist to the spot. The added pressure didn't help. The sharp edge of finality in Colm's tone cut to the bone. He was done with her. His position was clear. But she wasn't ready to be done with him. She was an idiot. An absolute idiot. She should have listened to Melody. Hell, she should have listened to her own conscience. But no, as usual, she hadn't listened to anyone or anything. Like a pirate, she'd barged right into the man's life, taken what she wanted, ignoring what was right. Or honorable. Honest.

The cab jerked to a halt in front of her place. She scrounged a twenty from her wallet and shoved the money through the partition, mumbling, "Keep the change."

The driver did a double take when he saw the bill. "You sure, lady?"

Monica roused herself from her stupor to look at the meter. The fare had come to seven dollars and forty-five cents. Automatically, her brain clicked and whirred. The balance from the bill would be about a one-hundred-and-eighty percent tip. Monica shrugged, reached for the door handle, and dragged her purse and briefcase across the cracked vinyl seat as she climbed out. "One of us needs to have a good day, and I don't think it's going to be me."

"Hey, thanks! Hope things get better for ya," he called as she let the door swing shut.

Monica acknowledged his well-wishes with a wave and trudged to her door. Once inside, she let her bags fall to the floor and tossed her keys into the glass bowl on the table. Shuffling into the kitchen, she realized she was home in the middle of the morning and didn't have the first clue what to do.

Was she supposed to watch daytime TV? She frowned at the tiny television mounted above the kitchen counter. Usually, she only powered the set on if she wanted to catch an early morning market report, or maybe check to see if a day's trading made the evening news for one reason or another. But this wasn't the time for talking about money; these were the hours when money was made. Or lost.

A surge of panic gripped her heart like a fist. She turned toward the front door but stopped. No. She'd done the right thing. She wasn't thinking straight, and the worst thing she could do to her team or her clients was pretend like she was. This was why she trained her people so rigorously, she reminded herself, so she could take vacations or the occasional day off. Smirking at her own capacity for self-delusion, she reached for the remote control. She *rarely* took vacations and *never* took days off.

She pointed the remote at the flat screen and hit the power button. Maybe there was a soap opera on. Did they still make soap operas? Maybe some daytime drama other than her own was what she needed. A little over-the-top acting to put her own little melodrama in the shade might be the ticket.

Monica flipped channels until she landed on one of the networks. A group of women were assembled in a variety of mismatched armchairs set to resemble some kind of eclectic living room. Between sound bites, photos of a Hollywood starlet caught in a variety of unflattering poses appeared. Monica caught the words "downward spiral," "unreliable," and "break-up." She turned her back on the chatty coven.

There was a little ice cream in the freezer. Very little, but she and Melody had shown a modicum of restraint when they had their wallow. Monica yanked open the door and a blast of super-cooled air hit her right in the face. She eyeballed the container of Chunky Monkey, wrinkling her nose in distaste. Ice cream in the morning didn't seem right.

She let the freezer door slam shut and turned her attention to the fridge. There, on the top shelf, were the six-pack of beer she'd bought for Colm and a bottle of crisp, dry chardonnay. She blinked to banish the tears threatening to fall and lunged for the slender green bottle. Ice cream might not be the answer this early in the day, but wine sounded perfect.

"Five o'clock somewhere," she muttered as she pulled the

corkscrew from a drawer.

The cork released with a satisfying *thwunk*. Monica smiled grimly as the liquid gold glugged into the bowl of a stemless glass. She downed half the glass. The ladies on the talk show moved on to the next topic—the red-hot actor who'd titillated all the residents of Ladyland by getting caught on film playing with his squealing kids in the Pacific surf. Cradling her glass with both hands, Monica sagged against the opposite counter as she took in the man's rippling muscles and crinkling smile.

He looked like Colm. She heard one of the women say something about the actor being Irish, and the next thing she knew, Monica had drained the contents of the glass. Gasping for breath, she gripped the edge of the counter to steady herself. The wine hit her stomach and her head at the exact same time.

What the hell was wrong with her? Was she having a stroke? Maybe a heart attack? More likely. Her chest felt compressed. As if she were folding in on herself. Or curling up like one of those furry little guys who balled up to protect themselves.

"Hedgehog," she blurted the moment her brain located the data.

Wincing, Monica set the glass aside and wrapped her arms around her roiling stomach. Her skin felt stretched too tight. Like she might burst out of her own face. Closing her eyes, she gave in to the pull of gravity and allowed herself to bend at the waist, curling her arms and shoulders in as she did. Maybe if she made herself as small as possible, she'd be able to keep from exploding. Or imploding.

Hard to say at this point which way she would go.

She opened her mouth to try some yoga breathing, but, to her shock and mortification, the only thing she managed was a big, heaving sob. Oh, no-no-no. Her mind raced to keep up with this new turn of events. She wasn't a sobber. She didn't cry. Particularly not over a man. She didn't need a man. Particularly not one with a kid. What did she think was going to happen, even if she had come clean? The three of them would live happily ever after? Like she'd wake up one day and suddenly be all…maternal and shit?

Not likely.

Pressing her palms to her knees, she forced herself to drag big gulps of air. She tuned out the diaper and baby food commercials playing in the background and stared hard at the hammered-nickel handle on the cabinet directly in front of her. Though she had told him she liked to cook, Monica couldn't say what might be in the cabinet. She did her best work in the office and the bedroom. If she'd been smart, she'd have stuck to her strengths.

She should never have let him into her kitchen.

Pushing away from the counter, she rushed down the hall to where she'd dropped her bags. Her phone was tucked into its usual pocket. Nicole must have put it there. Monica didn't remember gathering any of her stuff. As a matter of fact, she didn't recall leaving her office. Or most of the ride home.

Had it buzzed and she didn't hear? Maybe Nicole had turned the ringer off so she wouldn't be bothered?

Nicole was always thinking. Planning. She did thoughtful things. The little niceties always entered Monica's consciousness a second too late. Story of her life. Always a beat too late. Until today, she never minded too much.

Of course, she'd never had a delaying tactic bite her in the ass as hard as this asinine "pretend to be a mommy to get the hot daddy" ploy.

Patience was more than a virtue; it was a sound business practice. Waiting for others to make their move so she could respond strategically paid off for her time and again. The key was knowing the right moment. Fear had forced her to cling to a losing proposition. Her refusal to take the risk had cost her big.

But maybe sticking to the safe side didn't have to cost her everything. Or, maybe she wasn't too late to make the bold move.

She pushed the button to wake the device, a lump lodged firmly in her throat. No calls. No texts. She swallowed the last bitter dregs of willful optimism and swiped the screen. She stared at the photo for a long moment, then tapped the option to dial his number. For the first time since the afternoon they met, she was reaching out to him.

The call clicked over to voicemail, and she pulled the phone from her ear to scowl at the screen. The temptation to end the call was strong, but she refused to indulge the weakness. She'd hidden too much already.

The second she heard the beep, she pressed the phone to her cheek. "Hi. Colm."

She spit the words out like watermelon seeds—sharp, staccato. She gulped and tried again.

"Hi, Colm. It's me. Monica. I, uh…" Pausing to curl her hand into a fist, she pushed through in a rush of breath. "I'm sorry. I'm so sorry. I should have told you. I wanted to tell you—" She stopped herself. The last thing she wanted was to venture too far down the road of half-truths again. "Actually, I didn't. I didn't want to tell you because you liked me as Emma's mom, or thinking I was her mom, and I liked you. So I didn't tell you."

Pulling in a lungful of bracing oxygen, she barreled ahead. "I wanted you, so I lied to get you." A frown tugged at her mouth as she considered the veracity of her statement. Once she started, the compulsion to come completely clean won out. "But, technically, I didn't lie *to* you. I let you believe what you assumed was the truth."

Good God, this had to be the worst apology ever given. If any guy had tried to woo her with such weak arguments, she would have shot enough holes through him to make Swiss cheese. What was worse, she was giving this testimony on the record.

"Not what I meant to say," she rushed to assure him, though she was certain there was no redeeming the call at this point. "I just…I am sorry, Colm." She bit the inside of her cheek, gearing up to give him the bald-faced truth. "I never thought things would go this far. I didn't expect to like you this much. I only wish…" She shook her head in despair, even though she knew the motion wouldn't translate over the phone. "I'm sorry. More sorry than you can imagine."

Biting her lip, she searched her mind for a way to say what she wanted to say next without coming across as a pathetic girl who'd been dumped because she'd done something dumb. But there was no denying she deserved to pay the price. Even if that price was the last scrap of her pride.

"Please call me, okay? Give me a chance to explain." She winced at her own word choice. "And apologize. Because I am sorry." She gave a short huff of a laugh. "Sorrier than I've ever been, I think. If sorry counts for anything."

Tapping her fingers against the hard plastic shell of the phone case, she let the rest of her pride go on a long sigh.

"Call me. Please."

Monica ended the call, her eyes fixed on the screen until it went dark. There. She'd done her best. Invoked the magic word. Saying please had to count for something, right?

Chapter 10

Colm's phone buzzed for what had to be the fiftieth time. He didn't need to take it out of his pocket to see who was messaging him. The first forty-nine clued him in solid. Unfortunately, he couldn't turn the phone off. This was his work number. And the one the daycare called. And, if he did, he'd miss the chance to gloat while Monica groveled.

The problem was, gloating didn't feel so great. As a matter of fact, he'd felt nothing but crappy since he spoke to her. She'd left only one voicemail. Listening to her babble and ramble, it wasn't hard to figure out why she switched to texts. The woman truly sucked at apologizing.

Oh, her "I'm sorries" sounded genuine. And he could tell by the creak in her voice the sentiment behind them was sincere. What tripped him up was her reasoning. She'd knowingly, purposefully lied to him. How was he supposed to get past that?

"What are you doing?"

Colm jerked and swung his feet from his desk to the floor, feeling like a kid caught woolgathering during class. He spun around to find Mike braced in the open doorway, a puzzled frown on his face.

"I work here," Colm replied, unable to come up with more potent smart-assery on the spot. "How about you? Don't you have a spreadsheet to…spread?"

Mike fixed him with a bland stare as he pushed away from the doorframe. "I meant, I thought you had an on-site with a client today."

Colm nodded. "Yep. Done. Piece of cake."

At least, easy was his general impression. Frankly, he couldn't remember much about his on-site visit. The woman owned an adult-themed bakery called Getta Piece. Interesting, and a little uncomfortable. She'd had trouble with some vandalism, which, frankly, didn't surprise him. She made cakes and cookies shaped like genitals. The way Colm figured, the place was bound to attract the wrong kind of attention. But the business was apparently a successful one. When he'd mentioned the name of the bakery to their receptionist, Rosie, she'd nodded and blushed.

Mike raised an eyebrow. "Sampled the product?"

"Hell no." Colm gave a shudder he didn't have to enhance too much to show his distaste for the prospect. "You know what her best seller is? A two-foot long dick made out of red velvet cake. Called the Big Kahuna."

His friend gave an empathetic wince. "Yeah, no. I'll pass, too." He spared a glance at Rosie, then stepped into Colm's office. "Good business, though. I went over her credit app, and she's making a decent buck off selling the naughty stuff."

"Bet her mother is proud."

"James says most of her business is catering to bachelor and bachelorette parties and stuff."

"I can see there'd be limited appeal."

Mike frowned, vertical lines appearing between his brows and cutting deep. "There's nothing wrong with the business. Legally, I mean," he said, his tone disapproving but at the same time a little defensive.

"I didn't say there was," Colm replied, annoyance making his voice gruffer than usual. "I said I took the meeting. I'll have a proposal drawn up in a day or so."

"Are you okay?" Mike nudged the door partway closed for privacy. "You didn't have to get a triple root canal or anything, did you?"

Colm returned the squinty-eyed stare. "No. Why?"

"Rosie said you growled at her."

"I would never growl at Rosie," Colm objected.

He wouldn't. The three partners wholeheartedly agreed on one thing—their one and only employee was the lynchpin in the whole operation. As such, Rosie was accorded not only respect but a certain amount of deference.

"Have you ever heard me say anything even remotely rude to Rosie?" he demanded.

"No. Which is why I wondered what's going on with you."

"Nothing's going on with me. Why do you think something is going on with me?"

"I've texted you five times about the Anderson account, and you haven't responded. I figured the bakery lady had minced you up and put you in one of her penis cakes." He pushed his hands into his pants pockets and took a step closer. "Turns out, you've been sitting right here." He gave a casual shrug and rocked on his heels, but the grave expression of concern didn't change one bit. "Not like you to ignore texts. James ignores things all the time, but you? No."

The urge to tell his friend to piss off was strong, but nothing compared to the pressure of the hurt and confusion welling up inside him. Hell, his throat burned, and he had a sneaking suspicion the tickle he felt at the base of his skull might be more than the prickle of impatience.

He'd been so wrong about her.

So wrong.

Again.

Swallowing hard, he ignored the heat blazing up his neck and bleeding into his cheeks as he yanked his phone out of his pocket. The alert showed a mere nineteen texts messages awaiting his attention. Scowling at the number on the indicator, he set the phone aside without opening the application. "What did you need?"

Mike stepped closer, his gaze dropping to the cell laying face-up on the desk. The screen went black, but he gave a full head-tilt. "I was giving you a heads-up on two more prospects. James is on a hot streak."

Without waiting for an invite, Mike dropped into the single guest chair. Colm had moved the chair's mate to the reception area when he figured out his partners considered his office the optimal battleground for their disagreements. Thankfully, Colm didn't feel the need to be as tactful with the guys as they all were with Rosie.

"No need to get comfortable," he grumbled. He made a show of shuffling a few folders from one pile to another, then shook his mouse to wake his computer. "I'll look them over and get them set up."

"What's up with you?" Mike asked bluntly.

"Nothing."

"Something," his friend countered.

Colm shot him a filthy look. "Leave me alone."

"Make me." Mike added a smirk to the taunt. "I think we know we can both go on like this all night, so why don't we cut to the chase. What crawled up your ass?"

"I'm fine. Bad day, that's all."

Mike nodded, but the smirk stayed in place. A clear indicator he wasn't buying the B.S. Colm was pushing. "No good day starts with a trip to the dentist."

"She's his kid!" Colm threw his hands up in the air, every bit as surprised as Mike by the outburst.

"What?"

Sighing with a mix of frustration and resignation, Colm rubbed a hand across his eyes. He had no energy for this. This whole screwed up scenario was too much to be believed. What were the odds?

"Emma. She's my dentist's kid," he explained.

"Monica's kid? Monica is your dentist's baby mama?" Mike asked, as if slowly putting puzzle pieces together.

"Do people even use that term anymore?"

Mike shrugged. "Damned if I know."

Colm shook his head dismissively. "No. The kid is my dentist's kid." He paused, but Mike stared at him, his face a perfect blank. "She isn't Monica's kid at all. She's her niece."

"Her niece?"

"Yeah."

Mike took a moment to digest the information. "Wow. Well…" He hummed softly as he worked his way around the problem. "I guess that makes life a little less complicated."

Colm blinked, stunned by his friend's cockeyed take on the situation. "Less complicated? How do you figure?"

His friend tossed Colm's incredulity off with a shrug. "One kid, one babysitter. I mean, she's free as a bird, right?"

He snorted. "Yeah, I guess you could say so."

"Less complicated," Mike concluded.

"If I ignore the fact that she's been lying to me all this time," Colm interjected.

"Right," Mike murmured, almost to himself.

Colm could almost see his friend processing the data. The three of them were different this way. In Mike's case, the information would be broken down to the essentials and plugged into some kind of mental computer. He'd weigh every fact, recalculate possible outcomes, and spit out an opinion only when he'd had time to consider every angle. Mike was the polar opposite of James, who was quick to jump and not always inclined to ask questions later. Colm always figured he fell somewhere in the middle ground, but processing the situation, he wondered if he might be even more cautious than Mike. Giving his head a shake, he dismissed the thought. While he might not be as impulsive as James, he didn't analyze every angle like Mike. No, he wasn't overly cautious. More a believer in the old fool-me-once school of thought.

"Doesn't matter. I already told her we were done."

The declaration startled Mike from his contemplation of the situation. "What? Why?"

Colm snapped his fingers to get the guy's attention. "Weren't you listening?"

"I was. She's not the kid's mom."

"She's a liar."

Mike's brow beetled and he sat up a little straighter. "Yeah, well, yeah. Did she say why she lied?"

"Does it matter why?" Colm exploded. "I mean, what the hell? Do I have the word 'gullible' tattooed on my forehead or something? One of those weird UV tats people can only see in a certain light?"

"Whoa, hang on—"

Mike held up both hands to stop him, but Colm had a full head of steam worked up.

"What. The. Fuck. Why me?" His chair shot out as he stood. "Why do they always lie to me?"

He side-armed the cube of notepaper he'd been fanning. The pad hit the wall with a *thunk*, then descended in a flutter to the floor, the glue binding folded neatly in two, leaving the pad open like a tiny book. Running his hand through his hair, he exhaled in a blast. "I'm a decent guy. I try to do the right thing most of the time. I don't go around pretending to be something I'm not. Why can't they?" He swung his arm in an all-encompassing arc. "What's so hard about telling the truth?"

Mike stared up at him, understanding overriding the concern in his eyes. "You really want me to answer?"

"Yes." Colm gestured for him to hit him with his best shot. "Please."

"You don't want to hear the truth any more than you want to tell her the truth."

His friend made the statement with the kind of quiet firmness that makes a person wonder what he missed.

Colm rewound the conversation in his head, but for the life of him, he couldn't quite make the answer match up with his question. "What's that supposed to mean?"

"Did you tell her the truth? Tell her you wake up dreading whatever unseen catastrophe life has in store for you that day? That the majority of your social interactions revolve around cartoons and arguments over food?" He took a breath but forged ahead, warming to the topic. "Did you tell her you couldn't talk on the phone before eight because you're too busy doling out fruit snacks and sniffing Aiden's head to see if he actually shampooed or just got his hair wet?"

Folding his hands across his belly, he leaned back in the chair.

"Did you mention you'd forgotten what it feels like to touch someone other than your kid?" He stared Colm straight in the eye. "Did you tell her you go to bed every night terrified you won't be enough? That no matter how much you do, or how hard you try, you'll never be able to make not having a mom up to him?"

Colm scrubbed a hand over his face. "Christ, Mike."

"Did you tell her you fantasize about finding some woman willing to take the two of you on—and not for the whole happy family bit, but because you want someone else to do a fucking load of laundry, or decide whether you're having chicken nuggets or fish sticks for dinner?"

Colm sucked in a sharp breath, but Mike didn't let up.

"Because let's be honest here, Col, it's not all about the sex or even love anymore, is it?"

"Okay, all right." He raised his hands in surrender, but apparently his pal wasn't quite done yet.

"This girl liked you so much she lied to get you into bed. Shit. You should be down on your knees thanking her," Mike said, rising from the chair. "You fucking hypocrite."

Colm reared, stung by the accusation. "Hypocrite? Wait a—"

"How many women have you lied to, to get laid? We all did. We'd lie about our grandmothers if it meant we had half a chance," he corrected. "I can think of a dozen of my standard lines off the top of my head. Hell, I can probably name two or three of yours. I was standing right next to you when you told one woman you were S.W.A.T."

"Okay, okay."

"I couldn't believe she believed you," Mike continued, undeterred. "Like there's anything stealthy or tactical about you. You make the proverbial bull in a china shop look graceful."

"All right, fuck off."

Mike waved his protests off and turned to stomp toward the door, clearly pissed. Colm smiled a little as Mike jerked the door open and strode toward his office. Rosie looked up from her monitor when Mike slammed his door hard. The prints on the wall trembled, then settled. She turned to Colm, her eyes wide and worried. Standing in his own doorway, he blew out the dregs of a breath, feeling lighter than he had since he first spotted the photograph. He lifted a hand to assure the office manager all was well, but let his fingers curl into his palm as he retreated.

"Hey, Rosie?"

Her head popped up again. "Yes?"

"Men are nothing but lying scum. Stay away from them."

She smirked, her nose wrinkling as she peered at him through her glasses. "Even you?"

"Even me." He nodded to add a little oomph to the confirmation. He pointed to Mike's closed door. "Him, too."

The outer door opened and his pal James blew in. As usual, he held his cell phone pressed to his ear. He greeted them with a distracted wave, made a beeline for his own office, and kicked the door closed behind him. James treated the caller on the other end of the line to what could only be described as a lascivious chuckle.

Colm took a step into the safety of his own domain. "And him in particular," he called to Rosie. "Never, ever believe anything he says," he cautioned.

Closing his office door, he sighed. The warning came too late to be any use. Rosie had been moony-eyed over James since the day she first stepped foot in their offices. He hoped James remained oblivious. Maybe he could make Rosie believe James was single because he had a raging case of herpes or something. After all, it wouldn't take a huge stretch of the imagination.

Leaning against his door, he closed his eyes. "Well, what do you know? Mikey was right. Nothing but liars with their pants on fire around here."

His phone vibrated, skittering across his desk. The sustained urgency of the buzzing indicated an incoming call, not a text or email. He wished he could ignore the damn thing, but Mike's scolding and the ever-niggling worry of Aiden's daycare calling always won out. Mustering all his strength, he pushed away from the door and lunged for the desk.

His heart jumped up and lodged in his throat like a fist when he saw the caller displayed. Pawing at the screen, he fumbled the phone a little, then pressed it too hard to his ear. "Yeah. Hello?"

"Mr. Cleary?"

He closed his eyes, silently cursing himself for tempting fate. "Yes, this is Colm Cleary. What happened? Is something wrong?"

"This is Mrs. Bell at Jump Start."

"Yes, yes," Colm interrupted the daycare director impatiently. "Is Aiden okay?"

"Aiden took a spill on the playground today and hit his forehead. Ms. Seever has taken him to St. Vincent's to be looked at on the chance he may need stitches—"

Colm grabbed his keys from the desk and started for the door. "I'm on my way."

He ended the call, belatedly remembering he hadn't thanked the woman for keeping him informed or asked for any details of the accident. He didn't slow as he passed Rosie's desk. "Gotta go. Aiden's hurt," he managed to mumble. The moment he opened the exterior door, Colm broke into a dead run.

His stupid phone beeped, blerped, and buzzed the entire drive from their office to the emergency room, but he didn't risk a glance. His hands were shaking so hard he was scared to let go of the steering wheel.

By the time he parked and jogged his way to the urgent care entrance, twenty minutes had passed. Try as he might, it was hard to forget he'd lost Carmen in about the same short window of time. And almost lost his son.

Up until the day of the accident, Colm was convinced he had everything. A home. A job he loved. A baby on the way. And Carmen. Beautiful, tempestuous Carmen.

Whose name was actually Estella.

Breathless and sweating, he ran directly to the information desk. He hit the stylized glass and faux-granite countertop so hard, the young man seated on the stool jumped. "Aiden Cleary. His school brought him. Jump Start," he panted.

"Are you—?"

"His dad. I'm his dad. Where is he?"

The younger man's brow arched in such a way to imply Colm was perhaps a tad melodramatic, but he was beyond caring. All he wanted was his kid. Whole and healthy. Aiden was all he needed in his life. Now or ever.

He didn't need a woman in his life. He and Aiden were fine. They were perfectly fine on their own.

When the guy failed to answer right away, he leaned over the counter and rearticulated the question through gritted teeth. "Where is my son?"

The gatekeeper pushed away from his podium. "Exam three. I'll take you there."

Exam three. Carmen—or Estella Perez, as he discovered—had been in trauma four. Different hospital, same gut-wrenching trip down the hall.

Her head bloodied nearly beyond recognition, but her belly swelling with life. There'd been mere moments between his son's birth and her death. The woman he'd married, but hadn't known. A man showed up at the hospital claiming to be Colm's wife's brother. A guy named Adrian Perez. And he kept telling Colm his wife's name wasn't Carmen, but Estella. The man who spilled the whole story of his family's illegal immigration from Mexico, but Colm refused to believe him. How could he?

How could everything be a lie?

But Carmen had claimed she was from Colombia. She'd been working at Carita and Pablo's restaurant when they met, so he had no reason not to believe her. The older couple had been incensed when he told them what he'd discovered about his late wife. Angered by both the lie, and the fact that their good friend the cop had made the typical white guy mistake of thinking all Latinas were the same.

He skidded to a stop as the attendant pulled the edge of a curtain. Relief flooded through his veins the moment he saw Aiden sitting up on the exam table, a yellow freezer pop in hand. He looked up and almost immediately those big brown eyes filled with tears.

"Daddy."

"I'm here, bub," Colm assured him, flashing a quick glance at the young daycare teacher who'd been standing at Aiden's bedside.

The first big, glossy tear trickled over dark lashes. Colm was at his son's side in a heartbeat. His kissed the boy's head, tipping his face up for inspection. Aiden gave a hiccuppy little laugh and Colm hugged him tight.

"Jeez, if you wanted an ice pop, all you had to do was ask." He wiped at the drying tear tracks. "I bet the other guy looks worse."

"I fell off the slide."

Colm raised his head to look at the teacher. Ms. Seever grimaced. "There seems to have been a scuffle on the platform, but no one is talking…" She raised both eyebrows and craned around Colm's arm to peer at Aiden. "…Yet."

"Anyone else hurt?"

"No others bleeding. Some scrapes and crying," she assured him.

"Well, it's not a party until there are scrapes and crying." He reluctantly released the boy when the inevitable squirming set in.

"The doctor says the cut isn't too deep. He thinks they can close it with tape," the woman rushed to assure him. "He should be back in a minute."

Colm nodded and tore his gaze away from his son. Turning his full attention to Ms. Seever, he said, "I can take things from here."

"But, Mrs. Bell—"

"I'll call her and tell her he's okay." He blew out a breath as he watched Aiden suck half the frozen treat into his mouth. His expression puckered comically. "Go on. And thank you," he added, remembering his earlier rudeness to Mrs. Bell.

Ms. Seever moved to the bed and patted Aiden's leg gently. "You were really good, A," she assured the boy. "Super brave."

"Thanks," Aiden lisped, his swollen upper lip curling into a sneer-like smile.

"I'll see you tomorrow?" she asked, darting a glance at Colm.

"Tomorrow's Saturday," Aiden said, wagging his head emphatically.

"Oh. Right." The young woman laughed. "Well, I'll see you Monday, then." She smiled and backed out of the curtained cube. "His backpack is under the bed." Turning her attention to Aiden, she waved. "Enjoy your pancakes, okay?"

"I will." Aiden sent his teacher off with a cheery waggle of his fingers and returned his attention to the ice pop.

As always, Colm marveled at his son's resilience. He reached for his phone to call the school and his office. No service. No wonder it had finally stopped buzzing.

"Hey, bub?"

"Yeah?" Aiden looked up. With his upper lip swollen into a cockeyed sneer, the blindingly white square of gauze taped over his right eyebrow, and the frozen stick in his hand like a microphone, the kid looked like some kind of a miniature Elvis impersonator.

"What happened on the slide?"

His son turned his head and his gaze dropped to the rapidly liquefying tube in his hand. "Julissa pushed me."

"Julissa did?" Colm dropped into the guest chair and scooted a few inches closer to the bed. "I thought you and Ju were friends."

Aiden didn't meet his eyes. "We are."

"Did you say something to make her mad?"

A red flush flared in Aiden's cheeks and his head jerked up. "I didn't say nothing!"

"Anything," Colm corrected. "You didn't say *anything* to her."

But the lesson was lost on Aiden, who returned to sucking the last of the frozen treat from the plastic to avoid further conversation. He gently patted the boy's leg to assure them both all was well. And everything was. *Ish*. His boy was in one piece. A little banged up, but no guy escapes childhood without a few bumps and bruises. He waited, taking the time Aiden spent drawing each drop of sticky sweetness from the wrapper to try to bring himself into line. Not an easy task, considering this incident was the cherry on top of a truly fucked up twenty-four hours.

At last, he took the hollowed out husk of the freezer pop from Aiden's sticky hand and dropped the wrapper into the small wastebasket. He'd barely sat down when the kid ambushed him.

"Do you kiss girls?"

Colm blinked in stupefaction as his ass dropped into the seat. "Do I what?"

"Kiss girls," Aiden repeated, his eyes narrowing.

"Is that what happened with Julissa? You tried to kiss her?"

"Jamie says his dad kisses girls all the time."

Colm chuckled. "Haven't I always told you we don't do what Uncle James does?"

"He said you do, too," Aiden accused.

"Do what?"

"Kiss girls." The boy spit the words out as if they were contaminated.

"Is that what you were doing? Trying to kiss Julissa?" Colm persisted.

Aiden wriggled on the edge of the bed, drawing his bony little body up in indignation. "Do you? Do you kiss girls?"

"This isn't about me, it's about you." Colm raised an eyebrow. "You can't go around kissing girls who don't want to be kissed. That's how you get your block knocked off."

The curtain swung open and they both jumped.

"Truer words never spoken," a young man in a white coat answered jubilantly. He turned to Colm and offered his hand. "I'm Dr. Harby."

Colm rose from his chair and took the man's proffered hand. "Colm Cleary."

The younger man smiled conspiratorially, then turned his attention to the patient. "Kissing girls is fun, but dangerous." The doctor tossed the chart onto the bed as a nurse appeared in the opening to the cubicle, a sterile pack in her hands. Smiling down at Aiden, Dr. Harby chucked the boy's chin and started to remove the square of gauze. "Careful, Nurse Amy, we have a pirate here."

"Ooh, I love pirates," the nurse cooed.

Dr. Harby pulled a smirky face. "Sure, they all say they do, but you try to get one teensy kiss, and blammo!" He raised his chin and squinted at the cut through his glasses. "Yeah, not too deep, Dad. I think we'll put a little scotch tape on there and the two of you should be able to get to the evening's marauding."

"What's ma-raw-ding?" Aiden asked, his gaze darting from the doctor, to Colm, and back again.

Dr. Harby took the small strip of surgical adhesive the nurse handed him, carefully pinched the skin together, and applied the bandage. "The usual. Pillaging, plundering, trying to steal kisses from girls."

Nurse Amy gasped in mock horror. "You wouldn't! A nice boy like you?"

Aiden giggled and slid a sly look in Colm's direction. "My daddy does."

Stunned but pleased by the lightening of tone, Colm raised both hands to ward off further accusations. "I have never plundered anything in my life, and even if I had, you have no proof."

Aiden laughed again, pointing a grubby finger at his nurse. "Kiss Nurse Amy, Daddy," he crowed.

"Whoa. Ease up, Buccaneer," Dr. Harby chided, grasping the squirming boy by the shoulders and planting him where needed him. "I need you to hold still for a few more minutes."

Colm shook his head and nodded to the young woman's gloved hand. "I don't think Nurse Amy would like people trying to kiss her without asking." He shot the nurse an apologetic smile. "Like I said, you can't go around kissing people willy-nilly, bub."

As if a switch had been thrown, Aiden's dark eyes turned somber. "Did you kiss Emma's mommy?"

Licking his lips, Colm shifted uncomfortably. He could actually feel the doctor and nurse *not* looking at him, which was almost worse than his kid's unwavering stare. The boy needed to grow up to be a prosecutor or something. Then, he remembered he didn't have to evade the question. He could tell the truth. It wasn't the truth he and Aiden had thought it was, but technically...

"No. I have never kissed Emma's mommy," he stated unequivocally.

Aiden's eyes narrowed, but Colm refused to break the connection. Even though he was sure he heard Nurse Amy mutter, "Poor Emma's mommy," under her breath.

Dr. Harby placed the last strip over the cut and surveyed his work. After a moment, he nodded gravely and announced, "Nurse, I think this patient will live."

Nurse Amy's cheekbones nearly obscured her eyes. She pressed a gloved hand to her chest as if to calm her heart. "Oh, thank goodness you saved him, Doctor."

Peeling off his latex gloves, he gave an exaggerated shrug. "Yes, well, I am highly skilled with all forms of adhesives. Broke my mom's favorite vase in the fourth grade and glued the pieces together perfectly. She never would have known if I hadn't stuck my fingers together, too."

Aiden giggled and Colm gave a relieved chuckle as the doctor turned to face him.

"Amy will get you all lined out here." The doctor nodded to Aiden. "I'm afraid there's not much more we can do for the kissing bandit over there."

"Thank you."

Dr. Harby smiled and scooped the chart up from the bed. "See you later, Aiden. Try to keep your lips to yourself, okay? Much safer. Trust me."

The nurse bustled about, gathering a small kit of wound supplies and putting together the necessary discharge paperwork. After saying good-bye and thank you to Nurse Amy, the two Cleary men strapped into the car. Colm exhaled long and loud. Aiden's stomach gurgled. Colm snickered as he glanced into the rearview mirror. "Hungry, huh?"

"I missed snack."

Colm nodded. "I think we need mega-meals."

"Yes! Burger Boy!" Thrusting both fists into the air, Aiden executed a little victory dance at the thought of scoring dinner at the fast food restaurant with the largest children's play land in the area.

Colm's mind whirred as he navigated to the restaurant. He'd always reserved trips to Burger Boy as a splurge. Not because the place was expensive, but because eating there cut a little too close to eating in the center ring of a circus for Colm's tastes. He repressed a shudder at the thought of all those sweaty bodies crammed into what looked like a hamster trail. Naturally, the place was like crack for kids. But, by giving in, he'd get Aiden fed and keep him occupied while he returned the calls and messages accumulated on his phone.

The line at the counter was surprisingly short, considering how many little hellions ran loose in the glassed-in playground. Nearly every table in the place was taken. Most were occupied by abandoned trays and solitary men staring at their cell phones. Colm groaned inwardly as the situation swam into focus.

This was Friday evening. These were weekend dads.

The Saturdaddies.

That's what Monica said the women in the park called them. He'd wanted to snap at her, tell her he wasn't a weekend dad, but a full-time dad. The only parent on duty twenty-four-seven. The one who was there. All. Of. The Time.

He sat at the table, eating like an automaton as Aiden wolfed his meal down as fast as he possibly could. Colm admonished him to chew once or twice, but his mind was otherwise occupied. Frankly, he couldn't help observing his fellow Burger Boy inmates and wondering what being able to pick up and drop off his parental responsibility might feel like.

He couldn't imagine.

And from the expressions on most of the dads' faces, they never thought they'd be here, either. Most watched their children play attentively. Some wearing such stark looks of longing, Colm felt compelled to glance away.

Part-time dads.

In all honesty, he'd thought about these guys the same way. Watching them, the stereotyping made him feel ashamed. Most of these guys probably hadn't wanted to be separated from their children, maybe not even their children's mother. But many of them ended up on the short end of the visitation stick. Though progress had been made, the courts, and society in general, favored the mother unless the woman opted out.

The way Colm saw it, there seemed to be more guys like him these days. Guys who, through choice or circumstance, had picked up the roles most everyone in the world assumed fell to the mother. One rarely heard sob stories about the plight of the single dad, but they were out there. Guys like him, and Mike, and James.

Moms got all the press. And the perks, in some ways. Because when a woman walks out and actually leaves her kids behind, they're not as keen to work the shared custody schedule. At least, not in his experience. Nor were they big on making the child support payments ordered by the court. The press hardly ever railed on about deadbeat moms, but they existed. He knew for a fact James wasn't getting a penny of the court-ordered support Megan was supposed to pay, but his friend didn't bother fighting for his rights. The woman was the proverbial starving artist. Getting money for the twins' most basic necessities would be like squeezing blood from a stone.

"Can I go play?"

Colm dragged his attention away from his fellow inmates and focused on Aiden's hopeful face. Half his chicken nuggets were gone and all of his French fries. If Colm had been paying closer attention, the situation would have been reversed. But he didn't have a single ounce of bad cop left in him. No, he'd expended all his anger and frustration long before the call from Jump Start came.

Looking his son square in the eye, he sighed. "You know the lady we went to see? Monica?" Aiden opened his mouth, but Colm forged ahead. "She isn't Emma's mommy, she's her aunt. The day we met her in the park, she was just babysitting Emma for a little while."

Aiden started up at him, his eyes wide, his expression nonplussed.

His kid's lack of response sliced through another thread of his already barely-tethered self-control.

Curling his lip into a sneer, he stared straight into his boy's eyes. "And I kissed her. A lot."

Aiden's nose wrinkled and his mouth puckered as if he'd sucked a raw lemon. "Ew, Dad."

Colm raised his brows challengingly. "I'm not the one who got knocked off a slide when I tried."

"But I was only gonna kiss her once," Aiden reasoned. "You said you kissed her a lot." He inched closer to the edge of the bench. "Can I go play now?"

Huffing, Colm made a flicking motion with his hand. "Go. And keep your lips to yourself."

"Thirty minutes," Aiden reminded him of their usual time limit as he shot out of the booth.

"Thirty minutes," Colm confirmed, pulling his phone out and making a show of checking the time. "And don't run." The last time he turned him loose, Aiden had collided with a grandmother holding a tray filled with milkshakes. The result was not pretty. The boy waited by the edge of the table, his skinny body practically humming with repressed eagerness. Looking down at the phone, he pressed the icon to bring up the countdown timer. "Go!"

He smiled as he watched his son race-walk through the rows of tables. A blast of screams and laughter filled the restaurant as he opened the door to the play area. Like a herd of wildebeests scenting the air for danger, the dads looked up from their phones, tablets, or other methods of social blockading. The door closed, and Colm would swear the sigh he heard had nothing to do with the hydraulic hinge.

Smiling to himself, he returned to the home screen on his own electronic avoidance device and winced when he saw the number of notifications indicated. The first call he made was to Rosie. Thankfully, the call went to voicemail. He gave her a brief, detailed report of the accident, injury, and result, and concluded by asking her to pass the word to his partners along with a promise to check in with them later. Next, he called Jump Start. Half-expecting this call to go to a voicemail system as well, he jumped when a woman answered in a brisk tone.

As if she could see him, he sat up straighter and held the phone to his mouth. "Yes. Uh, yes, is Mrs. Bell in…please?"

"This is Mrs. Bell," she replied crisply.

"Oh. Uh, this is Colm Cleary. Aiden's dad."

"Oh, yes. Mr. Cleary. How is Aiden?" she asked, her tone gentling a little.

"He's fine, thank you. Bouncing back like a rubber ball." The moment the words were out of his mouth, he looked up and saw Aiden plunging headfirst into the ball pit. He cringed, not even wanting to imagine the antiseptic shower he'd have to give the boy when they got home. "Kids are crazy that way."

"They are very resilient," Mrs. Bell confirmed.

"I wanted to apologize for being so abrupt on the phone earlier. And to thank Ms. Seever for staying with Aiden. I know she's one of his favorite teachers."

"I understand, Mr. Cleary. You'd had a shock." She covered the phone and spoke to someone else. When she returned, her tone was slightly harried. "Is there anything else you needed?"

"Uh, no. Thank you." He grimaced when he realized he was calling during pick-up hours. They were probably eager to wrap up their day. "Thanks again."

"We'll see you and Aiden on Monday morning." A statement, not a question.

"Monday morning," he confirmed.

Those two bits of business completed, he glanced up to check on Aiden. He had climbed out of the ball pit of death and was scaling a rope ladder like the pirate the doctor accused him of being. Colm smiled. His kid apparently had at least one career path opening up to him already.

Sighing, he returned his attention to the phone. Opening his text folder, he scrolled to the ones received earliest in the day without letting himself peek at the latest. His jaw tightened as he read the first few from Monica. More lame explanations. A few excuses. One or two came across a little accusatory, even. Interspersed with these were Mike's messages. One warning him about the X-rated goodies he'd find at the Getta Piece, the next giving him the date and time of their next meeting with the bank about their line of credit, and the third simply asking where he was. James sent him a picture of Ron Burgundy. The caption said breaking a mirror is seven years of bad luck, but breaking a condom is eighteen.

Colm chuckled as he saved the meme. "True. So true."

Those messages cleared, he had only Monica's left. Unlike her earlier attempts, these were more subdued. Contrite. Apologetic. A shudder ran down his spine as he read the last one. The simple "please" she added to the demand he return her call came across as almost…needy. And he didn't like Monica sounding needy one bit. The Monica he knew was balls-to-the-wall. She didn't have a needy bone in her body. Greedy, yes, but never needy.

He scrolled down. The messages from Mike, James, and Rosie demanding updates on Aiden were much easier to deal with. They grounded him. Reminded him of exactly who and what he was. Their friend and partner. Aiden's dad. The guy who got his teeth cleaned then went to bakeries specializing in buttercream boobs.

And Monica?

She was little more than a blip. Or she would be once a little time passed. The sting of betrayal would mellow and fade as it had with Carmen. He'd get reacquainted with his right hand. The most excitement he'd have to deal with would involve trips to Burger Boy and those heart-wrenching moments when Princess Clarissa went missing.

Colm sat up a little straighter, blinking rapidly as realization dawned. Aiden hadn't had his doll with him at the hospital. They had his backpack in the car. Colm could only hope the doll was tucked inside as she was supposed to be during school hours. Otherwise, this could turn out to be a cluster-fuck of a weekend.

But Aiden had to have noticed he didn't have his trusty sidekick. He wasn't freaked out at the hospital, or when they were in the car. The doll had to be in his backpack; otherwise his son would have gone nuclear. For the life of him, Colm couldn't remember the last time the kid went anywhere without her. Including the play area at Burger Boy.

A screeching toddler was being forcibly removed from the play area by a frazzled-looking dad wearing suit pants and a ketchup-spattered dress shirt.

Colm's heart seized a little as he recalled doing the exact same thing with Aiden not so very long ago. He turned to the scene playing out in play land. Laughter, tears, triumph, and disappointment. He sat on the hard plastic bench watching all of life's dramas unfold in a temperature-controlled microcosm, and suddenly the events of the day didn't seem so life-altering.

Tomorrow, he and Aiden would wake up, go to the park. Maybe they'd join their friends for pancakes. Life would be normal again. Whatever normal was supposed to be.

Chapter 11

Monica was a complete train wreck by Saturday morning. The sound of a key in the locks managed to rouse her partway from the doze she'd finally fallen into after dawn. Her lips felt like cracked vinyl. A telltale crusty patch at the corner of her mouth seemed the likely explanation for her lack of moisture. She swung her feet to the floor as the alarm beeped to apprise her of the open door.

"If you're alive and ignoring my calls, I'm going to kill you," Melody called up the staircase.

A shower of foil wrappers fluttered to the floor. Monica stared down at them. Those little fruit snack things were addictive. She particularly liked the superhero ones. They were all bold colors and normal fruit flavors. The Princess Clarissa snacks were pastel colors and tasted like she was licking a My Little Pony.

"In here," she managed to croak.

Glancing around at her seldom-used living room dispassionately, she gave the thought of clearing up a bit momentary consideration. She jettisoned any thought of cleanliness. One look at her and the flattened couch cushions, and Melody would know she hadn't gone upstairs to bed. Her life was messed up. And if anyone had the right to bear witness to her downfall, Mel did. Living in the shadow of a super-achiever sister hadn't been easy, as Melody never hesitated to point out.

Mel stopped short at the entrance to the room. So short Emma walked right into her.

"*Mooooom*," Emma complained.

"Sorry, faulty brake lights," Melody responded distractedly, taking in every bit of the wreckage in a sweeping glance. With the data she needed collected, she patted her daughter's head. "I heard Auntie Monica is stocking string cheese and Clarissa's Carnival snacks these days. Go see if it's true."

"But, I—"

"And if there's apple juice, pour me a glass, will you?"

To Monica's utter surprise, the request lit the little girl up like a glow stick. "Really?"

"Be careful getting up to get a glass," Mel warned sternly. Whirling as the little girl scampered off, she called after her, "And use a chair, not one of the stools." Huffing, she dropped into a never-used armchair. "I swear I'm going to screw a helmet onto her head. She's becoming such a daredevil."

"Like her mother," Monica said as she made a grab for the empty wrappers strewn around her. "You were the original heart attack kid."

Melody settled into the chair, her gaze fixed on Monica but her expression soft and sympathetic. "So, the jig is up, huh?"

Monica flung herself across the couch, fruit snack wrappers clutched in her hand. She shot her sister a look of pure annoyance. "Who says stuff like that?"

"People who've been watching other people act like morons to get what they want when they could have had what they wanted very easily."

Mel shrugged, and Monica gaped at her, her brain whirring as she tried to work out the logic. "Care to boil things down to bullet points?"

She held up one finger. "You've been lying." A second popped up to join point number one. "You didn't need to." Melody raised a third finger, stared at the digit for a second, then made a show of folding it into her palm again. "I think I covered the pertinents."

"Thanks for lining things out for me," Monica said dryly. "Got any suggestions on what to do?"

Mel shrugged again. "Call him?"

"Not picking up."

"Text?"

"No reply."

Her sister nodded as if such roadblocks never occurred to her. "We have to get creative."

Emma skidded into the room, giggling as her sock-clad feet allowed her to sail across polished hardwood. "I've never been to your house with food, Aunt Monnie." She beamed as she held out the bounty clasped in her hands. The little girl had scored the last of the string cheese and at least three packages of the funky Princess Clarissa fruit snacks. "Look, Mommy!"

Melody smirked. "Yes, a veritable feast."

"Can we go to the park now?" Emma asked, dumping her loot into the enormous tote Mel had set on the floor. "You said we could go once we made sure we couldn't smell Aunt Monnie's body." Her freckled little nose as she shot a worried glance at Monica. "Though I can kind of smell her."

"Thanks, kiddo." Surreptitiously, Monica slid the empty wine bottle around the arm of the couch. "I'm fine," she said waving them off. "Didn't sleep well, that's all."

Melody turned to Emma. "Hey, sweets, will you go grab a couple bottles of water from the fridge, too? I forgot to bring some from home."

Emma scowled and pointed into the gaping bag. "No, you didn't. There's some right there."

Mel blew out a breath so emphatic the gust ruffled her hair. "Yeah, but those aren't cold. Will you go grab us some *cold* water from the fridge?" she repeated with exaggerated patience. "Pretty please."

"Since you asked nicely," Emma sing-songed as she skipped from the room.

The second she was gone, she swiveled to glare at Monica. "Get up. Get dressed. We're going to the park."

"The park?" The foil wrappers sprang from her hands when Monica unclenched her fists. "Me? Oh no. Nuh-uh."

In a flash, her sister was out of the chair and pulling on her arm. "Yuh-huh. Come on, get up." She retreated quickly when Monica exhaled a snort. "Whoa. You do stink."

Monica collapsed in a heap, throwing her arm up to cover her eyes. "Go. Leave me here to die."

Standing over her, Melody gave a pitying shake of her head. "Wow. What happened to my killer shark of a big sister?"

"She bit off more than she could chew."

"Bullshit." Mel spit the word out with startling vehemence. "You played the wrong strategy." She ran her hand through her hair. "I couldn't figure out why you did. It's never been your style to play games, Mon. You go out and ask for what you want, and, most of the time, you hit your goals. I've always admired your drive."

"I'm even more like Dad than we thought."

"Stop," Melody snapped. "That's only some ridiculous excuse you use."

Monica peeked at her sister from under her elbow. "Is it? We both know I haven't had the best experiences with relationships."

"Because you haven't met anyone you cared about, but now you have."

"Have I?" Her voice came out soft and tremulous. She met Melody's gaze and held. "How will I know? What if I'm caring enough? I'm not. What if I can't keep…caring?"

Silence fell between them like a heavy, wet fisherman's net. Pressing her lips together, Monica swallowed the surge of anxiety rising inside her.

"What if I am like Dad? Can I risk hurting Colm? Aiden?"

Mel grabbed her hand and peeled her arm away from her face. "You aren't."

Wetting parched lips, Monica gave her head a weak shake. "You don't know, Melly," she whispered. "I'd rather be at work than most anywhere else in the world."

"You've never had anything compelling to pull you away." She squeezed Monica's hand, perhaps a tad too hard. "You haven't let yourself have anything else. Look at yourself. How the mighty have fallen."

"I never said I was mighty."

Melody brushed the tangled hair away from Monica's eyes. "No, but you have fallen. The really strong ones figure out how to get up again."

"I screwed up so bad," Monica whispered, looking up at her sister dolefully.

"Go back, start over, and do things right," Mel insisted. "He wouldn't have pushed so hard if he didn't want you. You have the advantage already. Introduce him to the real you, and give this thing a chance." She dropped down on the end of the sofa and rubbed Monica's shin consolingly. "If the relationship works, it works. If it doesn't, at least you tried."

"I heard you cuss," Emma announced as she came into the room, three bottles of water cradled in her toothpick arms. She dropped two bottles into the tote and brought the third over to Monica. "You said a B-word. A fifty-cent B-word, too."

Monica darted a look from daughter to mother. "There's a sliding scale?"

"Based on syllables," Melody said with a grim smile. "Jeremy and I had a fight one night after we thought she was asleep, but no, little miss accountant was sitting in the hallway running up the tab."

Opening her eyes wide, Monica gave her niece an approving high five. "Way to work the system, kid."

"Thanks." Emma smiled brightly and turned her attention to her mother. "Can we go to the park now?"

Melody gave Monica one final pat, then sprang to her feet with the grace and agility borne from years of yoga practice. "Yes, we will leave your aunt here to wallow in her muck and go off to the park for a little fresh air and sunshine."

"Yay!" Emma darted forward to peck a kiss to Monica's cheek, but stopped short, her nose crinkling again. "See you later, Monnie!"

Monica waved them off. "See you later. Thanks for making sure the smell hadn't crept out from under the door."

"Not yet," Mel said as she shouldered her bag. "But a shower should be real high on the to-do list."

Covering her eyes with her hand, Monica made a vague nodding movement. "Recommendation noted."

She heard the jangle of a key ring and peeked out from between her fingers. Melody stopped in the living room doorway, her bottom lip drawn up between her teeth. When Monica lowered her hand a couple inches, she asked, "If we see him…do you want to know?"

Torn between yes and no, she hesitated. Colm was angry, as he had every right to be. If he spotted Emma, would he say something to Melody? Would he be rude? Ugly? The moment the thought popped into her head, she dismissed the notion. Colm wouldn't be a jerk. Particularly not in front of the kids. Or his friends. At last, she gave in to the weak side and nodded. "Yeah. Let me know."

Emma called out another round of farewells, but Melody said nothing as they let themselves out of the house. Monica lowered her hand and raised her head. The floor and couch were littered with wrappers. She wished with all her might she could blame the empty wine bottle for the pounding in her head, but the grapes weren't the culprit. The tears were. Bitter, salty tears ran down her face in a steady stream for hours. And she let them, because she didn't know what else to do. She had to let them out. Try to get him out of her system.

But they didn't help.

Her head hurt as much as her heart. Her eyes felt hot and scratchy. The muscles in her neck and back protested the evening spent on the sofa. But she couldn't bring herself to go upstairs. Sleeping in her own bed would mean she'd run the risk of missing him. And she didn't miss people. Because pining for someone meant you needed them, and she didn't need Colm Cleary. So they got along well. She'd always worked well with others. And the sex, well, she could get sex anywhere, right? She had appliances capable of giving her satisfaction without the messy complications.

But they wouldn't be Colm. They wouldn't smell like him. Their arms wouldn't feel like his. And his laugh. Was there another man on earth with such a laugh? Probably not. She'd accidentally stumbled onto one of the good ones when she wasn't even looking. Not a lot of guys would hop out of bed and hit the pavement because their kid had a nightmare. Sure, when it happened, she counted the ungraceful dismount as points against him.

But now… Now, she knew better.

She knew he had a hard time trusting others with his kid. Aiden was all Colm had in the world. And he'd been ready to share him with her. Not realizing she was the biggest, fattest of all big, fat liars. And talk about daddy issues. She was facing those coming and going.

He'd never trust her again. How could he? But the urge to explain was as strong as it was when she made her first phone call. Something in her, the part that believed in fair play and keeping things above-board, wouldn't let her rest until she had. Somehow, some way, she needed to make him understand why she let him believe what he wanted to believe for so long.

And she needed to do so as soon as possible, because she couldn't go on like this one day more.

She swung her legs off the sofa and lunged to her feet. The mess she'd made in her usually pristine living room would have to wait. She had bigger, badder messes to straighten out. With a frown of grim determination, she marched toward the stairs. Halfway up, she ran her hand over her hair and her fingers stuck in a snarl. Keeping her eyes averted from the bed, she made a beeline for the bathroom. A quick peek at the mirror confirmed the integrity of her sister and niece's assessments. She was a mess.

Reaching into the shower, she spun the knobs until the spray was set to her preferred temperature and velocity. She undressed automatically, letting the blouse and pants she'd worn to work the previous morning fall to the floor. Stepping into the glass enclosure, she reveled in the shiver that ran through her body the second the spray touched her skin. The water was cool but not cold. The perfect temperature for someone who needed a jolt of get-up-and-go.

* * * *

They'd skipped the park. And the guys. Colm didn't have the energy for grilling and ribbing. He'd taken a good dose during poker, but now they had the whole story, and he figured Mike and James were most likely mixing up a vat of sass to baste him in for weeks.

"Can we go to the park after?"

Aiden's hopeful question pulled him from his thoughts.

Colm was saved from answering by the appearance of a waitress carrying a loaded tray. "Elbows off, short stack," he ordered as the woman started to unload the bounty they'd ordered for breakfast.

The little boy bounced on the bench seat of the booth, beside himself with anticipation. In his weakened state, Colm had agreed to let him have chocolate chip pancakes. The big kind, not the kid-sized mini cakes. Colm envied his son's simple joy.

Aiden smacked his lips as he rose up onto his knees to grab the syrup bottle. Colm made a mental note to pick up lip balm, then snatched the dispenser from the boy's grabby hand. "No way. Last time, you made pancake soup."

Giggling, Aiden subsided onto the seat, his wide smile lighting his face. "So awesome."

"So gross." Colm drizzled the pancakes with a reasonable amount of syrup, then placed the bottle well out of his son's sneaky reach.

Three bites in, Aiden circled around again. "How come we didn't go to the park?" he asked without looking up.

Colm applied himself to the omelet on his plate. "I was hungry."

The little boy demolished a third of the stack in short order. "Did you hurt your heart?"

His head jerked up so fast he almost choked on the bite he'd taken. The food turned to gravel in his mouth. Slowly and with extreme effort, he managed to chew and swallow before speaking. "What?"

Aiden shrugged but didn't pause in his systematic destruction of the pancakes. "Uncle Mike said you hadda broken heart."

A wave of anger and embarrassment rose inside him. This was exactly the reason why he kept his dating life—such as it was—separate from Aiden. Considering the source, he tamped down on his indignation. Mike might have been discussing his love life with someone, but certainly not with his kids. This was most likely a case of little pitchers having big ears. "He did?"

Aiden nodded and shoved an enormous forkful into his mouth. Colm set his silverware down and waited patiently. He winced when Aiden swallowed what looked like a painful gulp.

"Who'd he say that to?"

The boy shrugged again.

Colm made another mental note to work on making Aiden use his words. "Did you hear him say so, or did someone tell you he said it?"

"He *tole* Uncle James, and Jamie *tole* me and Tyler."

Colm blew out a breath. He should have known. Little Chrissie might be the only girl in the mix, but the boys gossiped like women. He watched as Aiden prepared another syrup-sodden bite. His son looked up, pinning him with a startlingly direct gaze.

"Is it?"

Lost in his son's bottomless brown eyes, he asked, "Is what?"

"Is it broken?" He blinked a couple times in rapid succession. "Do we hafta go to the hospital? Maybe they can put tape on you like they did me."

Colm couldn't answer for a moment. His throat was too tight, his tongue thick and as lifeless as a slab of porterhouse steak. Was his heart broken over Monica? No, probably not. They hadn't gotten to know one another on a deep enough level. At least, not yet. But he was hurt. And disappointed. Disheartened.

So, yeah, maybe there was a little bruising around his heart, but not broken. But after all the lies Carmen had fed him…To his way of thinking, shattered trust was one hell of a lot harder to fix.

"No, buddy. My heart's not broken. No need to rush to the ER for some superglue," he added with a wan smile. "I just…I liked Monica. The lady we thought was Emma's mommy. But turns out she's not Emma's mommy. She's her aunt, and she didn't tell me. Hurt my feelings."

Aiden's eyebrows pulled together as he puzzled the problem out. "You can't like her because she isn't Emma's mommy? Don't you like aunts? Jamie and Jeff's mommy is Tyler and Chrissie's aunt. Didja know?"

"I did. And I like aunts fine," Colm assured him.

"Maybe she's not Emma's mommy, but she could be someone else's mommy. You could like her, and you wouldn't hafta be so crabby all the time."

The hopeful speculation on Aiden's face nearly tore Colm's heart out. "I'm not crabby all the time," he retorted in a voice gruff with emotion.

"Are, too," Aiden mumbled as he gathered more pancake.

"I don't mean to be."

"Butcha are."

Before Colm could comment on the kid's smart mouth, Aiden filled it again. He waited and watched until the coast was clear, then covered Aiden's hand with his.

"I'm sorry. I'll try not to be crabby all the time."

Aiden nodded and he released the boy's hand with a squeeze.

"Maybe you should go tell her you're sorry and make up with her."

A flash of indignation heated Colm's blood, but he ignored the impulse to argue. Giving up on his breakfast, Colm pushed his plate aside. "Things are more complicated than that, buddy."

Aiden blinked owlishly. "Why?"

"Well, first, I'm not the one who needs to be sorry," he said patiently.

Aiden shifted from eating to mutilation mode in the blink of an eye. He'd stabbed the remainder of the stack repeatedly. Colm reached over and plucked the fork from his hand.

Unfazed, Aiden looked up. "Did she say she was sorry?"

"Yeah, but—"

"A 'pology is a 'pology," Aiden said in the same stern tone Colm had used on him countless times. "Shake hands and be friends again."

Colm bit his lip and turned away. This wasn't the first time his son had thrown his own words at him, but, for some reason, this particular message stung. He sat stunned for a moment. Bored with the conversation, Aiden had pulled out his Princess Clarissa doll and was having the doll do death-defying backflips off the table onto the seat.

Cocking his head to the side, he stared at the boy across from him, wondering why he'd thought he needed to hide anything from him. Aiden was his best friend. Had been since the day the doctors placed him in his arms. Once, his infant son had been the keeper of all the worries of a frightened father. His midnight confessor. Aiden was the one person on Earth who knew every single truth about him…and loved him anyway.

Because everyone had secrets. And things they were afraid to say out loud for fear of losing something or someone they wanted desperately.

Swallowing the lump in his throat, Colm reached across the table to save the doll from yet another harrowing tumble. "So, you think I should go talk to her?"

Aiden shrugged again, but this time Colm didn't mind as much. This shrug looked like a stamp of approval to him.

Taking is as such, he snatched the ticket from the table and started to slide from the booth. "Okay. Let's go hose you down, then we'll see if Monica wants to shake hands and be friends again."

Aiden craned his neck as he practically fell out of the booth. "After, can we go to the park?"

Chapter 12

Monica camouflaged the circles under her eyes as best she could, and blow-dried her hair into submission. Phone clutched to her ear, she stood in front of her closet, trying to decide what kind of outfit a woman wore to eat a heaping helping of crow. "You're sure he's not there?" she asked for the fourth time.

Her sister didn't even sigh. With the kind of patience that was a testament to the power of "om," she replied, "I'm sure."

"You remember what he looks like?"

"Tall, dark, and Irish, like a good glass of beer. He's not here, Mon."

"Did you check by the sand pit thingy?"

Mel chuckled. "Yes, I checked the sand pit thingy. He's not here. And before you give me three more suggestions, let me give you a little more info to lay grounds for the deductive reasoning which has led me to this conclusion. There are no guys here today."

"None?"

"Well, not the tall one with the redheaded twins, or the one with the little girl. I checked in with the Mommy Mafia and reports are the Saturdaddies are a no-show today." She paused for a beat. "At least, the hot ones aren't here. A couple who aren't as decorative are, but there's no fun in checking them out, according to Kandi Kardashian."

Monica yanked the first shirt she groped from its hanger. "Kandi Kardashian? Is there a secret sister?"

"Okay, she's not really a Kardashian, but she did tell me her name was Kandi with a K, and with a little black hair dye, we could drop her into the mix. Ten bucks says no one notices."

"Wow. And here I was thinking you were the Queen of Zen. Can I pour you a saucer of milk?"

"No, thank you," Melody answered primly.

Monica sighed and looked down at the shirt in her hand. It was a plain black T-shirt, but she could have bought her sister a half-dozen champagne brunches for what the brushed cotton cost. Or fed a few dozen hungry kids pancakes. God, what an utterly selfish creature she was. She swallowed the lump clogging her throat, but the faint taste of regret lingered on her tongue.

"I have to go. Ems is tired of playing super-spy and wants to hit the swings."

"Okay. Thanks for checking for me. I'd totally vote to make you the next Bond."

Her sister snorted. "I don't have the bikini body to be a Bond girl anymore."

"Not a Bond Girl—Bond. James Bond." She paused to let the concept sink in. "Melody Bond. The kickass international spy who infiltrates the upper echelons of national security by posing as a mild-mannered mommy."

"Jeremy would laugh his behind off if he heard you describe me as mild-mannered."

"No, he wouldn't. He's too scared you'll crush him between your powerful thighs."

"They are strong," Melody mused, huffing a little as she walked.

Knowing delay tactics weren't going to help her out in any way, Monica forced a weak smile, because she had no doubt her sister's super-spy powers meant she could see through the phone. "Thanks again."

"I love you, Mon, even if you are a giant fibber."

"I love you, too. Even if you shake your martinis instead of stirring them." She paused. "You shouldn't, by the way. Shaking bruises the gin," she said in her best know-it-all voice.

"Hanging up," Melody sang into the phone. "Go forth and try to be a productive member of society. And lay off the fruit snacks. They aren't really fruit, you know," she added, mimicking Monica's uppity tone.

The call ended, and Monica let her hand fall to her side as if the phone weighed a hundred pounds.

Clad in only a bra and panties, Monica pursed her lips as she studied the overpriced designer T-shirt. What in the world had possessed her to spend so much on one top? Unable to reason away her impulse buys, she yanked the shirt from its hanger. A pair of slim-fitting jeans, a long sweater, and some loafers completed her ensemble. She turned toward the mirror in her walk-in closet. She looked casual, but chic. The colors were even subdued. She had atonement on her mind. And atonement meant she needed to spring into action. Or shuffle. She didn't really have the energy for springing.

Shoving her phone into the pocket of the jeans, she left the walk-in without adding so much as a necklace or a pair of earrings. Only the worthy accessorized. The leather soles of her shoes slapped the polished wood stairs. Her briefcase and handbag lay exactly where she'd left them. She should pull out her tablet and make up for a little of the work she'd blown off, but the prospect didn't appeal. She looped her hand through the straps of her purse and pulled her keys from the fragile glass bowl she treated so cavalierly.

One way or another, she had to get Colm to at least listen to her apology.

Hiking her purse high on her shoulder, she flipped the locks on the door, reset the alarm system, and backed out of the house, the beeping becoming more insistent as she slid her key into the lock. She gave the deadbolt a hard twist, but rather than the *thunk* of the tumbler falling into place, she heard a bright, chipper, "Hi!"

Monica whirled to find Colm and Aiden standing at the foot of her steps. Pressing her hand to her racing heart, she leaned against the door. "Oh!"

The little boy's smile started to fade as his hand fell to his side, and she stumbled over herself in her rush to reclaim the happy greeting.

"Hi!" she blurted too loud. A blip of a laugh escaped her as her gaze darted from son to father and back again. "You startled me."

Aiden nodded in silent acceptance of her explanation, but his expression clearly read, "No, duh."

Straightening away from the door, she gave the hem of her shirt a nervous tug. "Hi! Hello," she babbled. Drawing a steadying breath, she tried to tap what composure she owned, but any calm she might claim was nowhere to be found. "What are you…?" She stopped, not wanting to scare them off with questions. Reeling, she ran her fingers through her hair, tried to hitch her purse even higher, then gave up, letting her hand flutter uselessly to her side. "I'm glad to see you."

Colm said nothing, which totally freaked her out. Shouldn't he be saying something? After all, he and his trusty sidekick showed up at her door, not the other way around. Sure, she'd been heading to his house, but maybe she should go ahead and start—

"We came to 'pologize and shake hands," Aiden announced, breaking into her frantic thoughts and trampling his father's stony silence.

Monica watched, her heart in her throat, as the beautiful boy turned to look up at Colm.

"Right, Daddy?"

Time stood still for a second. Colm nodded, his eyes never straying from Monica. "Right."

"Apologize?" Monica shook her head so hard her hair whipped her face. "No, I should—"

Colm climbed three steps and extended his hand. "I'm sorry. I should have given you a chance to explain."

Tears scorched Monica's eyes, but she blinked to keep them at bay. Rushing down a couple steps, she grasped his hand in hers. "No, I'm sorry. I should have told you who I am. The whole thing was stupid."

He didn't loosen his grip, so neither did she.

"Now you can be friends again," Aiden informed them gleefully.

Monica looked down to find him hopping from step-to-step, his favorite doll clutched tightly in his hand. She chanced a look at Colm. "Can we?"

"Yep!" Aiden interjected. "And now we can go to the park." He paused on the top step and looked down at her. "You wanna go, too?"

"To the park?" She repeated the invitation without moving. The last thing she wanted was for Colm to notice he hadn't let go of her hand. "Sure," she said cautiously. "If your dad is okay with me coming along."

"Fine by me," Colm answered, preempting Aiden's prod.

"Yay!" Arms stretched over his head in victory, Aiden bent his knees, his eyes gleaming bright in anticipation of a massive jump. "Watch thi—"

"Don't even," Colm snapped.

He snatched his hand from her grasp to corral his kid, but Monica was feeling too relieved to be annoyed by the loss. If Colm hadn't, she would have grabbed Aiden herself.

Once he placed the little boy safely on the sidewalk, he looked up and offered his hand to her again, his green eyes bright as spring leaves. "Shall we?"

"Yes." She tossed her keys into her bag and flew down the stone steps. "Melody and Emma are there. If we hurry, maybe you guys can play a while," she told Aiden in a rush of breath.

The little boy nodded. "Cool."

Aiden danced around, clearly antsy to get the show on the road. But when she reached the sidewalk, Colm changed the offer of his hand to a shake.

"Hi. I'm Colm Cleary." He reached over, and without taking his eyes off her, stopped Aiden's whirling with a palm planted atop his head. "I'm a single dad, and this is my son, Aiden."

Baffled, Aiden said, "But she knows us already."

Monica nodded, a small smile curving her lips. "Right, but you guys don't know me." Squaring her shoulders, she looked Colm directly in the eye. "Monica Rayburn, single workaholic with a sister who thinks she's Jiminy Cricket and a fairly awesome niece."

"Emma," Aiden interjected. He tugged hard on Colm's arm to get his father's attention. "Her niece is Emma, and *she's* at the park."

"And we're off," Colm announced, gesturing for Aiden to lead the way.

Monica's cheeks burned with pleasure when he shifted her hand to his other and held fast as they fell into step behind the excited boy. Monica watched with amused bewilderment while Aiden skip-hopped over cracks in the sidewalk and twirled at unmarked intervals. "I don't know much about kids," she said in a low voice, "but I think I like yours. What you see is what you get, huh?"

"Calls 'em like he sees 'em." Colm chuckled, but in the next breath, he was on the job. "A big whoa at the corner, buddy," he called to Aiden.

"I *know*, Dad," Aiden called, his voice dripping with impatience.

"That's new," Colm murmured to Monica.

Turning to look at him, she found him frowning. "The tone?"

He nodded. "Yes, and the 'Dad' instead of 'Daddy.' I'm not sure I'm ready for the change."

"Happens fast, huh?"

Colm's steps slowed as he turned to look straight at her. "Seems like all the best things happen fast."

Her breath caught in her throat, but he didn't give her a chance to weigh in on his observations.

"Life has one hell of a learning curve."

She nodded as they stopped at the street corner. "Yeah, it does."

They checked both ways, then herded Aiden safely to the other side. As if he had an inner GPS urging him on to his destination, Aiden picked up his pace even more. They covered the remaining three blocks in silence, but with her hand tucked firmly in Colm's.

Aiden pranced in place while they waited for the traffic light to change. When the walk signal finally illuminated, Colm grabbed the neck of Aiden's sweatshirt to restrain him. "Says walk, not run."

"Dad-dy," Aiden whined, straining against their more sedate pace. "*Leggo*."

"Nope. Never. You're mine forever," Colm answered, a smile in his voice.

The second they reached the opposite curb, Aiden twisted from his grip and took off running through the carpet of autumn leaves. He stumbled, fell, and tumbled laughing through the crisp foliage, calling for them to do the same.

"Wow, such a fast never," she commented, grinning at the little boy's antics.

"Never always comes too fast, and forever isn't always built to last."

Stopping, she turned to face him. "But here we are."

"Here we are," he concurred.

"I know next to nothing about kids, Colm, but I'm smart…I can learn."

He smiled and stepped closer, sliding his hand onto her hip to draw her in. "I'm glad you're so smart. Do you know how many people have called me an idiot lately?"

"No," she whispered.

"Almost everyone I know."

"Do you know a lot of people?" she asked, his nearness leaving her breathless.

"Enough."

"Do you want to get to know me?"

He sighed. "I've been trying to all along, Monica."

She ducked her head, heat creeping up her neck into her cheeks. "So maybe I'm not as smart as I think?"

"I think we've got a lot to teach each other."

Relief warmed her insides while big piles of leaves were plowed up around her feet. "I'm going to need a crash course on this kid thing. I haven't exactly been the most hands-on aunt."

"I think we could set one up."

"You'll be teaching, right?"

He grinned and lowered his head a fraction of an inch. "Right."

"Maybe you can tell me why Aiden is trying to bury our feet in leaves?"

"He's practicing for a job with the mafia. You know, cement shoes and all."

She laughed. "Glad he has a career plan in mind." Tipping her face into the side of his neck, she whispered. "When do we cover the lesson on kissing?"

"Oh, we'll have to wait until later. Kissing is gross and must be done when no one is looking."

"You're killing me."

"Welcome to parenthood training. Lesson number one: you only get what you want after he gets what he wants."

Aiden cried out a protest as Colm scattered the leaves he'd gathered around them. Swooping down, he scooped up the scowling boy and set him on his feet. "Playground, ho!" Pointing to the play area swarmed with children, he patted Aiden on the head. "Take no prisoners, matey."

With an excited yelp, Aiden kicked into high gear and ran helter-skelter for the massive playground structure. Spotting something glittery among the leaves, Monica plucked Princess Clarissa from the crackling pile.

"Hey, wait, Aiden!" she called out, but the warning came too late. He'd hit the ladder leading to the hamster tube. Turning to Colm, she held up the doll. "He almost lost her."

"Again."

"Again," she amended.

He snaked an arm around her waist and pulled her hard against him.

"I guess it's a good thing I was here after all. I'm apparently a Princess Clarissa magnet."

He chuckled. "Wish I'd met you a year ago. This one is number five."

She blinked. "You mean he's lost her before?"

Colm nodded. "After number three, I bought six more, rubbed them around in some dirt to make them not-so-new, and stashed them in my closet. Each time one disappears, I'm ready."

Monica gaped at him. "Wow. I really do have a lot to learn."

He let one shoulder rise and fall. "Parenting is mostly basic self-preservation."

"And the rest?"

He lowered his head until she could feel his breath against her lips. "The rest is winging your way through."

"I could learn to wing," she whispered.

Colm nodded. "Good. Now, kiss me quick, while no one is looking."

Rising onto her toes, she pressed her mouth to his. The kiss was more enthusiasm than finesse, but Colm didn't seem to care. He wrapped her up tighter and took the kiss deeper. They broke apart, breathless and flushed. He brushed her hair from her face with his knuckles.

She cocked her head. "Can I get six of you?"

"Do you need more than one?"

"What if I lose you?"

He looked surprised. "I'm a lot harder to misplace than a doll."

Monica took a deep breath and plunged in. "I'm not very good at this falling in love stuff."

He stared at her, his lips moving slightly but no sound coming out at first. "Is that what we're doing?"

Her heart lodged in her throat, she gave a hesitant nod. "I think I am. At least, Melody tells me I am."

Colm wet his lips and darted a glance at the playground. "So, Melody is really the smart one?"

She conceded a smile. "When it comes to some things."

"Don't lie to me, Monica. I can take a lot of bad, but I can't take lies."

"I won't," she promised.

Colm took her at her word. "I'm falling for you, too, even if you are a big liar."

She wanted to refute his claim, but he took her mouth again, kissing her long, slow, and deep. Her fingers curled into the lapels of his jacket. She pulled him closer, and was fighting the urge to shimmy right up the trunk of him when the first shriek pierced their bubble.

Colm's head jerked up, his eyes open wide, his muscles tensed to spring into action.

She heard a familiar giggle and whirled. Emma and Aiden peeked out at them from behind a tree. The very tree Colm had leaned against the first day she saw him.

"Ewwww," someone added with exaggerated revulsion. Seconds later, Melody and Jeremy stepped into view. "They were kissing!" Mel exclaimed, her hands covering both eyes.

"Gross," Jeremy added with gleeful relish. "I hope they brushed and flossed first."

Monica rolled her eyes at her brother-in-law's dentist humor, but gently disentangled herself from Colm. "Ha. Ha."

"Monnie never thinks jokes about her are funny," Melody said archly. Offering her hand and a warm smile, she said, "You must be Colm."

He returned her grin. "And you must be Emma's mommy."

Her sister nodded gravely. "An unwieldy first name, but I seem to be stuck with it."

"Melody," Monica interjected. "Mel." Recovering her manners, she turned to Jeremy. "And her husband, Jeremy."

"We've met," Jeremy reminded her. "Good to see you again."

Colm nodded. "You, too."

Monica cringed, remembering the day she'd been caught out in her lies. Melody must have seen the look because she jumped in. "So, we're heading to La Maison for crêpes, and I'm sure you two have a lot to talk about. Can Aiden come with us?"

Colm sensed an ambush. "Oh. Uh, we just ate pancakes."

"But I'm *sooooooo* hungry," Aiden cried, clutching his stomach for added emphasis. "I ran 'em all off, and I'm starving."

Rolling his eyes, Colm turned to look at Monica. She answered him with a shrug. After the fiasco of the fake flu, she determined she didn't have the skill set for arranging play dates.

Yet.

"Sure. Okay," he said at last. "Should I pick him up at your house, or—"

"We'll come by Monica's. Say, in about an hour?" Mel raised an inquiring eyebrow. "Give you two kids some time to hash things out."

Monica and Colm nodded in unison.

"Great. Come on, gang," Jeremy called to the kids. "Let's get crêpey."

They stood in silence, watching all their buffers walk away. Pulling in a bracing breath, Monica cocked her head and peered at him. "So, a whole hour…What should we do?"

To her surprise, Colm took her hand and started to pull her along. In the opposite direction of her house. When she spotted the weathered wooden bench, understanding dawned. She sat next to him, a wry smile twisting her lips. "No sex, huh?"

He hooked an arm over the bench. "Not until the sixth date."

Her jaw dropped and her brows shot up. "Sixth? Isn't the third date the charm?"

"You have to pay some price for lying to me."

"Wow. Talk about being *penal*ized."

He snorted. "Another joke like that, and I'll hold out for seven."

"Three," she retorted.

"Eight."

Monica grinned. "Four, final offer."

"Five it is," he said with a nod.

She relaxed into him and his arm curled around her. Blinking up at the vibrant blue sky, she sighed. "I am sorry, Colm. I never meant for things to go so far."

"I know," he said quietly. "Truthfully, neither did I."

Twisting, she met and held his gaze. "But they did. For me, at least. And by the time I knew what was happening, I didn't know how to get out of it without, well, losing you."

"I understand." A moment passed. He nodded once. "I do."

Settling into his embrace, Monica let the breath she'd been holding seep out. "So…this dating thing. I think we might need a chaperone for the first four. Make sure we don't lapse into…shenanigans."

Colm pressed a kiss to the top of her head. "Lucky for us, I know the right guy for the job."

The End

Enjoy this preview of the first book in the Coastal Heat series by Maggie Wells!

Going Deep

MAKING HEADLINES

Brooke Hastings almost won a Pulitzer Prize for her hard-hitting reportage. Now she's sitting on the story of a lifetime and wants to prove she's not a one-hit-wonder. But in order to get the world to take notice, she'll need the help of the one person she loves to hate—Brian Dalton.

Brian Dalton stumbled into celebrity when he landed a show on the Earth Channel. But the hunky marine biologist never forgot the serious, studious boy who left Mobile a decade before. Now back in Alabama, he's looking for the quiet life he always wanted and hoping for a chance with the girl he always loved. When Brooke asks him to help expose some of the lingering effects of the Gulf oil disaster, Brian jumps at the chance to help preserve the place both call home . . .

Chapter 1

"If I didn't have Harley Cade and his ten million ways of making a girl happy on the hook, I'd cling to that man's hull like a barnacle."

Brooke Hastings drowned a smirk in her martini glass. Twenty years of friendship did little to lessen the shock value of Laney's declarations. Brooke took a cautious sip. The cocktail was pinker than a My Little Pony, but the triple sec and vodka packed a punch that more than made up for the girly color.

Dragging her gaze from the former classmate-turned-television-hunk she was here to stalk, Brooke turned to face her best friend. "*That man* told Mrs. Wise you had your Spanish conjugation written on your thigh."

Laney refused to be put off by something as fickle as fact. "If I'd known he'd grow up to be rich, famous, and hot as Hades, I would have let him conjugate whatever he wanted on my thigh."

"You told your mother you'd drown yourself in the ocean if she made you invite him to your birthday party in third grade."

The feisty redhead at her side pursed her lips and made a great show of scanning the room. "She invited him anyway."

Revisionist history or no, Laney wasn't one who took being thwarted lightly. Nearly twenty years had passed since that birthday party, but the sour expression on her face said the sting of her mother's betrayal hadn't yet faded.

"*Do* you have Harley Cade on the hook?"

"I could," her friend said, eying the crowded room. "I'd only have to give that line a little old tug."

Brooke smiled. She admired Laney's confidence, but she wished they could be having this conversation anywhere but in the middle of one of Mobile's most popular social gatherings.

Glittering jewels and porcelain veneers shone in the light of the ancient chandeliers, adding sparkle to the mansion's faded glory. The first floor of Putnam House, one of the ruthlessly preserved mansions that graced Mobile's historic district, was crowded—every square inch packed with potential donors. Saints Preserve Us was the premier fundraising event for their alma mater, St. Patrick's Academy, and one of Brooke's mother's pet projects. Her mother and her merry band of fundraising fiends plied their victims with Guinness, Jameson's, and heaping helpings of flattery in hopes of getting them to write big, fat checks.

Thursday night television programming may not be what it used to be, but Brooke had a reason for being here. She wasn't in a position to donate the scraps of cash left over after she stretched her paycheck to the max. Frankly, she wasn't interested in whether the football team could afford new jock straps or if the Drama Club had to—insert shudder here—*rent* costumes for their spring production. She wasn't here because her mother insisted she come. No, she was trussed up in her Spanx for a reason. A motive she shared with 99.9 percent of the women in that room. She was there for Brian Dalton.

"Any Tucker sightings yet?"

The question jerked Brooke from her mini-sulk. The possibility of running into Jack Tucker was exactly what kept her miles away from the Gulf Shore's social whirl in the last few weeks. News of Jack's return to Mobile after his divorce had lit a spark of hope inside her. The possibility of rekindling their romance seemed to lighten the miasma of loneliness that covered her like a heavy blanket. Alone in her bed, she allowed herself to spin a fantasy of marriage and family that was not only attractive but convenient, as well. Then she ran into him at her parents' club and her thinking shifted from possibly-maybe to never-gonna-happen.

Unfortunately, her mother had hopped onto the Jack Tucker bandwagon the minute the man crossed the city limits. Emmaline Hastings wasn't a woman whose mind was easily changed. That meant Brooke's best course of action had been to avoid Jack altogether. Eventually her mother would find a project more promising than the daunting task of marrying off her almost-thirty-year-old daughter.

"No. Thank goodness."

"You used to get all twitterpated at the thought of seeing old Jack Tucker," Laney drawled.

"And you used to spend your entire study hall plotting ways to torment Brian Dalton."

Laney remained as impervious to criticism as she'd been in high school.

It was one of her greatest charms. "He brought it on himself."

Hard to argue that logic. Back in those days, Brian did earn a good bit of his torment. His fall from social grace started the day he displayed a clock powered by a potato for second grade show and tell. His position as class pariah was written in the stars before Brooke scored the blue ribbon at the eighth grade science fair, but he cemented it in high school. Brian Dalton was worse than a nerd. He was a nerd who thought it was cool to be arrogant and condescending to anyone he considered his intellectual inferior. This meant practically everyone.

He might have redeemed himself if he'd stuck to delivering the world's shortest valedictory address. But then he planted a kiss on the salutatorian that shook the entire auditorium.

Brooke never forgot the way her kiss-swollen lips tingled as he whispered the Alabama fan's mantra of "Roll, Tide, roll" into her Auburn-bound ear. Nor would she forgive him for the scalding rush of humiliation he left in his wake as he walked away.

The hell of it was, nearly a decade later, she could still taste him. Salty and sweet. The brainy boy seemed to have ocean water in his veins and coconut-scented sunscreen embedded in his pores. She pressed her glass to her bottom lip, sternly reminding herself that a kiss could not linger for ten years. No matter how much pent up passion a guy put into it.

Laney broke into her thoughts. "I always thought your mama might be convinced to give up on her dream of you marrying Jack Tucker if a bigger fish came swimming along."

"If Brian's the fish you're referring to, I'll remind you that you used to want to see him flopping on the floor gasping for breath."

"We've grown up. Matured. Besides, nerds are hot these days. Didn't anyone tell you?"

That was where Laney's assessment went wrong. Brian's hotness wasn't simply a trend. It was a matter of perspective. As a teenager, he might have been quiet, bookish, but he'd always been good looking. If one could get past the annoying arrogance.

He stood in the center of the room like he'd ruled the school all along, and the sight of all the other Laney-come-latelys flocking the boy they once snubbed irked Brooke to the bone. The fact that she was the only one who saw it used to make her feel superior to the rest of the world. Now, she wondered if she'd missed out on something when she watched him walk away.

Miffed by the train of thought, Brooke turned and gave her friend the hairy eyeball. "I can't believe you're lusting after Brian Dalton. What's the world coming to?"

Her friend's chuckle was genuine. "I was talking about you, not me."

"Me?"

"The world we once knew came to a screeching halt the day that boy kissed you."

"It did not."

"You might sell that to someone else, sugar, but not me. You lost all interest in Jack Tucker the minute you locked lips with the delectable Mr. Limpet."

"Incredible," Brooke murmured into her glass. She took a quick sip, her eyes locked on her quarry. "The movie was *The Incredible Mr. Limpet*."

Laney huffed. "It could have been *The Incredible Hulk* for all I care."

"How about *The Incredibles*?"

"As long as you're not trying to deny he kissed you senseless and it was incredible."

"He kissed me, it was incredible, then he left," Brooke said flatly. "He left. Period. The end."

"And you still think he's incredible." Brooke started to shake her head but Laney raised a hand to ward off further protest. "Shelbrooke Hastings, are you trying to tell me that you have absolutely no interest in spawning with Aquaman?"

"I prefer Batman. Maybe Superman. Hell, I'd even take Captain America, though I suspect he's a prig in bed."

Her friend barked a short laugh. "I'm betting Superman has a stick up his ass, too."

"Yes, but he has that ice castle thingy. I always thought that looked awesome."

Laney nodded, the corners of her mouth pulling down as she gave the argument due consideration. "Beats the hell out of a damp, musty cave."

"Yes, but Batman has the black cape. And all the cool toys."

"Can you imagine the vibrator Wayne Enterprises could manufacture?" Laney clutched imaginary pearls. "A Bat-brator. Exactly what every single girl needs."

Brooke frowned and shook her head. Listening to her friend verbally fondle Brian was more than vaguely disturbing. Sure, Brian had the looks, the money, and his picture printed in *People*, *US Magazine*, and on the cover of the tabloids, but that shouldn't make him fair game for everyone. Especially not here. This was supposed to be his home. But a star was a star, even if he was a little burned out, and everyone in the room seemed to be caught in the man's gravitational pull.

Not many women would pass on a chance to de-pants Brian Dalton these days. If she felt like being scrupulously honest, Brooke would number herself among them. But she didn't want to hear it from Laney. Or anyone else, for that matter. Her relationship with Brian, whatever it might have been, was always separate from everyone else in her life. Their odd friendship had been as fascinating as exploring an uncharted island—intellectually stimulating, undeniably appealing, but treacherous as high tide.

Judging by the sardonic smirk on his face, this new and improved Brian would be equally challenging. And intriguing. He was undoubtedly mouthwatering.

The cut of his jacket showcased the broad-shouldered, narrow-hipped perfection of a body that spent hours in the water. Days working in the sun threaded his brown hair with hints of gold. A minimalist flash of white teeth evoked a visceral reaction in females from eighteen to eighty. The suit screamed matinee idol rather than marine biologist. It was no wonder a bevy of elegantly dressed women flocked to him like seagulls after a saltine. Grown-up Brian might still spend his days talking about plankton and marsh grass and amoebas, but the idea that he could spend his nights with his pick of women seemed more a given than a hypothesis.

Brooke held her breath when he scanned the room, torn between wanting to step forward and the urge to shrink away from his probing gaze. Oxygen seeped from her lungs when she spotted the familiar flash of arrogance in his eyes. Curious, she dragged her attention from the knot of back-slappers that closed around him and surveyed the room, trying to see it all through his eyes.

Brian turned and bestowed a dazzling smile on the woman next to him. The kind that made normally sane women flibbertigibbety. That weapon wasn't even turned on her, and Brooke went weak in the knees. Darting a glance at Laney to see if she'd witnessed the same phenomenon, she found her friend's dreamy-eyed gaze turned in the opposite direction.

Pitching her voice low, she jabbed an elbow into Laney's ribs. "Don't you dare ditch me."

Laney had the good grace to grimace when she was caught ogling her millionaire. "I won't." She tore herself from whatever crazy eye sex mojo Harley was using on her and turned back to the task at hand. Clearing her throat, she gave the bodice of her dress a surreptitious tug. "Brian Dalton. Did I mention wanting to be his barnacle?"

It was Brooke's turn to grin. "Liar."

Cradling her drink in both hands, Laney darted one last wistful glance at the bar area. "Okay, fine. But I'm telling you, if Mr. Cade so much as blinks you'll be scraping me off Brian's...hull."

"I'm starting to think *you* might be hooked on Harley." Raising her glass in a mocking toast, she smiled sweetly. "But if it makes you feel better, I still think you're a hussy."

Laney grinned. "Thank you."

At that moment, Brian turned his head and their gazes locked. Her breath snagged when he took a step in her direction, but she refused to show any sign of weakness. Taking a casual sip of her drink, she rolled her shoulders back, edged one foot in front of the other, and arched her back ever-so-slightly. A trick that her mother, like any former Miss Alabama worth her salt, passed along to her daughter the moment she left the cradle.

Brooke learned the power of the pose long before she'd had any assets to display. By the time she finished puberty, she'd honed it to sharp perfection. It never failed to rile Emmaline Hastings's that her daughter chose to wield the power of the written word rather than the ceremonial sash. Wearing a smile to cover the uncertainty that twanged her nerves, she surveyed the room with studied nonchalance.

It seemed she'd been doing this her whole life. Measuring, testing, and gauging. Checking herself against the competition. From her first Little Miss Mobile crown to the Pulitzer Prize nomination she'd garnered at the tender age of twenty-six. To her mother and the world outside the microcosm of print journalism, she was a wunderkind, a prodigy, a savant. But those on the inside knew the glow of that nomination faded the second someone used her story to line their parrot cage. And one of those people was her boss.

Despite the critical acclaim her series garnered in the aftermath of the Gulf Oil Spill crisis, *The Courier,* like many other print news outlets, was suffering an acute case of declining circulation. The sinking numbers put a lot of pressure on the paper's management and reporting staff. Her boss wasn't only the news editor, he was the publisher's son and heir apparent.

She needed a big story and she needed one bad. And to that end, she also needed Brian Dalton, but not in the way that Laney or Emmaline might hope.

Her pulse beat a frantic strobe when she saw her mother snare Brian's arm and pull him into the slipknot of people eddying at the edge of the dance floor. Blond and beautiful as the day she was crowned thirty-three years before, people naturally gravitated to her mama. Brooke's father liked to say Emmaline was a force of nature. One that left the people in her wake reeling and off-kilter. Like the hurricanes that battered the coast with disheartening regularity, Brooke had learned long ago that the best course of action when caught in her eye was to hunker down and wait it out.

Laney sighed as she watched Emmaline work her magic. "I swear she made a deal with the devil."

"Don't kid yourself. My mother *is* the devil."

Joking or not, it was a plausible explanation. Emmaline looked obscenely good for a woman who'd hit the half-century mark and barreled right past it. The dress she wore clung to curves disciplined by hours on the elliptical and skimmed the long, lean legs that nabbed first place in every swimsuit competition she'd ever entered. If Brooke didn't love her mother so damn much, she wouldn't have bothered hating her. She would have gone straight to putting glue in her shampoo bottle.

Lifting her glass, she tossed back the remainder of her drink then plopped the empty glass onto the tray of a passing waiter. She fought the urge to stomp her stiletto-clad foot as she watched her mother bathe Brian in the spotlight of her attentions. Then he blinked and gave his head a bewildered shake. Emmaline's eyes narrowed a millimeter, and the side-to-side wag morphed into a weak nod.

Her mother out-sparkled the chandelier above their heads. Familial pride rippled through Brooke. A woman wearing a blue and green plaid kilt pressed a glass of stout into Brian's limp hand. Emmaline patted his arm, marking the end of negotiations. The man's befuddled expression confirmed a direct hit.

"Damn, she's good," a deep voice drawled.

Blatant admiration dripped from each word. Brooke didn't need to glance over her shoulder to know her father was standing behind her. "The best."

Henry Hastings pressed a kiss to his daughter's cheek, an indulgent smile creasing his time-worn, but still handsome, face. Seizing the chance for escape, Laney murmured her excuses and headed straight for the bar and Harley Cade.

A speculative gleam lit her father's forest green eyes. "How much do you think she got him for?"

Brooke let a shoulder rise and fall before she returned her father's conspiratorial grin. "Five?"

Her father snorted and rocked back on his heels as he wet his lips with what was surely very good bourbon. "Chump change. She got at least ten large out of that boy."

She couldn't help but smile when her daddy smacked his lips, clearly savoring the splash of eau de banned booze that lingered there. Emmaline only allowed him one drink a night these days. Henry made certain it was exceptional and nursed it through the entirety of whatever social event he was forced to endure that week. Her father would have happily ponied up ten grand to get out of the room, but after three decades of marriage he knew better than to try.

Her parents had what genteel society might call an understanding. He was allowed to shoot, stuff and mount as many woodland creatures as he desired as long as the trophies remained in his garage or the hunting cabin his granddaddy built. She could buy as many pretty party dresses and accept as many invitations as she pleased, but her husband would serve as an accessory no more than once a week.

Her father was far more approachable. Affable and indulgent, he masked his sharp intellect with a smooth Southern gentleman veneer. As dark as her mother was light, the two of them were a striking and formidable pair. The tartan plaid of his tie might have been a concession to the occasion, but the effect played up the roguish features of his Scots-Irish heritage.

Brooke chuckled. "What was I thinking? Of course she got ten."

Her reward was a kiss on the cheek and a one-armed squeeze. "You look awful pretty, pumpkin."

The familiar scent of her daddy's aftershave was all she needed to reinforce the steel in her backbone. Henry Hastings was her biggest fan and staunchest defender. They were a unit, a team, a mutual admiration society made for two.

Lifting the glass of rationed mash, he toasted her. "Thank you for comin'. You made your mama very happy, and you saved me from utter and complete boredom."

"It's the least I could do. After all, you allowed me to get a top notch education without having to resort to smearing Preparation H under my eyes."

"Now, now. Don't mock your mama's scholarship programs," he warned, a smile quirking his lips.

Knowing they'd arrived at an impasse, she reached for two of her most effective weapons—distraction and deflection. "What's this I hear about you buying a new boat?"

His answering huff confirmed a direct hit. Her parents' latest struggle for marital control revolved around a news magazine article on funding retirement and what her mother considered an excess of unnecessary discretionary spending. His.

"It's a johnboat, for Christ's sake, not a cabin cruiser."

Squeezing her father's arm, Brooke darted a glance around the room, checking to be certain none of St. Pat's few remaining nuns stood nearby to hear her father blaspheme. "Hush, Daddy. I was teasing you."

Henry took a hasty gulp of his beloved bourbon. "It's not funny. I tell you it's a crying shame when a man who works as hard as I do wants to buy himself one little toy and he ends up getting nothing but a bellyful of guff."

"Damn straight."

The words were soft-spoken but heartfelt enough to break into the conversation. Brooke jumped and whirled, but the butterflies in the pit of her stomach identified the owner a heartbeat before their gazes met.

A smug smile played at the corners of Brian's mouth. The same one he wore when she missed the Advanced Chemistry review due to an impacted wisdom tooth. He'd refused to lend her his notes, the bastard. For months after that graduation day kiss she stewed and simmered, wondering if whatever precious data he captured in his Mead three-subject spiral cost her the chance of giving the Valedictory address.

"Hello, Brooke."

Meet the Author

Maggie Wells is a deep-down dirty girl with a weakness for hot heroes and happy endings. By day she is buried in spreadsheets, but at night she pens tales of people tangling up the sheets. Fueled by supertankers of Diet Coke, Maggie juggles fictional romance and the real deal by keeping her slow-talking Southern gentleman constantly amused and their two children mildly embarrassed. For more please visit www.maggie-wells.com.

CPSIA information can be obtained
at www.ICGtesting.com
Printed in the USA
FFOW03n1222230817
39163FF